D0990471

An Amish Barn Raising

AN AMISH BARN RAISING

THREE STORIES

AMY CLIPSTON
KELLY IRVIN
KATHLEEN FULLER

THORNDIKE PRESS
A part of Gale, a Cengage Company

Thorndike Press, a part of Gale, a Cengage Company.

Thorndike Press® Large Print Amish Fiction.
The text of this Large Print edition is unabridged.
Other aspects of the book may vary from the original edition.
Set in 16 pt. Plantin.

**LIBRARY OF CONGRESS CIP DATA ON FILE.
CATALOGUING IN PUBLICATION FOR THIS BOOK
IS AVAILABLE FROM THE LIBRARY OF CONGRESS.**

ISBN-13: 978-1-4328-8783-4 (hardcover alk. paper)

Published in 2021 by arrangement with The Zondervan Corporation LLC, a subsidiary of HarperCollins Christian Publishing, Inc.

Printed in Mexico
Print Number: 01 Print Year: 2021

CONTENTS

GLOSSARY*

ach: oh
aenti: aunt
appeditlich: delicious
bedauerlich: sad
bopli(n)/boppli: baby
brot: bread
bruder: brother
bruders: brothers
bruderskinner: nieces/nephews
bu: boy
buwe: boys
daadi: grandfather
daed: father

* The German dialect spoken by the Amish is not a written language and varies depending on the location and origin of the settlement. These spellings are approximations. Most Amish children learn English after they start school. They also learn high German, which is used in their Sunday services.

danki: thank you
dat: dad
dawdy haus: grandparents' house
dochder: daughter
dochdern: daughters
dummkopp: moron
Dummle!: hurry!
eck: corner table at a wedding reception reserved for newly married couple
Englischer/Englisher: English or non-Amish
fraa: wife
freind: friend
freinden: friends
froh: happy
gegisch: silly
geh: go
gern gschehne: you're welcome
Gmay: church district
Gott: God
Gude mariye/guder mariye: Good morning
gut: good
Gut nacht: Good night
haus: house
hund: dog
Ich liebe dich: I love you
jah: yes
kaffi: coffee
kapp: prayer cap or head covering worn by Amish women

kichli: cookie
kichlin: cookies
kinn/kinner: child/children
kumm: come
lieb/liewe: love, a term of endearment
maed: young women, girls
maedel: young woman
mamm: mom
mammi: grandmother
mann: husband
mei: my
mudder: mother
naerfich: nervous
narrisch: crazy
nee: no
onkel: uncle
rumspringa: period of running around
schee: pretty
schmeir: peanut butter, corn syrup, and marshmallow fluff spread
schtupp: family room
schweschder: sister
schweschdere: sisters
sohn/suh: son
vatter: father
Was iss letz?: What's wrong?
Wie geht's: How do you do? or Good day!
Wunderbaar/wunderbarr: wonderful
ya: yes
yung: young

BUILDING A DREAM

AMY CLIPSTON

With love and appreciation for DeeDee. Your friendship is a blessing, and I'm so glad our kids introduced us.

FEATURED CHARACTERS FROM THE AMISH MARKETPLACE SERIES

DARLENE M. HARVEY GINGERICH

Bethany | Anthony

NELSON M. SUZETTA BEILER

|

Kathryn

Chapter One

Kathryn Beiler tapped her chin with her finger as she surveyed the folding table filled with bowls of pretzels, chips, popcorn, trail mix, a variety of dips, a fruit salad, a vegetable plate, and plastic containers of lemonade and iced tea.

"We forgot the *kichlin,*" Kathryn said.

"And where do you suggest we put the cookies?" Maria Swarey gave a little laugh as she pushed the ties from her prayer covering over the shoulders of her red dress. Kathryn smiled at her best friend. She had always thought that red made Maria's bright smile, dark brown hair, and milk-chocolate-colored eyes look even prettier.

"Maybe get another table? After all, we have plenty of *freinden* here that will be hungry for snacks soon."

Kathryn shielded her eyes from the bright June afternoon sun as she looked out over her father's rolling green pastures dotted with cows and then toward the dairy barn where her friends played volleyball and laughed. Her golden retriever, Fred, sat by the volleyball nets, wagging his tail as her friends played. Every so often, someone would reach over and rub his head, causing him to look up at them, his tongue lolling. She grinned and shook her head. Fred had never met a stranger!

It was Kathryn's turn to host the youth gathering, and Maria had come over the day before to help clean and prepare. Since today was an off-Sunday without a church service, a few young men from youth group had arrived early to put up the volleyball nets before the rest of their friends arrived.

"Do you want to ask a few of the *buwe* to help us get another table out of the utility room?" Maria asked.

Kathryn smiled as her eyes found Anthony Gingerich laughing beside his best friend, Dwain Bontrager, who prepared to serve the volleyball to the opposing team. Not only was Anthony friendly and thoughtful, always seeming to go out of his way to talk to Kathryn and lend a hand at youth gatherings, but he was also handsome.

"I'm fairly positive I know who you'd like to ask to help with another table." Maria's singsong voice was next to Kathryn's ear.

"Stop it." Kathryn felt her cheeks heat as she waved off her best friend's teasing. "We don't need another table. We'll just rearrange everything to make room for the *kichlin.*"

Maria's dark eyes sparkled with teasing as she began moving the bowls of chips. "Whatever you say, Kathryn, but I think making room on this table will be like solving a puzzle."

"We'll make do." Kathryn stole one more glance at Anthony and then began pushing the serving platters and bowls closer together.

"Why don't you try talking to him and telling him how you feel?" Maria whispered as she pushed a bowl of dip toward the end of the table.

"Shh!" Kathryn peeked up to make sure the group of six young women standing near the table hadn't heard Maria. When they continued with their conversation without looking over, she breathed a sigh of relief. "Anthony and I have been friends our whole lives, and we talk all the time. You know that!"

Maria jammed a hand on her small hip. "But he won't know that you have a crush on him unless you tell him."

Kathryn shushed her again. "We have food

to bring out. Let's discuss this later." *Or not at all!*

"I'll get the *kichlin,* and you get the cups." Maria headed into Kathryn's house to gather up the supplies.

Kathryn glanced around the small kitchen and then pointed to the four containers of cookies she and Maria had baked yesterday. "There they are. I can't believe we forgot them."

"I'll take them out." Maria picked up the containers and headed back out the door.

Mamm stepped into the kitchen from the family room. "How is everything going?"

With *Mamm*'s bright smile and easy laugh, Kathryn considered her one of her best friends. Blonde hair peeked out from her prayer covering, and the wrinkles around her eyes were clues that her mother was close to fifty, but the sparkle in her deep brown eyes gave a hint of her young and fun demeanor.

"Fine." Kathryn opened the cupboard and retrieved a large stack of cups. "Maria and I were trying to make room on the table for the *kichlin* and cups. We were discussing setting up another table."

"Oh. Should I ask your *dat* to get one for you?" *Mamm* pointed to the family room. "We're just reading in the *schtupp.*"

"No, *danki.* We'll be fine." Kathryn balanced the package of cups and then started for the back door. "Enjoy your reading."

She descended the stairs and walked toward the table, where a group of young men and women were filling plates with the snacks as conversations buzzed through the air. Fred sat nearby, begging for attention, and Kathryn shook her head.

"Come here, Fred," she called, and the dog trotted over to her. She pulled a dog treat from her apron pocket. "Sit."

He sat and lifted a paw to her.

"Here you go." With her free hand, she gave him the snack, and he chomped it with delight. "Now, go sit on the porch like a *gut bu.*"

The dog complied, bouncing over to the porch and sitting in his favorite spot, where he could watch all of the action around the yard.

Kathryn walked to the end of the table, and after setting down the cups, she rearranged containers of cookies to make more room.

"Please tell me you made oatmeal raisin."

She felt a flutter dance in her stomach when she peeked up at Anthony standing beside her. "I did."

"Danki." With his light-brown hair, bright

blue eyes, and angular jaw, Anthony towered over her by nearly nine inches. And he always sent her pulse pumping when he aimed his electric smile at her. "You made them for me, right?"

"Maybe." She gave him a coy smile as he took a bite. She *had* made the cookies with him in mind, but she chose to keep her response more flirtatious than direct.

"Wow. *Appeditlich.*" He finished the cookie and then grabbed two more.

"I'm glad you like them. I have more oatmeal raisin *kichlin* stashed away. If you like, I can put together a container for you to take home."

His smile widened. "That would be amazing."

Dwain smacked Anthony on the arm as he lumbered past him. "Hey, Anthony. Let's get back to the volleyball game." He nodded at Kathryn and headed to the group of young people standing by the volleyball net.

"I guess I have to go." Anthony swiped another cookie. He winked at her and then jogged toward his friends.

Kathryn felt her lips turn up in a smile as she watched him dash over to Dwain and smack him on the arm before laughing at something someone said.

"I saw that wink," Maria said as she sidled

up to Kathryn. "I told you he likes you. It's so obvious."

Kathryn hugged her arms over her waist as she tried to imagine what it would be like to date Anthony. To call him her boyfriend. To plan a future with him.

Then her shoulders drooped as facts brought her back to reality. Those dreams would never come true.

Because her father didn't approve of Anthony.

"I think you need some practice serving the ball," Dwain quipped as he helped Anthony roll up the volleyball net later that evening.

"Uh-huh." Anthony snorted. "Because you're the expert. How many bumps did you miss?"

Dwain shrugged and then pushed his hand through his sweaty, dark hair. "A few."

Anthony couldn't stop his laughter as he recalled his best friend's blunders during their games that afternoon. "*Ya,* a few. That's a great way to put it."

He hefted the net in his arms as Dwain picked up the ball. Then he glanced over his shoulder as they made their way to the supply barn to stow the net and the ball.

Above them, the sky lit with bright streaks of orange and yellow as the sun began to set. The cicadas began their evening chorus, and lightning bugs started to make their appearance. While the other members of their youth group had left for the evening, Anthony and Dwain stayed to help clean up.

Anthony's pulse ticked up when he spotted Kathryn and Maria gathering up bowls and plates at the snack table. Fred guarded the table, waiting for someone to drop a piece of food. Anthony grinned. How he enjoyed that dog!

Kathryn looked beautiful today clad in a yellow dress that complemented the sunshine-kissed blonde hair peeking out of her prayer covering. He'd had a difficult time keeping his eyes off her when he'd first seen her this afternoon. And when he'd had an opportunity to talk with her at the snack table, he'd longed to stay there all day, continuing to flirt and make small talk about the cookies.

Anthony had always felt drawn to Kathryn, even when they were children attending the same school. They'd become fast friends on the playground in first grade, and that friendship had blossomed over the years during youth group gatherings. She was the friend he sought out when he needed advice or he craved someone with whom to share happy news.

And now that they were both twenty, he wanted to take their friendship to the next level. He just had to muster up the courage to ask her father's permission to date her.

But he found himself pondering if Kathryn would even want to date him after knowing him so long. Did she harbor the same growing feelings for him, and if so, how could they turn their friendship into something more meaningful?

After stowing the volleyball net and ball, Anthony and Dwain headed toward the house, where they folded up the empty table that had held their snacks. Anthony headed up the steps toward the back door, and Fred trotted beside him.

"How's it going, Fred?" he asked the dog, who panted and smiled up at him. "I had fun today too."

As Anthony reached the top step, the door swung open, revealing Kathryn. Fred sat down beside him and wagged his tail, which thumped against the porch floor.

"*Danki* so much for bringing in the table," Kathryn said. "It's heavier than it looks." She pushed the door open wide as her smile brightened. "Maria and I were just discussing carrying it in."

"We thought we'd stay and help you," Anthony said as he hefted the table past her, stepping into the kitchen, where Kathryn's mother, Suzetta, washed dishes and Maria dried.

"Oh, thank you for bringing the table in, you two," Suzetta said, her smile bright as she rinsed a serving platter.

"Of course," Anthony responded before nodding toward the door that led to the utility room. "It goes in there, right?"

"That's right," Suzetta said.

Maria scampered toward the utility room. "Oh! Let me get the door for you." She pushed it open and flipped on the overhead propane-powered light fixture.

"Thanks," Anthony muttered as he moved past Maria and set the table down beside a shelf full of cleaning supplies and the wringer washer.

"Did you have fun today?" Dwain asked Maria.

"I did. You?" Maria fiddled with the hem of her black apron as she smiled up at him.

"*Ya,* I was just telling Anthony that he needs to work on his volleyball skills. If he improves, we might win more games."

Maria tittered, and Dwain's grin widened as his green eyes seemed to glint in the propane light above them.

Anthony blinked. His best friend was flirting with Maria! He hadn't seen Dwain flirt since he had broken up with his last girlfriend nearly a year ago.

When had this development taken place? And how had Anthony missed it?

"Anthony?"

He spun toward Kathryn, who was standing in the doorway watching him. She held up a container. "As promised, I have your *kichlin.*"

"Danki." He rubbed his hands together and moved into the kitchen. "I'm going to hide them from my family. If not, then *mei dat* will try to eat them all."

Kathryn laughed as she placed the container in his hands. "Maybe just offer him one and then hide the rest."

"How are your folks?" Suzetta asked as she faced him while drying a large bowl.

"*Gut. Danki. Mei dat* and I are staying busy, and *Mamm* tries to keep us in line," he joked, and Suzetta and Kathryn laughed.

"I guess your business is booming this time of year," Suzetta said.

"*Ya,* it is." Anthony leaned back on the door frame.

"How is it going with Micah?" Kathryn asked about Anthony's older sister's boyfriend, Micah Zook.

"It's been *wunderbaar* ever since Micah combined his patio furniture business with our gazebo business. We don't seem to have a moment between orders, which is nice, though a bit hectic."

"What a blessing," Suzetta said. "How is Bethany doing with her Coffee Corner?" Bethany, Anthony's older sister, ran a coffee and donut booth at the Bird-in-Hand Marketplace.

"Her booth has been busy since tourist season is in full swing. She comes home exhausted each day, but she loves it."

"I need to stop by there," Kathryn chimed in. "She has the most *appeditlich* flavored *kaffi.*"

"We should go there together sometime," Anthony told her.

"Ya." The intensity in her pretty brown eyes sent his blood pounding.

"Please tell your folks hello for me," Suzetta said.

"I will." Anthony turned to Kathryn. "Would you please walk me out?"

Her eyes widened for a split second as if she were surprised or excited by the suggestion. "Of course."

"Great." He turned toward the utility room, where Dwain and Maria continued to talk and laugh. "I'm heading out. *Gut nacht.*"

"I'll be there in a minute." Dwain gave

him a half wave before returning to his conversation with Maria.

Anthony swallowed a snort. He was eager to ask Dwain about his sudden interest in Maria.

He turned his attention back to Kathryn and held the back door open for her. She picked up a lantern from the counter and then stepped out onto the porch, where Fred still sat, his tail thumping.

Anthony gave Fred a pat on the head as he walked by. "*Gut nacht,* buddy. Hopefully I'll see you soon."

Fred responded by thumping his tail harder, and Anthony chuckled.

"Fred had a great day, and I did too. The youth gathering was really fun today," he commented as he followed Kathryn out into the warm night air. He looked over at the pasture, which was now cloaked in darkness.

"Fred always loves when we have company. I agree it was a great day." Kathryn set the lantern on the porch railing and then wound a tie from her prayer covering around her finger as if she were nervous. Fred came to sit by her, smiling up at her with his doggy grin.

"You never played volleyball with me. I missed having you on my team."

She gestured over toward where the snack table had sat this afternoon. Earlier in the evening, Maria had helped her fill the table with trays of sandwiches for their supper. "I was busy worrying about the snacks and making sure everyone had what they needed. I guess I owe you a game."

"I'm going to hold you to it."

"Okay."

They stared at each other for a moment, and he felt a strange stirring in his chest. It was as if everything between them had shifted and come into clear view. He cared for her and wanted to date her, if only he could find the words to ask.

The storm door opened and clicked shut, yanking Anthony back to the present.

Dwain pulled a flashlight out of his pocket and then loped down the steps. "You ready to go, Anthony?"

"Ya." Anthony held up the container of cookies. "*Danki* again."

"*Gern gschehne.* I'll see you soon," Kathryn said.

"*Danki,* Kathryn." Dwain walked toward his horse and buggy. He and Anthony had hitched them up before they began taking down the volleyball net.

"Bye, Dwain." Kathryn gave one last wave and then headed back into the house with

Fred in tow.

Anthony pulled a flashlight out of his pocket as he quickened his steps to catch up to his best friend. "So, you and Maria, huh?"

Dwain's smile widened. "She's so *schee.*"

Anthony grabbed Dwain's arm and spun him to face him. "When did you develop this sudden interest in her?"

"I don't know. I just sort of woke up one day and realized that I cared for her. Does that sound *narrisch*?"

Anthony shook his head. "No. It doesn't sound crazy at all."

Dwain leaned back against his buggy. "Do you think she'd go out with me if I asked?"

"I think so."

"I feel like I'm meant to be with her, and the feeling came out of nowhere. Maybe God is leading me to her." He yanked open the door to his buggy.

Anthony understood because his feelings for Kathryn had also caught him unawares. As he looked back toward Kathryn's porch, he felt called to ask her father's permission to date her. But first he had to find out if she would even consider the idea. If she said no, he'd be crushed — and he'd be sad to lose her as a friend too.

But his heart skipped a beat at the idea of

her saying yes. Perhaps there was a chance that they could be together. And maybe, just maybe, he'd have a chance to plan for a future with his beautiful friend if the Lord saw fit.

CHAPTER TWO

"I think Dwain likes me," Maria gushed after Kathryn stepped back into the kitchen. "He's so handsome — especially his *schee* green eyes. And he's so nice and funny."

Kathryn blinked as she studied her best friend. Fred sat down beside her and divided a look between Kathryn and Maria. Kathryn glanced behind her and noticed that *Mamm* had disappeared. She could hear her parents talking softly in the family room as she took a step closer to Maria. "You like Dwain?"

Maria bit her lower lip as she shrugged. "Why not? He goes out of his way to talk to me at church and at youth group gatherings. I think he would be a nice boyfriend." She elbowed Kathryn in the side. "What about you and Anthony? You seemed to be getting awfully close today."

Kathryn peeked toward the doorway as her parents' voices had seemed to come closer to the kitchen. "I don't know . . ." She tried to wave off Maria's comments.

"Are you kidding? I saw him flirting with you at the snack table more than once today. And he and Dwain didn't have to stay and help us clean up, but they did. It's obvious that they're up to something." Maria's eyes widened. "Wouldn't it be amazing if Dwain asked me out, and Anthony asked you out? The four of us could go on dates together." Then Maria started counting off on her fingers. "We could go on picnics, go swimming, have dinners together . . ."

Then Kathryn's parents stepped into the kitchen, and her father's frosty expression sent a chill down her back. "Maria, we'll talk about this later, okay?" Kathryn said quickly.

Maria's brow furrowed, and she glanced over her shoulder at Kathryn's parents before looking back at Kathryn. "I suppose I should get going. It's late." Her pretty smile returned as she waved at Kathryn's parents. "Have a *gut* evening."

"You too," *Mamm* said.

Maria gave Fred a pat on the head, gathered up her purse and tote bag, and then retrieved her flashlight from the bottom of her bag. "See you soon."

Kathryn let Fred out the door, and he ran

off to do his business. Then she walked Maria out to the porch and gave her a quick hug. "*Danki* for helping me today."

"Gern gschehne." Maria's brow pinched once again. "Is everything okay?"

"*Ya.* Why?"

"I don't know." Maria looked back toward the house. "I know your *dat* is serious, but he seems almost annoyed tonight. Did something happen?"

"He just gets that way when we have youth gatherings at our *haus.* He's always anxious to get to bed since he has to get up early to take care of the cows. I'm certain your *dat* is the same way." She hoped her response was believable.

"Right. Of course." Seemingly satisfied with that explanation, Maria hefted her tote bag and purse higher on her shoulder. *"Gut nacht."*

"Be safe walking home."

Maria headed down the rock driveway toward the street, the beam from her flashlight bumping along the ground as she walked. Fred ran back up the porch steps and joined Kathryn.

Kathryn squared her shoulders and turned back toward the door, where Fred sat looking in through the screen. Her hands trembled as she awaited another lecture. Her father had warned her once before to stay away from Anthony Gingerich.

She tried to steel herself. Maybe this time, she could convince *Dat* that Anthony was worthy of a chance to prove himself as her friend and possibly more.

Kathryn's confidence began to crumble when she entered the kitchen, and her gaze landed on her parents sitting at the table, her father with a disapproving frown.

"Sit, Kathryn," *Dat* barked.

Mamm shot Kathryn a sympathetic look as Kathryn dropped into a chair across from her father. Fred walked over to his bowls and began noisily lapping up water.

"Ya, Dat?" Kathryn longed for the quiver in her voice to disappear. "What did you want to talk about?"

Dat rubbed his graying brown beard. "I overheard your conversation with Maria earlier. She implied that you have feelings for Anthony Gingerich."

Kathryn opened her mouth to respond and glanced at her mother, who frowned.

"Do you care for Anthony?" *Dat* asked, his dark eyes assessing her.

"We've been *freinden* our whole lives." She looked down at the tabletop and began drawing invisible circles on the wood-grain with her fingernail. "We get along well, and

I enjoy his company." She took a deep breath and then looked up at her father again. "I do care for him, and I think he might care for me."

Dat huffed. "You know I don't approve of Anthony Gingerich's occupation, and I wouldn't allow you to date him."

Kathryn held her hands up. "Could we please discuss this, *Dat*? You know Anthony's family. His *schweschder* runs her own business. They're all hardworking people. Just because they don't live on a farm doesn't mean they aren't truly Amish."

Mamm shot her a warning look as *Dat*'s expression hardened.

"Their gazebo business is frivolous and caters to *English* people. Selling *kaffi* and donuts to tourists is the same. I can't respect it." He gestured around the kitchen. "Taking care of animals and the land is what we're called to do."

He tapped his finger on the tabletop for emphasis. "But building impractical gazebos and patio furniture for *Englishers* is not God's work. I will not allow you to waste your time on a man like him."

Disappointment clogged her throat, and she tried to clear it. "*Dat,* Anthony is a *gut* man." Her voice quavered. "He's a talented carpenter, and he works hard alongside his *dat* and Micah. He's not a frivolous person, and I know he feels he's doing what he's called to do with his life."

Dat shook his head. "You will not see him. End of discussion."

"But what if I feel called to be with him? What if God wills it for me to date him and have a future with him?"

"Kathryn . . ." *Mamm*'s warning came in a whisper. "You need to stop."

"You should listen to your *mamm,*" *Dat* snapped. "You will not disobey me by pursuing a relationship with Anthony. You need to look for a man who does God's work. I can't allow my only *kind* to marry a man whose job is worldly."

He pushed his chair back and stood, his expression suddenly calm as if he hadn't just ripped Kathryn's dreams to shreds. "I'm going to bed. We need to be up early to work."

"I'll be there in a moment, Nelson," *Mamm* said.

Dat picked up a nearby lantern and left the kitchen, his boots echoing as he made his way up the stairs toward the second floor.

Kathryn clasped her hands together and tried to calm her jangling nerves.

Mamm reached across the table and

touched Kathryn's arm. "Are you okay?"

"Ya." Kathryn nodded, but inside her heart was breaking.

"You have to obey your *dat.*"

"I know."

"He only wants what's best for you. Anthony is a nice young man, but you'll find someone who better suits your *dat*'s idea of what a Plain man should be."

Kathryn pursed her lips as she studied her mother's serious expression. *Mamm* would never go against *Dat*'s wishes, and normally, neither would Kathryn.

But this decision felt wrong to the depth of her core.

"Get some sleep." *Mamm* pushed her chair back and stood. "It's late, *mei liewe.* And tomorrow is laundry day."

"Ya, Mamm." Kathryn stood and picked up a lantern from the counter. "*Kumm,* Fred."

The dog scampered to life, his nails clicking on the linoleum as he followed Kathryn and her mother to the stairs.

As they headed to the second floor, Kathryn sent up a quick, silent prayer:

Lord, I believe in my heart that Anthony and I might be called to be more than freinden. *Help us find a way to be together if that's your will.*

When she reached her bedroom door, she said goodnight to her mother and then slipped inside. Fred plopped down onto his cushion, and Kathryn sank down on the edge of her bed. As she hugged her arms to her chest and closed her eyes, Anthony's handsome, smiling face and bright blue eyes filled her mind. With God's help, they would be together. She would have faith.

"With God all things are possible, right, Fred?" she whispered before gathering up her nightclothes.

Fred glanced over at her and set his chin on his paw.

"Right," she said as she got ready for bed.

Anthony stowed his horse and buggy in the barn and then headed toward the back porch of the large farmhouse where he'd been born and raised. The bright beam of the flashlight guided his way.

He glanced up at the sky and marveled at the bright stars glittering above him and smiled. It had been the perfect day. He looked down at the container of cookies and his chest warmed. He couldn't wait to see Kathryn again.

When he spotted a warm, yellow glow on the porch, he quickened his steps and waved the container of cookies in greeting to his older sister, Bethany, and her boyfriend, Micah, sitting on a glider together.

"Wie geht's!" Anthony called.

"You're finally home," Bethany said. "How was the youth gathering?"

At twenty-four, Bethany was four years older than Anthony. While he had many friends who complained about their siblings, Anthony could count on one hand the times that he and his sister had argued. With her golden-blonde hair, clear blue eyes, and chatty demeanor, she was as bright and sunny as a June day, and Anthony was grateful God had blessed him with her for his sister.

"It was *gut.*" Anthony climbed the steps and leaned back against the railing. "We played volleyball and visited. Then I stayed to help clean up."

Micah grinned as he pointed at the container. "Did you bring us snacks?"

"Uh. Well, I don't have many to share." Why hadn't he just gone in the house and avoided having to share his special cookies from Kathryn?

Micah clucked his tongue and then leaned over toward Bethany. "Did you hear that, Bethany? Anthony doesn't want to share his snacks. I'm offended."

Bethany grinned at Micah. "I am too. I'm

not going to share my leftover donuts from the Coffee Corner with him anymore."

Anthony groaned. "You two are so dramatic."

"That's why we're together," his sister quipped while gazing at Micah.

Anthony took in the love they had in their eyes for each other, and he felt a twinge of jealousy. If only Kathryn would look at him that way. Was such a thing even possible?

Micah was three years older than Bethany, and they had started dating officially a couple of months ago. After his grandfather died, Micah had discovered that his grandfather's patio furniture business — the business they had shared — was drowning in debt. He had considered selling the business and moving away, but Bethany convinced him to combine his patio furniture business with the gazebo business that Anthony and their father had built. Now sales were booming, and Bethany and Micah's relationship also seemed to be moving along. Anthony expected his sister to be engaged soon.

Anthony set his flashlight on the porch railing and then opened the container. "Here. You can each have one. Just one."

"Oh!" Bethany rubbed her hands together

as he held out the container. "I love oatmeal raisin."

"My favorite," Micah said.

"They're mine, too, so don't eat them all," Anthony warned.

Bethany and Micah each chose a cookie and then took a bite. Then they gasped and smiled.

"Amazing," Bethany said.

"The best I've ever had," Micah said, and Bethany shot him a look. "Other than yours, of course."

Anthony snickered and then replaced the lid.

"Who made them?" Bethany asked.

"Kathryn." Anthony tried to hold back his smile as he said her name.

"How nice." Bethany finished the cookie. "Did she host the gathering today?"

Anthony nodded and picked up his flashlight.

"How's she doing?" Bethany asked.

"Fine." He nodded toward the door. "I'm going to get ready for bed. *Gut nacht.*"

Anthony stepped into the house. He headed through the mudroom and kitchen to the family room. When he found the house completely dark and quiet, he assumed his parents had already gone to bed.

With quiet steps, Anthony made his way

upstairs to his room. He set the tin on his dresser, opened the lid, and smiled as he pulled out another cookie. He took a bite and wondered if Kathryn was thinking of him tonight, just as he was thinking of her.

As Anthony showered and prepared to sleep, visions of Kathryn kept him company. When he crawled into bed, he tried to turn his thoughts away — but her pretty face filled his mind as he waited for sleep to find him.

Chapter Three

The following morning, *Mamm* handed Kathryn a pair of *Dat*'s trousers, and Kathryn pulled a couple of clothespins out of her apron pocket before hanging them on the line.

As she pushed the line farther out, she glanced up at the blue, cloudless sky and squinted at the bright sunlight. Across the yard, Fred rolled around in the grass and then settled onto his side. If only Kathryn's life were as easy as Fred's.

The early-morning birds serenaded her as her thoughts turned to her disappointing conversation with her father. She'd stayed awake last night trying to think of ways to change her father's mind about Anthony, but she'd tossed and turned and come up empty.

Kathryn took a damp shirt from her mother and hung it on the line. Then she paused. "*Mamm,* could I ask you a question?"

"Of course." *Mamm*'s expression was warm.

"Why is *Dat* so hard on Anthony's family's businesses?" She reached for more laundry and then moved along while awaiting her mother's response.

"I think it's just how your *Dat* was raised. He comes from a long line of dairy farmers. This land has been in his family for generations, and his *dat* believed that farming was God's work."

"But why isn't being a carpenter God's work? Aren't we called to use the gifts that God gives us? Anthony and his *dat* are both skilled woodworkers, and they're using their gifts the way they know best. Micah is the same. And *Dat* said that Bethany's work isn't worthy either. She has the gift of not only making the donuts and *kaffi* but also talking to the customers. She's never met a stranger, and she brings joy to the people who give her their business. I've seen her have conversations with people who look as if they're having a terrible day. She makes them smile and brings some light into their lives."

Mamm clucked her tongue. "I understand what you're saying, but we have to respect your *dat.* He is the head of our family, and we have to abide by his rules."

"What if I don't agree with his rules?" Kathryn muttered as she hung another one of her father's shirts on the line.

"Kathryn!" *Mamm* snapped. "You need to stop talking that way. You've always been a dutiful *dochder.* Don't let this situation change you."

"I won't." She felt her shoulders droop as she reached into her apron pocket for more pins.

She couldn't even get her mother to be on her side, but she'd find a way. She just hoped that Anthony cared for her the way that she cared for him. If not, then all of her hopes and prayers were in vain.

Anthony swiped his hand across his sweaty brow Friday afternoon as he walked around the large cinder block shop on his father's property. He walked past the line of work-benches cluttered with tools and the large pieces of wood that would become the gazebos their customers had ordered. The sweet, familiar scent of cedar and sawdust filled his lungs.

Dat had left to go to town earlier in the day to talk to one of the business owners who sent orders for his customers, and

Anthony didn't expect him to be back for at least another hour.

Anthony walked past the diagrams and posters of gazebos on the wall and stopped by the large cooler he kept stocked with cold bottles of water on hot days like today. After grabbing two bottles, he entered the back part of the shop, where Micah worked on sanding a large piece of wood that looked as if it would become one of his benches.

"How's it going?" Anthony asked as he hopped up on a nearby stool.

"Gut." Micah stood up tall and swiped the back of his arm across his forehead. "Hot."

Anthony held out a bottle of water. "Need a drink?"

"Danki." Micah took the bottle and sat on another stool. "Is your *dat* back?"

"Not yet. He said he might stop for supplies after his meeting, so I assumed he'd be a while." Anthony studied his bottle of water as the questions he'd wanted to ask Micah all week filled his mind again. He looked up and found Micah watching him. "Micah, since you're the expert on this . . . How do you know when it's the right time to ask for a father's permission to ask out a *maedel*?"

Micah let out a bark of laughter that echoed through the shop, and Anthony cringed as his face burned hot. He took a long drink of the cold water, hoping to cool his humiliation.

"You're asking me for dating advice?" Micah pointed to himself. "I am the worst person to ask. You know what I put Bethany through earlier this year. You were there when she found me in my shop after a night of drowning myself in my sorrows. I'm still astounded that she gave me another chance."

Anthony took another drink of water. "You made amends for your sins, completed your shunning, and then you and Bethany were able to build a relationship together with God's help."

Micah nodded and then took a long drink of water. "That is true."

They were both silent for a moment, and Anthony's embarrassment only grew.

"Who's the *maedel*?" Micah asked.

Anthony hesitated.

"Is it Kathryn?"

"How did you know?"

Micah grinned. "The *kichlin* that you refused to share on Sunday were my first clue."

"I shared a few. I just didn't want to share *all* of them." Anthony smiled. "*Ya,* it's Kathryn. I've known her my whole life, but recently I started seeing her in a new light. Now I want to be more than just her *freind*, but . . ." He looked down at his lap. "I don't know how to make the transition from *freinden* to something more. How do I know if she's even interested in me that way?"

"Follow your heart. And rely on God. Pray about it and see where he leads you. That's what I did, and I couldn't be happier."

Anthony nodded. *"Ya."* He stood. "Well, I better get back to work. Thanks, Micah." He started for the door.

"Hey, Anthony," Micah called, and he spun to face him. "If she makes you *kichlin*, I would imagine she cares about you too. *Maed* like to bake for the men they care for. Your *schweschder* did for me. You came with her when she delivered meals to me, remember?"

"That's true." Hope lit in Anthony's chest.

"It will all work out."

Anthony smiled as he made his way back to the front of the shop. He hoped Micah was right.

Later than afternoon, Dwain stepped into the workshop. "Hey, Anthony!" he called out.

"Dwain." Anthony stopped painting a picket for a gazebo and walked over to him.

"What are you doing here?"

"I forgot to grab my lunch this morning, so I had to run home. I thought I'd stop by on my way back to the store." He looked past Anthony and waved. "Hello, Harvey."

"Good to see you, Dwain," *Dat* said before returning to painting.

"How's your week been?" Anthony asked as they walked to the door and stepped outside into the hot June afternoon air.

"Gut." Dwain grinned. "I think I'm going to ask Maria to ride home with me after the youth gathering on Sunday."

"Really?"

"*Ya,* I've been thinking about her all week, and I feel led to ask her out." He grimaced. "I just hope her *dat* gives me permission."

"Please." Anthony snorted and gave Dwain's shoulder a push. "Why would he say no? We've all been in the same church district our whole lives. We all grew up together. Her *dat* knows you're a *gut* man."

Dwain rocked back on his heels. "We'll see."

Anthony thought about his conversation with Micah earlier in the day, and he squared his shoulders. He was ready to confess his feelings about Kathryn to his best friend. "Speaking of *maed,* I'm thinking about asking Kathryn out too."

Dwain's eyes widened. "You and Kathryn?"

"Maybe." Anthony rubbed at a tight muscle in his neck. "I care about her, and I'm hoping she cares about me."

"That's fantastic news." Dwain rubbed his hands together. "If this all works out, we could double date!"

"*Ya,* it would be great."

And it certainly would be.

On Sunday afternoon, it was the Glick family's turn to host the church service in their barn, and Kathryn had helped the women serve the meal before she sat down to eat with Maria and the rest of her girlfriends.

After helping clean up the dishes, she told her mother she was going to go out with her friends and then hurried into the warm June afternoon air to head to the youth gathering.

She'd anxiously waited for Sunday to come in hopes that Anthony might ask her to ride with him to the gathering and then offer her a ride home. Normally an offer of a ride home would lead to dating, and her stomach dipped at the thought!

Kathryn quickened her steps when she spotted Maria standing with Dwain and

Anthony by the line of horses and buggies near the pasture fence. She shielded her eyes from the bright sunlight as she approached them.

"Hi, Kathryn." Anthony gave her a wide smile, and his handsome face lit up like the sun above them.

"Hi." She tried to stop her heart from beating out of her chest as she smiled at him. "Are you heading to Gretchen King's *haus* for the gathering?"

"We were just talking about it," Dwain said.

"Are you going?" Anthony asked Kathryn as he leaned back against the fence.

"I am." She held her breath, waiting for him to offer her a ride.

"Great." He pushed himself off of the fence. "I'll see you there." Then he started toward his horse and buggy.

Kathryn's lips pressed into a thin line as Anthony stopped in front of a buggy and began talking to one of his friends. Her shoulders slumped, and her hopes of riding with him were dashed.

Kathryn heard someone call her name and spun around. She froze when she found her father glaring at her while beckoning her to walk over to where he stood with her mother next to their buggy.

She slowly made her way over to her parents as worry gripped her. *"Ya, Dat?"*

"What did I tell you about staying away from Anthony Gingerich?" he hissed through clenched teeth.

"We were only discussing going to the youth gathering." With a shaky hand, she gestured toward the group of young people climbing into their buggies. "We're all heading to Gretchen King's *haus* to —"

"I've told you to stay away from him. You need to limit your time with him, or you'll have to stop going to youth group."

Kathryn's eyes burned with anger and humiliation as she looked around, hoping her friends couldn't overhear them. Thankfully, Anthony, Maria, and Dwain were engrossed in their own conversations and didn't seem to notice her. "*Dat,* I've known them my whole life."

"That doesn't matter." He shook his head. "I spoke to my cousin Arlan in Lititz earlier this week, and he told me about a young farmer out there named Jeremiah Fisher who is single and looking for a *fraa.* I'd like you to meet him. He'd be a *gut* match for you."

Kathryn stared at him as her heart began to pound. "You're trying to set me up with a farmer?"

"Kathryn . . ." *Mamm* warned.

"If you want to keep coming to these Sunday gatherings, then I want you to promise me that you'll agree to meet Jeremiah," *Dat* said.

Kathryn glanced behind her to where Maria smiled up at Dwain, who seemed just as smitten with her. Why couldn't her father allow her to choose her own boyfriend instead of interfering? She wanted to be as happy as Maria seemed to be.

Squaring her shoulders, she looked back at her father. She'd agree to meet Jeremiah just so she could have a chance to talk to Anthony again. "Okay. I'll meet him."

"Gut."

"I'm going to go see *mei freinden* now."

"Fine," *Dat* said.

With frustration pressing down on her shoulders, Kathryn made her way back to where Maria and Dwain stood together. She hoped she could get Maria alone to tell her what her father had just said.

"Do you want a ride to the gathering?" Dwain asked Maria.

"*Ya,* that would be nice," Maria gushed.

Kathryn turned back toward where Anthony stood laughing while his friend seemed to share a story. Now she was stuck without a ride. She couldn't possibly ask

Anthony, either, for fear of her father seeing them together.

"Could Kathryn ride with us?" Maria asked.

Kathryn swallowed a groan. She didn't want to interfere with Maria and Dwain's time.

"Sure." Dwain's smile seemed forced as he turned toward Kathryn. "That would be fine."

"Oh no." She shook her head as she stepped away. "I'll find a ride." She spun and spotted Gretchen standing with a few of their other friends. "I can go ask Gretchen if —"

"No, no." Maria grabbed Kathryn's arm and gave it a tug. "Ride with us."

"But I don't want to be in the way." Kathryn tried to convey her thoughts with her expression.

"Ride with us," Maria said, emphasizing her words. "I insist."

Kathryn felt her brow pinch as her friend seemed to plead with her. Why would Maria want Kathryn to intrude on their time together?

"Let's go." Maria took Kathryn's arm and then smiled at Dwain. "*Danki* for giving us a ride."

"Happy to do it." Dwain opened the buggy's passenger side door.

Kathryn peeked over her shoulder at Anthony one last time and found him still talking to his friend. Her heart crumbled as she recalled what her father had said. Would he force her to marry this stranger named Jeremiah? How would she ever get over her feelings for Anthony?

Reluctantly, she climbed into the back of the buggy as Maria took her place beside Dwain. Kathryn stared out the back while Maria and Dwain discussed the weather and their busy weeks during the ride to Gretchen's farm.

While she was happy to hear her best friend and Dwain bond during the ride, her heart ached at the memory of how easily Anthony had walked away from her. Between her father's ultimatum and the way Anthony had dismissed her, she was certain her heart was doomed.

Before long, she spotted Gretchen's family farm ahead. She pushed her disappointed thoughts away and took a deep breath. She would ignore Anthony and try to forget her father's threat. Instead, she would spend her time today helping Gretchen with the snacks and enjoying the other women's company.

Kathryn was strong. She could make it

through this afternoon and hopefully keep her spirit intact.

Chapter Four

Anthony glanced around the pasture as he walked up toward Gretchen's house after stowing his horse and buggy. He felt like a complete idiot for riding to the youth gathering alone.

He'd spent the entire church service trying to keep his eyes from watching Kathryn while she sat beside Maria in the unmarried women's section of the congregation. His eyes kept defying him and finding her, locking on her beautiful face as she stared down at her hymnal or at the bishop. It was as if an invisible force was pulling him to her, and his feelings for her seemed to grow each time he saw her.

While he ate lunch with Dwain and the rest of their friends, he'd convinced himself that he was going to be brave and ask Kathryn to ride with him to the youth gathering. He'd hoped to talk to her after he finished his lunch, but she had rushed off to the kitchen with the rest of the women. He waited by the pasture fence and made small talk with Dwain and a few friends while they waited for the women to finish their lunch.

When Kathryn had finally approached him while he talked to Dwain and Maria, Anthony had thought he was ready to ask her. He'd mentally prepared what he was going to say, but his courage had dissolved when he looked into her pretty brown eyes. He couldn't form the words.

By the time he finally mustered up his courage, he had missed his opportunity. Kathryn was busy speaking to her father, and before long, she was already leaving with Dwain and Maria.

You're a coward, Anthony!

Now he was determined to make it up to her. If he moved quickly enough, maybe he could talk to her around the snack table again. So long as another man didn't have the chance to talk to her in his place!

Anthony looked toward the field where two volleyball nets had been set up and two groups of players had formed. He searched the sea of faces for Kathryn but didn't spot her.

He looked over toward a few smaller groups of young people and found Dwain and Maria sitting by a tree together and sharing a plate of snacks. He smiled. His friend had planned to seek out Maria, and it looked as if things were going well.

Now, he had to find Kathryn.

He'd thought he'd seen her riding in Dwain's buggy, but what if he'd been wrong? What if she'd decided to go home instead of going to the youth gathering? Worry threaded through him.

Turning toward the house, Anthony spotted a table of snacks. When he caught a glimpse of a young woman in a pink dress walking up the back-porch steps, he picked up speed. His pulse kept pace with his feet as he dashed toward the porch.

"Kathryn!" he called.

The young woman stopped and turned toward him. And when he found himself face-to-face with Kathryn, the knots in his shoulders began to relax.

"Hi, Anthony." Her pretty expression seemed full of hesitation as she stood on the top step. "I'm going to bring out more snacks."

"Do you need help?"

She shrugged, and her expression softened. "Sure."

"Great." He jogged up the steps and followed her into the kitchen, where Gretchen and a few of their friends were busy putting food into bowls and onto platters.

Anthony waved to the women and then picked up two platters of cookies. He stood by the door and waited while Kathryn shook two bags of potato chips into a large bowl and then picked up a container of dip.

He studied her face, admiring her pink lips and the way her beautiful face lit up when she smiled and laughed. She was stunning. Why had it taken him so long to notice?

He tried to imagine having Kathryn by his side as his girlfriend — riding places together in his buggy and sitting on the glider on her parents' porch late at night while sharing secrets, holding hands, and maybe stealing kisses. His heart turned over in his chest.

He prayed he could find the courage to ask her and then be blessed with her response of yes.

Kathryn carried the bowl of chips and dip over to him. "Think you could get the door?"

"Of course!" Balancing the trays of cookies in one hand, Anthony wrenched open the screen door and pushed it open wide with his arm. He held it while Kathryn moved past him and then down the porch steps.

He followed her down to the tables, where they placed the food in an empty spot.

"Are you hungry?" she asked him.

He shrugged. "A little." He pointed to the tray of chocolate chip cookies. "They smell *gut.*"

"They sure do." She handed him a plate. "Take a few."

He filled his plate with a few cookies, along with some chips and popcorn. She did the same and then walked over to an empty cluster of folding chairs.

"Would you like to sit?" he asked.

"Sure." She seemed hesitant again, almost uncomfortable, as they sat down beside each other.

He studied her expression as she tasted a cookie. She kept her gaze focused on her plate, and when she didn't seem anxious to speak, Anthony began to worry. Had something changed between them? Had he done something to upset her?

"How was your week?" he asked, hoping to start a conversation.

She finished chewing and then wiped her mouth with a paper napkin. "It was *gut* and busy. I did the usual chores — laundry, cleaning, sewing, and cooking." She took a bite of another cookie and then swallowed. "How was yours?"

"Very busy. *Mei dat* received a contract for two gazebos and several pieces of patio furniture for a new retirement home that's going to be built in Lancaster."

"Wow." Her pretty caramel eyes sparkled. "That's fantastic."

"Danki." He popped a chip into his mouth.

"What kind of patio furniture do they want?"

"They're looking for benches, picnic tables, and rockers." He talked on about their order, and she seemed to listen with interest. Still, he worried about boring her.

"I saw Maria and Dwain sitting over by the trees," he told her when he finished talking about their big order. He pointed in the direction of the trees.

"I know." She gave a little sigh, which piqued his interest. "They're getting awfully close."

He opened his mouth to ask her opinion on their best friends' budding relationship, but she cut him off by standing and reaching for his empty plate.

"Would you like to play volleyball?" she asked.

"I'd love to."

"Great." She dropped their plates into a nearby trash can. "Let's go."

He smiled as they walked to where their

friends were gathered by the two volleyball nets. Soon they were picked to be on the same team, and Anthony grinned as they began playing together.

Time disappeared as they played, laughing and teasing each other as they jumped for the ball. He couldn't wait to ask her to be his girlfriend so that they could spend more time together like this.

The afternoon went by too quickly as Kathryn enjoyed every minute playing volleyball with Anthony by her side. When it was time to give another team a chance to play, they sat on the grass and talked with their friends.

Kathryn had a difficult time taking her eyes off Anthony as he talked. She enjoyed the warm, rich sound of his infectious laugh and the way his bright blue eyes glinted in the afternoon sun. She studied his strong jaw and his chiseled cheekbones. He was the most handsome man she had ever known. She tried to imagine having him by her side forever.

What she loved most about Anthony was that he was the complete opposite of her father. Anthony was warm, kind, and thoughtful. When she was with him, she felt like she could be herself and not worry about upsetting him or being corrected for doing or saying something wrong.

She chided herself at such indulgent thoughts. Every time her imagination strayed toward Anthony, she had to ignore her father's words. She worried he would insist she marry a farmer — possibly this stranger that his cousin knew — and the chances of Kathryn changing her father's mind seemed less and less likely every day.

But here Anthony was — talking to her, laughing with her, making her feel special. And she could never have him. Chagrin threatened to swallow her whole.

Why was she punishing herself by allowing her heart to get attached to him? She needed to put distance between them. She needed to tell him the truth. Her hands trembled at the thought of telling him she wasn't permitted to spend time with him anymore, especially after so many years of friendship.

The sun began to set, and the women started walking toward the house while a group of men began taking down the volleyball nets.

"I guess it's time to clean up." Kathryn stood and swiped her hands down her dress and apron to wipe off the grass.

She hesitated as Anthony stood and

brushed his hands down his trousers. Now was the perfect time to tell him that her father had forbade her from being his friend. But when she opened her mouth, she froze. The words wouldn't come.

"I'll help them with the nets," he said.

"Okay." Kathryn made her way up to the house and carried in a few empty trays before helping to dry the clean serving trays. She placed the last serving tray in the cabinet as Maria sidled up to her.

"Kathryn!" Maria grabbed Kathryn's arm and pulled her over to an empty corner of the kitchen. "Dwain asked me to ride home with him."

"Oh. That's so exciting." Kathryn was happy for her friend.

Maria's smile faltered. "Will you be okay to find a ride home?"

"Of course."

Maria's expression became hopeful. "Maybe Anthony will ask you if you want a ride."

"I doubt that." Dat *would be so angry!*

"I'll let you know what happens." Maria gave her a quick hug.

"You go have fun." Kathryn gave Gretchen the dish towel and thanked her for hosting the youth gathering before walking outside with Maria.

■ ■ ■ ■

"I asked Maria to ride home with me," Dwain told Anthony as they walked back toward the house.

They had helped stow the volleyball equipment and then hitched up their horses and buggies.

"Are you going to ask her out?" Anthony asked.

"Not yet. I still need to talk to her father and ask permission. I'm hoping to go see him sometime this week since I didn't get a chance to talk to him at church today."

"That's *wunderbaar.*" Anthony looked toward the porch, where Kathryn and Maria stood talking with a group of friends.

Dwain bumped Anthony's arm. "You should ask if you can drive her home. We brought her here, so I know she'll need a ride."

Anthony sucked in a breath. "You're right. I need to just do it. Then I'll find out if she really wants to date me."

Dwain snorted. "I think it's obvious. She seemed to hang on your every word earlier."

Had Dwain imagined that?

"You need to ask her out before someone else does," Dwain said.

Anthony was stuck on that for a moment. How would he feel if Kathryn decided to date someone else? He'd be crushed!

Dwain was right. It was now or never. Kathryn had always been important to him, and he had to act before she slipped through his fingers.

Maria walked down the porch steps and sauntered over to them. She smiled at Anthony and then turned to Dwain. "Are you ready to go home?"

"Ya." He smiled at Anthony. "Have a *gut* week."

"You too."

Anthony turned back toward the porch, but Kathryn was gone. He spun and found her walking with her friend Ruthie and Ruthie's older brother, Leroy. Anthony started toward them and then stopped when Kathryn climbed into the back of Leroy's buggy.

Anthony silently chastised himself. He had missed his chance yet again.

Chapter Five

"Dwain came to see me last night," Maria announced Thursday morning.

She and Kathryn walked side by side on the sidewalk down Old Philadelphia Pike in Bird-in-Hand toward their favorite fabric store. It was another warm, beautiful June day with the sun kissing their cheeks and the sky a sparkling blue above them.

"And . . ." Kathryn coaxed her.

Cars drove by on the road, and Kathryn looked up as they moved past her favorite bookstore and then approached a gift shop that sold Amish Country souvenirs such as dolls, quilts, horse and buggy figurines, and T-shirts.

Maria stopped and faced Kathryn in front of the ice cream shop. The delicious smells of ice cream invaded Kathryn's senses, causing her stomach to growl.

Then Maria's face broke into a wide grin. "He asked me out."

Kathryn gasped and then pulled her best friend in for a hug. "That is amazing! I'm so *froh* for you!"

"Danki." Maria sighed. "I'm so *froh* too."

"That is *wunderbaar.* When did he ask your *dat*?"

"He said he stopped by the farm earlier in the day. I must have been inside doing chores. After *mei dat* said yes, Dwain came by again later in the evening. I was so surprised." She started walking toward the fabric store again. "How are things with Anthony?"

Kathryn shrugged. "There's really nothing to tell."

"What do you mean?" Maria asked as they reached the entrance to Lydia's Fabrics.

"We talked on Sunday at Gretchen's, and that was it. I guess I'll see him at the youth gathering Sunday."

"Wait a minute." Maria stopped Kathryn and motioned for her to step away from the door. "You spoke to him at Gretchen's, but he didn't give you a ride home?"

Kathryn shook her head. "I got a ride from Ruthie and Leroy."

Maria blinked. "He didn't ask you if you wanted a ride home?"

"No." Kathryn fingered the strap of her purse. "He must only want to be *freinden,* and I've decided I'm okay with it."

"That doesn't make any sense to me."

"It's for the best, really." Anxious for a change of subject, Kathryn nodded toward the store. "Come on. Let's do our shopping."

They headed into the store and browsed the prints and cotton broadcloth until they found the fabric and notions they needed. After they paid for their supplies, they headed back outside. Kathryn's eyes moved to the long, one-story building that housed the Bird-in-Hand Marketplace across the street.

"Do you need to go home soon?" Kathryn asked Maria.

"No, I have some time."

"Then why don't we get a cup of *kaffi* and a donut at Bethany's booth in the marketplace?"

"*Ya.* That would be a treat," Maria agreed. "She has the best flavored *kaffi* around."

Kathryn and Maria waited for the cars to clear and then crossed the street. They walked past the line of horses and buggies sitting at the back of the parking lot and then past the lines of cars clogging the spaces.

"This place is always busy," Kathryn commented.

"That's true."

They made their way up the front steps, passing the planters full of colorful, cheery flowers that seemed to smile up at the sun above them. Kathryn stepped into the marketplace behind Maria, and delectable smells of chocolate and coffee assaulted her senses. Conversations buzzed around them as Amish and *Englisher* customers visited the different booths.

They ambled down the center aisle, past a lunch meat counter, a candy booth, and a jewelry booth. They weaved past a group of customers standing by the used book booth and then into the Coffee Corner, where customers sat at high-top tables while eating donuts and drinking coffee.

Kathryn and Maria made their way to the counter, where Bethany handed a teenage Amish couple their cups of coffee and strawberry iced donuts.

Kathryn peered at the shelves of donuts, taking in the flavors — cinnamon sugar, chocolate, strawberry iced, chocolate iced with sprinkles, vanilla iced with sprinkles, and plain glazed. "The donuts look and smell delectable," she muttered.

"I know." Maria sighed. "I want one of each."

"Me too." Then Kathryn looked up at the

blackboard where Bethany had written today's specials — coconut almond, bananas foster, butter pecan, regular, and decaf. "And the flavored *kaffi* sounds just as *wunderbaar.* Which one should we have?"

"I want to try the coconut almond," Maria said.

"I will too." Kathryn pulled out her wallet.

The teenagers gathered up their coffee and donuts and then moved to a nearby table, where they hopped up on the stools and sat.

"Kathryn! Maria!" Bethany greeted them with her usual bright smile. *"Wie geht's?"*

"We're doing well," Kathryn said. "We were out shopping and thought we'd stop by for some *kaffi* and a donut."

"Great. What would you like?" Bethany made a sweeping gesture toward the shelves of donuts and the blackboard listing the specials.

"I'd like a chocolate iced donut with sprinkles and a cup of coconut almond *kaffi,*" Kathryn said.

"Make that two, please," Maria said.

"Coming right up." Bethany poured the coffee and handed them the cups. Then she moved to the shelves and set two donuts on waxed paper.

After paying, Kathryn and Maria thanked Bethany, added creamer and sweetener to their cups, and snapped on a lid. Then they found the last empty table. Kathryn sat facing the counter while Maria perched on the stool across from her.

Kathryn sipped the coffee and groaned. "It's so *gut.*"

"Bethany is amazing." Maria took a sip. "I don't know how she comes up with these flavors, but they are phenomenal. Her booth is always busy, and you can tell she loves it."

"Ya." Kathryn looked up at the counter as Bethany smiled and greeted a group of middle-aged *Englishers.*

"Running your own business takes a lot of work, and she's done such a great job. Her parents must be so proud of her."

Kathryn's eyes darted to Maria's as her father's words about Bethany's business filled her mind. How could her father not see how special and talented Bethany was and how her kindness reflected so well upon their community?

Maria leaned forward. "What is it? Did I say something wrong?"

"No." Kathryn shook her head and looked down at her donut. She picked it up and took a bite. Just like the coffee, it was delicious.

"Was iss letz?" Maria's pretty face filled with concern. "I can tell you're upset. Does it have something to do with Anthony?"

Kathryn shushed her and then looked up toward the counter, grateful that Bethany was still talking to customers and not aware of their conversation. "Let's not talk about him here, okay?"

"Why not?" Maria pressed her lips together. "You've cared about him for so long. What has changed?"

Kathryn gave a half shrug and took another bite of donut.

Maria sat up a little taller. "I think Anthony cares for you. Maybe you just need to give him a chance."

Kathryn confirmed Bethany was still busy with customers, then faced Maria once again. "It's more complicated than that." She took a sip of coffee and then another bite of donut.

"You like him, and I think he likes you. How is that complicated?"

Kathryn swallowed her donut and shook her head. "You have no idea."

Maria lifted an eyebrow. "I can't stand it when you talk in code. Just tell me what you're talking about."

"There's something I haven't told you about Anthony."

Maria looked past her, and her eyes widened. "Kath—"

"*Mei dat* thinks that Anthony's —"

"Kathryn," Maria hissed. "He's here! Stop talking."

"Don't tease me." Kathryn peeked over her shoulder as Anthony, his father, and Micah walked into the Coffee Corner and past the tables.

While his father and Micah continued to the counter to see Bethany, Anthony turned toward their table. Kathryn's cheeks felt as if they might explode when his eyes met hers and his handsome smile broke out on his face.

Oh no! Had he heard her talking about him?

"Kathryn." He sauntered over to them. After nodding a greeting to Maria, he turned his gorgeous blue eyes on her. "What brings you two here today?"

"We had to go to the fabric store." Kathryn pointed to the bag on the stool beside her and then felt like a complete *dummkopp.* Why had she pointed to her bag? And why did he make her so flustered? He'd never made her feel self-conscious before!

"Oh." He pointed to her cup. "Is that

coconut almond flavored?"

Kathryn nodded. "It is."

He grabbed his chest. "That's my favorite. I always appreciate when Bethany brings me home a cup."

Maria grinned at Kathryn, and Kathryn kicked her under the table.

"Ow." Maria glared at her before looking down at her half-eaten donut.

"Are you out getting supplies?" Kathryn asked.

"*Ya.* We also had to talk to one of our clients." Anthony glanced over his shoulder to where his *dat* and Micah spoke to Bethany. "Micah wanted to stop by to see Bethany, and I never turn down a cup of her *kaffi* or one of her donuts."

Kathryn took in the warm smile on Bethany's face as she listened to Micah speak. The love between them sent envy slithering through her. Oh, how she wanted to share a love like that with Anthony!

Then her envy transformed to disappointment and despair as she recalled how her father disapproved of him. Even if Anthony cared for her, they had no path forward.

"Anthony," Bethany called. "Would you like anything?"

"*Ya,* please," he answered. "A cup of coconut almond and a chocolate donut."

When his father and Micah glanced over at their table, Kathryn gave them a wave and then turned back to Anthony. "Well, it's a nice surprise running into you."

"It sure is." He leaned his elbow on the table and kept his eyes focused on Kathryn. "What are your plans for the rest of the day?"

"We're heading home after we finish our snack," Kathryn said. "I have chores to do."

"Me too," Maria chimed in.

Anthony's father walked up behind him and handed him his coffee and donut. "Are we ready to go?" he asked his father before taking a bite of the donut.

"*Ya,* I want to say good-bye to Bethany." Harvey, Anthony's father, nodded at Kathryn and Maria again. Then he returned to the counter, where Micah and Bethany seemed to be engrossed in a conversation.

"Well, I guess I have to go." Anthony sipped his coffee. "*Mei schweschder* makes the best *kaffi,* doesn't she?"

"She does," Kathryn agreed.

Harvey reappeared behind Anthony, and Anthony's smile faded slightly as he nodded at Kathryn and then Maria. "You two enjoy your *kaffi.*"

"Bye." Kathryn waved at the men as they headed toward the booth exit with Micah trailing behind them.

Kathryn groaned and covered her face with her hands after Anthony was gone. "Oh, I hope he didn't hear me."

"He didn't." Maria touched her arm. "He only looked at you while he spoke. I might as well have been invisible."

"Ugh." Kathryn took another sip of coffee to try to drown her anxiety.

"What are you upset about? It was obvious he didn't want to leave."

"Even if he does care for me, I can't date him."

"Why not?"

Kathryn ate the last crumbs of her donut while Maria stared at her. "*Mei dat* won't allow it. He doesn't approve of Anthony's family's business." She felt a cold lump form in her chest as she said the words aloud.

Maria blinked and then her brow furrowed. "What do you mean?"

While staring down at the empty plate, Kathryn kept her voice soft as she explained the conversations she'd had with her *dat*. "He says I'm not allowed to date a man with a frivolous job."

She glanced up at Bethany and found her waiting on another customer. "He also said that Bethany's job is frivolous."

"You're kidding." A look of surprise rippled over Maria's face.

"No, but I wish I were." Kathryn sighed. "As much as I tried to change his mind, he shut me down and told me that his words were final. *Mei mamm* said the same thing when I tried to get her to help me convince *Dat* to change his mind."

She rested her elbow on the table and then her chin in her hand. "To make matters worse, *mei dat* wants me to stay away from Anthony, and he wants me to meet a farmer named Jeremiah who lives in Lititz. *Dat* thinks Jeremiah will be a good husband for me."

Maria gasped. "Your *dat* is going to force you to date a farmer from Lititz?"

"Ya." Kathryn nodded as despair wafted over her. "So, it really doesn't matter if Anthony cares for me or not since I can't date him."

Maria blinked and leaned forward. "Why didn't you tell me?"

"I guess I was in denial. I kept thinking that maybe Anthony would tell me that he cared about me and then we could convince *mei dat* to allow us to be together. But my hope has dwindled. *Mei dat* is stubborn and set in his ways, and without *mei mamm's* support, there's no way I can convince him." She sniffed. "My heart is broken. I can't stop thinking about Anthony, but I can't be with him."

"Don't give up that dream." Maria gave Kathryn's hand a squeeze. "Just remember the verse from Proverbs. 'Trust in the Lord with all your heart, and do not lean on your own understanding.' Trust God."

Kathryn nodded, but her hope continued to sink.

Chapter Six

Anthony couldn't stop his smile as he climbed into the back of his driver's van. He finished his donut and thought about how beautiful Kathryn had looked today in her purple dress. He looked out the window at the patchwork of green, lush farm fields speeding by as the van bumped down the road toward their workshop.

Thoughts of Kathryn had floated through his mind all week, and he'd been thrilled to run into her and Maria at the marketplace. At first, he wondered if he had imagined her there! It was as if God had prompted Micah to convince them to stop at the Coffee Corner just so Anthony had a chance to talk to her.

Thank you, God!

"Have you asked her out yet?"

"What?" Anthony looked up at Micah grinning at him.

"Did you ask Kathryn out yet?" Micah

sipped his coffee, and the aroma of bananas foster filled the van.

Dat shifted in the front passenger seat so that he was looking at Anthony. "You're going to ask out Kathryn?"

Anthony swallowed a groan. Now that *Dat* knew, he'd for sure tell *Mamm* and Bethany, and they would nag him relentlessly until he did ask her out. *Thanks, Micah!* "I'm thinking about it."

"Don't think about it," Micah said. "Just do it. If you wait too long, it might be too late."

Dat's expression was cautious. "She's a *wunderbaar maedel,* but you know her *dat* is strict," he said.

"You don't think Nelson would approve?" Anthony bit his lower lip as worry washed over him.

"I don't know," *Dat* said. "I've heard that he only respects farmers. He's not too supportive of carpenters, especially ones like us who make gazebos and furniture."

"Is that so?" Micah took a long drink of coffee.

Dat nodded. "I once heard him say that farming was the only respectable profession for an Amish man."

"Huh. That can't possibly be true," Anthony said. He would wait for the perfect moment and then he would talk to Nelson and ask for permission to date Kathryn. Surely Nelson would say yes when he asked. After all, he'd known Nelson his whole life.

He just had to wait for that moment to come.

"How was shopping?" *Mamm* looked up from her cookbook as Kathryn set her bag from the fabric store on a kitchen chair later that morning.

"It was *gut.*" Kathryn retrieved an oatmeal raisin cookie from the jar on the counter and took a bite. "Maria and I went to the Coffee Corner after we were done in the fabric store."

"Oh, how nice! What kind of *kaffi* did you have today?"

"Coconut almond. It was so *gut.*" Kathryn reached for another cookie, handed it to *Mamm,* and then sat down across from her. "Anthony stopped by for coffee and a donut while we were there."

Mamm's smile faded as she lifted the cookie to her mouth.

Silence stretched between them as the Scripture verse from Proverbs filled Kathryn's mind:

Trust in the Lord with all your heart, and do not lean on your own understanding.

Kathryn took a deep breath and rested her hands on the table. "I care for him, *Mamm.* I've known him for years and care for him deeply."

"Kathryn, you already know how your *dat* feels. He wants you to meet Jeremiah in Lititz, and he means it. Jeremiah is a hardworking farmer, and he would be *gut* for you. You need to respect your *dat* and obey."

"*Mamm,* please just listen to me." She held her hand up. "What would you have done if *Daadi* hadn't permitted you to date *Dat*? Wouldn't you have tried to convince him that you felt God leading you to him?"

Mamm shook her head. "You can't compare the two situations."

"Why?"

"Because *mei dat* was a dairy farmer. I knew that we belonged together."

Kathryn clucked her tongue. "Why should that matter?"

Mamm pushed her chair back and stood. "This conversation is over. You are going to do what your *dat* says, and that's it. No more discussion."

Kathryn sniffed as despondency whipped through her. While she longed to hold onto Maria's optimism, she had little reason to hope. Still she began to pray silently:

Please, Lord, lead Anthony to me. Find a

way for us to be together if it's your will.

Anthony's palms began to sweat as he stood with Dwain, Maria, and Kathryn after the church service three weeks later.

While he had hoped to ask Kathryn if she wanted a ride home after the last few youth gatherings, his plans had fallen through each time. On the first Sunday, he wound up with a stomach bug and had to skip the youth gathering altogether. The next Sunday, Kathryn had managed to get a ride from friends before he had a chance to ask her. And then last Sunday, it had rained, and the youth gathering at the lake was canceled.

Today, however, the mid-July sun was hot and cheerful, and birds in nearby trees seemed to sing their afternoon song to the bright blue sky above. Today was the day that Anthony was finally going to ask Kathryn to ride with him.

"Are we all going to Ruthie's *haus*?" Dwain asked.

Maria gazed up at Dwain and then threaded her fingers through his. "We are, right?"

Dwain smiled down at her. *"Ya."*

"I'd like to go," Kathryn said.

"Would you like to ride with us?" Dwain asked.

"No," Anthony said louder than he meant to, and they all turned to look at him, their expressions seeming either surprised or shocked.

Kathryn's pretty brow puckered as she studied him with her caramel eyes.

"I'm sorry." Anthony cleared his throat. "What I meant to say was — would you like to ride with me, Kathryn?"

Her eyes widened, and he held his breath. *Please don't reject me. Please don't reject me!*

"*Ya,* I'd like that." She nodded, but her smile seemed almost hesitant.

"Gut." He felt his shoulders relax as he nodded toward his buggy. "Then let's get going." He looked over his shoulder at Dwain and Maria, both grinning as he led Kathryn to his buggy.

Kathryn smoothed her hands down her green dress and black apron as Anthony guided his horse down the road toward Ruthie's house. The clip-clop of the horse, the whirring of the wheels, and the roar of the passing traffic filled the buggy.

She glanced over at his handsome profile and her heart sank. She was finally riding alone with Anthony, which meant that he most likely cared for her as more than a friend. But it was time for her to tell him the truth — she couldn't be with him. She had to obey her father.

Still, she would cherish this one ride with Anthony. After all, she would never be able to call him her boyfriend. But how could she bring herself to tell him that her father didn't approve of him when the words would hurt him and also tear at her soul?

"Dwain and Maria seem *froh,*" he said, breaking through her thoughts.

"They do. I was honestly surprised when she told me that she liked him."

Anthony gave her a sideways glance. "I was surprised when Dwain told me that he liked her. It seemed to come out of nowhere."

"*Ya.* I guess you never know what God has planned."

"You know what I was thinking about the other day?"

"What?"

"That time we went sledding on Eli Yoder's farm."

Kathryn smiled as the memory filled her mind. "Oh my goodness! How old were we? Maybe ten?"

"Ya." He halted the horse at a light and

angled his body toward her. "I had *mei schweschder*'s long sled, and you rode on the back of it, holding onto my waist."

"And when we went down the hill, it was so much faster than we thought it would be."

"And you screamed in my ear the whole time." He chuckled. "I was deaf in one ear for a week."

"Oh no!" She cupped her hand to her mouth. "You never told me that."

He waved it off. "I obviously recovered. But when we reached the bottom of the hill, I hit that bump, and we went flying!"

She cackled. "We landed in that snowbank, and we were covered in snow. I had snow caked in my hair and in my boots."

"It was so much fun."

"It was." She wiped her eyes and then stopped laughing as his expression became intense.

They were still sitting at the red light when he leaned over and cupped his hand to her cheek. Kathryn's mouth dried and her skin prickled, and her gaze lifted to meet Anthony's.

He's going to kiss me!

Then a horn tooted behind them, and Anthony quickly turned back toward the windshield. Silence filled the buggy once again as the horse started down the street.

Anthony cleared his throat. "What about that time we went ice skating on the pond behind your pasture?"

"I think I still have bruises from all the times I fell."

"I had some too." He chuckled. "And I was the one trying to teach you to skate."

She turned toward him. "You've always been there."

He nodded slowly. "And you have too."

She sighed. "I never had to worry about being alone and not having anyone to talk to when you were around."

He tilted his head as he looked at her. "I know."

Disappointment filled her as he guided the horse up Ruthie's driveway and then over to the field where the other buggies were lined up. She wanted to ride around all day and talk to him.

Anthony halted the horse and turned toward her. "You've been my best *freind* for as long as I can remember."

"And you've been mine."

He pushed his hand through his thick hair. "I have something to tell you, but I don't know how to say it."

"You can tell me anything," she said, her voice trembling.

He swallowed and took a deep breath. "I care for you deeply."

She gasped as tears filled her eyes. "I care for you too."

"You do?" His eyes were wide as he shifted closer to her.

"I have for a long time."

His expression seemed to relax. "I've been so *naerfich* to tell you how I felt. I was afraid you wouldn't want to be more than *freinden* after knowing me for such a long time."

A tear dripped down her cheek as she shook her head. "I would love that more than anything, but . . . I just can't, Anthony."

His brow pinched as he seemed to search her eyes. "What do you mean?"

"It's *mei dat.*" Her voice was raspy as if she'd screamed for hours. "He wouldn't approve of the match."

He took her hands in his, and when their skin touched, she felt sparks dancing up her arms.

"I don't understand." His voice was husky.

"He knows that I care about you, but he's warned me to stay away from you. He even threatened to limit my time with the youth group. He wants me to meet a farmer who lives in Lititz."

Anthony's expression hardened. "He's trying to get you to be with a man who lives in Lititz?"

She nodded and sniffed as more tears poured down her hot cheeks. "*Ya,* and I'm miserable. I care about you, Anthony, but *mei dat* won't allow it because . . . Oh Anthony, I hate to even repeat it! He says he doesn't respect your line of work. I'm so sorry, and of course I don't agree with him . . . But he's *mei dat.* I shouldn't even be here with you. If he knew I had ridden with you, he would forbid me from going to youth gatherings altogether."

"I — I don't understand. Why does he disapprove?"

"He thinks your work is frivolous and believes Plain people are only called to be farmers."

"Frivolous?"

She nodded, and his hurt expression made her chest ache. "That's not how I feel at all. I disagreed and told him how you're called to be a carpenter. But he wouldn't listen."

He brushed his hand down his face. "That doesn't make any sense. Plenty of Amish men are carpenters."

"I know."

"There has to be a way to change his mind. He can't truly believe that."

Kathryn longed to believe in the hope she

found in his eyes. "You know how stubborn he is."

"Maybe so, but I can't give up on us."

She sniffed.

"I *won't* give up on us, Kathryn. Please don't worry . . . I'll find a way for us to be together." He reached up and gently brushed away a tear, and when he leaned closer to her, Kathryn closed her eyes. He brushed his lips across her cheek, and the touch sent her stomach fluttering.

She opened her eyes and found him staring at her, his eyes intense. And for a moment, she clung to hope again.

But then the memory of her father's warning reclaimed her. She could never be with Anthony. She had to let go of this moment, this dream.

"We should join everyone at the youth gathering," he said. "We'll talk about this more later."

She pushed the buggy door open, and as Anthony unhitched his horse, she sent a silent prayer up to God.

Please, Lord, please change Dat*'s heart and mind. If it's your will, may* Dat *accept Anthony and his family, and let him see that Anthony's work is just as important as his.*

Later that evening, Anthony couldn't stop

his wide smile as he walked into the family room and found his parents sitting side by side in their matching dark brown recliners while they each read a book.

"Anthony." *Mamm* looked up and smiled. "How was your afternoon?"

He dropped onto the sofa and sighed. "Just perfect."

And it *had* been perfect. Anthony felt as if his soul had taken on wings when Kathryn told him that she cared about him. His face hurt from smiling all afternoon.

He and Kathryn had spent the day together — playing volleyball with their friends and then sitting by a tree and talking. He felt closer to her than he ever had. Now he had to ask her father's permission to date her. Once he convinced Nelson, then he could hold her hand, visit her at night, and steal kisses on the porch in the light of the lantern. He couldn't wait!

Surely Nelson didn't truly want to keep Kathryn from him. Anthony would find a way to convince Nelson to give his blessing.

Dat set his book down. "Did you tell Kathryn how you feel?"

"I did," Anthony said.

"And it went well?"

"Not exactly."

"Wait." *Mamm* held her hand up. "You

have feelings for Kathryn Beiler?"

"I do." Anthony rested his ankle on his opposite knee. "I finally told her how I feel, and she said she feels the same way. The only problem is her *dat.*"

Dat gave him a knowing expression. "Let me guess. Kathryn told you that her father doesn't approve of you."

Anthony felt his jaw clench. "It's worse than that. Not only does he not approve but he told her he wants her to meet a farmer who lives in Lititz." He shook his head. "I need to find a way to convince Nelson that I'm the right choice for Kathryn and I can provide for her even though I'm not a farmer."

Dat shook his head and sighed. "I admire your determination, but I've known Nelson a lot longer than you have. He's not easily convinced."

Mamm's expression was equally somber. "Your *dat* is right. Nelson Beiler is stubborn and set in his ways."

Anthony sat up taller. "Maybe so, but I'm going to find a way. Kathryn means a lot to me, and I can't just give up."

"I can tell that you care for her," *Mamm* began, her tone cautious, "but I don't think Nelson will budge on this. Once he makes up his mind about things, he doesn't bend.

I'm afraid you're going to wind up heartbroken if you try to pursue this."

"Your *mamm* is right." *Dat*'s expression was gentle.

Anthony pointed to his chest. "Surely if I make a case for myself, I can convince Nelson that I care for Kathryn and want to be with her. I'll make him see that I'm serious and won't take no for an answer."

His parents exchanged unconvinced expressions, which sent irritation burning through his veins.

Anthony stood. "I'm going to go to bed. I'll see you in the morning."

After his parents said goodnight, he started up the stairs, his heart thumping with optimism despite everything his family had said. When he reached his room, he sent a prayer up as he got ready for bed.

"*Danki,* God, for giving me the courage to tell Kathryn how I feel about her. Please grant me the courage to find the right words to ask her *dat*'s permission to date her and convince him that I am the man for her."

As he climbed into his bed, he imagined sitting on the porch with Kathryn late at night, holding her hand as they looked up at the stars. Oh, he couldn't wait!

Chapter Seven

Anthony's hands shook as he tied his horse to the fence post outside the Beilers' dairy barn the next morning. Above him, the sky was clogged with dark gray clouds and the air smelled of rain.

He looked toward Kathryn's house and imagined her inside helping her mother washing clothes in the utility room or scrubbing the floors. He closed his eyes. What if he stumbled over his words and her father laughed at him? Or what if her father refused to even talk to him since he wanted Kathryn to date someone else?

Then his thoughts turned to how she'd told him that she cared for him, and he felt a surge of confidence fill him.

He stood up straight and then walked into the dairy barn. The aroma of animals and hay filled his nostrils as he searched for her father. He heard a collar jangle, and Fred bounded over to him, his tongue hanging out as he approached.

"Hey, buddy." Anthony rubbed the retriever's head. "Where's Nelson?"

Fred barked and then panted.

Anthony nodded toward the back of the barn. "Back there, huh? *Danki.*" He walked past the rows of cows and found Nelson standing by the large tank that stirred the milk. "Hello, Nelson. *Wie geht's?*"

Kathryn's father turned toward him, and his eyes widened. Then they narrowed as he frowned. "What are you doing here, Anthony?"

"I wanted to talk to you. Do you have a few minutes?"

Fred sat at attention beside Anthony.

"Why didn't you talk to me yesterday at church?"

"Uh . . ." Anthony grasped for his words. "I — I wasn't ready to talk to you then."

Nelson's expression seemed to harden. "What do you want to talk about?"

Anthony jammed his hands into his pockets as he felt his confidence deflate.

Please, God. Please give me the right words! Please, Lord!

"I wanted to talk about Kathryn." Anthony hated the tremble in his voice. "I've known her nearly all my life, and she's important to me."

Nelson folded his arms over his wide chest.

"We've always cared about each other, and we've realized that we want to be more than *freinden.*"

When Nelson's expression remained impassive, Anthony spoke faster, trying to fill the awkward space between them.

"I want to date her and see where our relationship goes. I will cherish her and always treat her with respect." Anthony paused, but Nelson remained silent and stoic. "So, I am here to request your blessing. Would you please give me permission to date her?"

"No." Nelson nearly spat the word at Anthony and then turned and headed out of the barn toward the pasture.

Anthony winced as if Nelson had punched him in his stomach. Had he heard Nelson correctly? Had her father truly just refused him outright?

When Nelson continued walking, Anthony ran after him.

"Nelson!" Anthony called. "Nelson, please stop."

Her father turned toward him and shot him a sour expression. His eyes were like thunderclouds on the verge of rain. "Why are you still here? I've given you my answer."

"Please, Nelson. Give me a chance." Anthony held up his palms. "I care about your *dochder,* and I want to date her. You know me. You know my family."

"Are you deaf, *sohn*?" Nelson's lip curled into a snarl. "I said no. Stay away from *mei dochder.*" His words were equivalent to the slice of a razor.

Anthony gaped at him. Then he looked at his skin to see if it was black and blue from his bruised pride.

"Now I have work to do. Please be on your way."

Anthony stood frozen in place. He felt as if the ground would open up and swallow him whole. Nelson, however, continued stalking toward the nearby supply barn and stable as if nothing had happened.

Anthony's anger turned to hurt before slowly fading into oblivion. What had he done to deserve such treatment? He looked up toward the sky as cool raindrops began leaking from the clouds, sprinkling his face and wetting his straw hat and blue shirt. He thought he might choke on his confusion.

His dreams had disappeared in a puff of smoke. He felt as if his chest had cracked open and his heart had turned into a block of ice.

"Why, God?" he whispered. "Why would

you put love in my heart for a *maedel* I can't have? I don't understand. Please guide me."

Anthony looked toward the barns again, but Nelson was nowhere to be seen. After untying his horse, he climbed into his buggy and started toward home, his soul twisting with every clip-clop of his horse.

Kathryn hurried out of the sewing room and down the stairs toward the kitchen. "Did I hear a buggy outside?"

Slipping past her mother, she stepped onto the porch and was greeted by the smell of rain and the pitter-patter of the raindrops bouncing off the roof above her.

The back door opened, and *Mamm* stepped outside. "What did you say?"

"I thought maybe I heard a buggy." She spun toward her mother. "I was almost certain I heard horses, but I didn't see anything out the window. I rushed downstairs to check."

"Were you expecting someone?"

"No." Kathryn leaned forward on the porch railing. She looked out toward the barns and then pushed herself off the railing and started down the steps into the rain. "I'll go ask *Dat.* Maybe someone came to see him."

Kathryn jogged out to the barn and began

looking for her father. Fred caught up to her and joined her as she continued her search. She found *Dat* in the farthest barn, where he kept their two horses, his tools, and supplies.

"Dat," she said. "Did I hear a buggy here earlier?"

Her father turned toward her and gave her a curt nod. "*Ya,* Anthony Gingerich was here."

Her pulse skittered. "Anthony?"

Fred sat down beside her and panted up at her, seeming to smile.

"He didn't stay long." He studied her. "Did you know he was coming by to see me?"

"No." She fingered a broom leaning against the barn wall. "What did he want?"

Dat pinned her with a hard look. "Did you know that he had planned to come here to talk to me?" he repeated.

"I didn't." A chill crept up her spine despite the muggy July air. "What did he say?"

Dat glowered. "I have a feeling you already know what he came to discuss with me. And I told him no."

She dropped the broom and took a step toward him as frustration caused her throat to swell. "Did he ask you if he could date me?"

Dat pointed a finger at her as his eyes went cold. "You knew I would tell him no. You shouldn't have led him on." His words shredded her insides.

"I didn't lead him on," she croaked. "He told me that he cared about me, and I admitted to him that I care about him too. But I also told him that you would never allow us to date. I think he believed we could still have a chance."

"You knew how I felt about him, but you continued to see him and talk to him anyway? You even told him that you cared about him?"

She nodded. "I want to see where God leads our relationship. Why won't you allow me to do that?"

"The answer is no, Kathryn. Now you need to obey me. Stay away from him. You are not to talk to him at all. Do you understand?"

She nodded.

"It's time for you to meet Jeremiah. You should go to his church gatherings instead of your youth gatherings."

"You can't take my *freinden* away," she said, her voice trembling.

"Fine! I will allow you to continue to attend your youth group as long as you avoid Anthony Gingerich! That's it, Kathryn! No more discussion!"

As *Dat* walked away, Kathryn felt a sob burst from her throat. She covered her face with her hands and dissolved into tears. Above her, the rain beat a hard, steady cadence on the barn roof. Her sorrow weighed her down as she worked to control her sobs. She ran back through the rain, dodging puddles as she made her way toward the porch steps. Fred followed her, trotting at her heels.

Once inside the house, she found her mother sitting at the kitchen table.

"What happened?" *Mamm* asked.

"It was Anthony who came by to see *Dat.*" Kathryn's throat felt like sandpaper and ached for water. "He asked permission to date me, and *Dat* told him no."

Frowning, *Mamm* shook her head. "You knew your *dat* was going to say no. Why did Anthony even bother?"

Kathryn dropped into the chair across from her, and Fred appeared in front of her, resting his chin on her thigh. She absently rubbed his ears. "I guess Anthony believed he could change *Dat*'s mind. Now *Dat* says I can only go to youth group with *mei freinden* if I avoid Anthony." She sniffed and wiped her eyes and nose with a paper napkin. "So now *Dat* is taking away Anthony. It's too much to take, *Mamm*!"

Mamm sighed. "I'm sorry, *mei liewe,* but there's nothing I can do."

As Kathryn stared down at her sweet dog, she closed her eyes and sent up an urgent prayer:

Please, God, help Anthony and me find a way to be together. Only you can help Dat *see that Anthony is a* gut *man. Please help us, Lord.*

Anthony felt the weight of the world in his steps as he walked back into the workshop. Both *Dat* and Micah looked up from workbenches when he stepped inside.

"Oh no," Micah groaned. "From the look on your face, it didn't go the way you'd planned."

Shaking his head, Anthony dropped down onto a bench by the door. "He told me no." He felt a pang in his chest as he said the words out loud.

"*Ach,* no." *Dat* rushed over to him with Micah in tow. "I'm so sorry. What did he say?"

Anthony held up his hands. "He said no and then left me standing there. I went after him, and he asked me if I was deaf. He instructed me to stay away from Kathryn. I'm completely flummoxed."

Dat and Micah shared a confused expression as a wave of awkward silence rolled in.

"He didn't give you an explanation?" Micah asked.

Anthony shook his head before scrubbing his hand down his face. "No, but Kathryn told me that he thinks our profession is frivolous."

"I'm sorry. I had hoped Nelson would change his mind about us," *Dat* offered.

"It's ridiculous that Nelson is keeping Kathryn from me just because I'm a carpenter who sells gazebos to *Englishers,*" Anthony said as frustration and anguish whipped through him.

Dat's expression was somber. "He once told me that my profession wasn't Amish enough. I assume that's why he's convinced you're not *gut* enough for his *dochder.*"

"This is just insane." Anthony pushed himself up from the bench. He needed a distraction before he drove himself crazy with his doubts and confusion. "Let's get back to work."

"You sure you don't want to talk about it?" Micah asked.

"No, but thanks. I'll figure it out. With God's help." As Anthony turned his attention to his work, he sent up another prayer.

Lord, lead me to a solution. Help me find a way to convince Nelson that I will cherish Kathryn and treat her well. Help me show Nelson that I am a gut *match for his* dochder *and that my work can be godly in your sight.*

Chapter Eight

"That lemon meringue pie smells *appeditlich,*" *Mamm* said as she walked into the kitchen Thursday morning. "What's the occasion?"

"I made it for Maria." Kathryn placed it gently in the pie carrier, careful not to nick the crusts. "Since we're caught up on chores, I was hoping I could walk over to give it to her."

Mamm nodded. "Of course. You've been stuck in the house doing chores all week. I'm sure you're anxious to get out."

That was an understatement. Ever since her father had sent Anthony away, Kathryn had been anxious to talk to Maria. She felt alone and rejected in her own home, and she'd run out of tears. She found herself praying constantly, begging God to change *Dat*'s mind. So far, that prayer had not been answered.

Although talking to God helped to calm

her, she still craved a sympathetic ear to listen to her. She needed her best friend.

"Danki." Kathryn felt herself smile for the first time since Monday. "I'll be back soon."

"Take your time, *mei liewe,*" *Mamm* said as Kathryn headed out the door.

Holding the pie in her hands, she hurried up the street to Maria's farm next door. She made her way up the rock driveway to the porch steps, then knocked on the back door.

Maria swung the door open and grinned. "Kathryn! What a nice surprise."

"I brought you a pie." She held up the carrier.

Maria rubbed her hands together. "Oh! Is that lemon meringue?"

"Your favorite."

"Danki." Maria tilted her head. "Are you okay?"

Kathryn shook her head. "Not really. Do you have time to talk?"

"Of course. My parents went out for supplies, so we have the *haus* to ourselves. Come in. I'll make some tea."

Maria boiled water while Kathryn gathered up plates and utensils. Soon they were sitting at the kitchen table drinking tea and eating pie.

Maria pointed her fork to the large piece of pie on her plate. "This is spectacular."

"Danki." Kathryn sipped her tea.

"Now. Tell me what's wrong."

Kathryn sniffed and shook her head. "Everything I predicted happened."

Maria gasped as Kathryn described Anthony's visit and how her father had reacted.

"To make matters worse, *mei dat* said I'm not allowed to see Anthony at all. I have to stay away from him, so I've lost his friendship too. I can go to our youth group as long as I avoid Anthony." Kathryn's voice sounded like broken glass. When she felt her lip begin to tremble, she cleared her throat and forced the tears to remain at bay.

"*Ach,* no." Maria took Kathryn's hand in hers. Then she leaned back in her chair and folded her arms over her chest. "We need to come up with a plan to make your *dat* see that Anthony is a *gut* man."

"It's impossible. He won't change his mind, and *mei mamm* won't support me. There's nothing I can do."

"Don't say that." Maria swatted toward her. "There has to be something we haven't thought of . . ."

Kathryn shook her head. "I've lost him, and it hurts so much I can't breathe." The now-familiar ache overwhelmed her, and she looked down at her uneaten piece of pie.

"I'm sorry."

Kathryn looked over at her best friend. "It's not your fault."

Maria shook her head. "I feel like it is. I kept encouraging you. I believed that if Anthony asked for permission, your *dat* would realize that he was the one God had chosen for you. I'm sorry for giving you false hope."

"You were just being a *gut,* supportive *freind.* You made me realize that I needed to keep praying for God to change *mei dat*'s mind, and I am still praying for it. I talk to God constantly."

"Gut." Maria smiled. "I will keep praying too."

While Maria took another bite of pie, Kathryn drank more tea. Silence filled the kitchen, and Kathryn longed for Maria to say something. The quiet made her feel hollow.

"How's Dwain?"

Maria's dreamy expression sent envy coursing through Kathryn's veins. "He's *gut.* He and his parents are coming for supper tonight. They're going to come after they close the store."

"That's great." Kathryn cupped her mug in her hands and tried to relax as Maria talked on about how happy she and Dwain were.

While she was thrilled for her friend, Kathryn also prayed God would somehow find a way for Anthony and her to forge a relationship together.

Kathryn sat at a picnic table with Maria, Ruthie, and a few of their other friends Sunday afternoon. While the July afternoon was humid, the blue sky was clogged with clouds that seemed to mirror her mood. Since it was an off Sunday without a church service, she and a few of her friends gathered at the Esh farm. She just prayed Anthony would decide to join them so she could steal a few minutes to talk to him. The idea of never speaking to him again nearly broke her in two.

She had ridden to the gathering with Gretchen, and she couldn't stop her mind from recalling riding with Anthony in his buggy last weekend and how she'd enjoyed not only the conversation but the chaste kiss he had placed on her cheek.

She reached up and touched the spot where his lips had been. Oh, how she longed for more of those kisses! She missed him so much that her heart ached.

Why had her father taken her best friend

from her? It just didn't make sense!

"Kathryn?"

She glanced behind her and found Anthony staring at her. The storms in his blue eyes nearly ripped her in two. Did he miss her as much as she missed him?

"Could I please talk to you for a minute?" His handsome face seemed to plead with her to say yes.

Kathryn bit her lower lip and turned to Maria as if for permission. Should she break her father's rule and talk to him?

Maria nodded. "Go," she whispered.

Kathryn climbed off the bench and walked over to him. "*Ya.* Where should we go?"

"How about we take a walk around the pasture?" He pointed toward the fence.

"Perfect."

Kathryn fell into step with him as they made their way around the pasture, walking in silence. She glanced out to where the horses frolicked in the lush, green field. If only her life were as carefree as the horses'!

Anthony pointed to a bench ahead of them. "Why don't we sit there?"

"Okay."

She walked over to the bench and sank down beside him.

"Kathryn," he began. "I'm so sorry. I thought —"

"No," she interrupted as she angled her body toward his. "*I'm* sorry." She pointed to her chest. "None of this is your fault. I'm sorry that you spoke to *mei dat,* and I'm sorry he hurt you. I'm sorry that we can't be together. I'm sorry for everything." Her voice broke, and tears rushed down her cheeks. She pulled a tissue from the pocket of her apron and began wiping her eyes and nose.

"Hey." He reached over and wiped away a tear with his fingertip. "It's not your fault."

"It is my fault for thinking that we might be able to find a path forward. *Mei dat* won't allow it."

"I was crushed when he told me no. I thought for sure I could convince him that we belonged together." He shook his head. "I just don't understand why your *dat* wants to keep us apart because of my profession. It's crazy."

"*Ya.* I know, and I agree with you. I've tried talking to him and convincing him that you do God's work too." She sniffed and looked down at her lap. "I told him that you, your *dat,* and Micah are talented, and you are using your gifts the way you feel God has called you to use them. I even talked about how Bethany's gifts are making the *kaffi* and donuts and how she brings joy to her customers. He wouldn't listen." Her tears began anew, and Anthony touched her arm and then pulled his hand away.

"*Mei dat* and I aren't the only Amish men in the area who build gazebos. Jesus was a carpenter. How is it not respectable?"

"I don't know." She wiped her tears with a tissue. "I even tried to convince *mei mamm* to help me talk to *Dat,* but she won't. She said *mei dat* comes from a long line of farmers, and he only respects that work. I'm so sorry, Anthony." She reached over and touched his sinewy bicep, which sent a spark of excitement through her blood. "Please forgive me."

He shook his head. "Why would I be angry with you, Kathryn? This wasn't your decision."

"But I wanted to believe that we could be together."

"I wanted to believe it too." He touched her cheek, and she leaned into the touch, closing her eyes.

"I'm sorry." She reached for his arm again and then pulled her hand away as pure sadness drowned her from the inside out. "I just kept praying God would help *mei dat* accept you."

Anthony looked out toward the horses for a moment, and then he sighed, his expression relaxing slightly. "He told me to stay away from you. Does that mean we can't be *freinden*?"

She swallowed against her dry throat. "I'm supposed to avoid you. He wants me to see that farmer in Lititz. He's making plans for me to meet him, but I don't want to." Then she whispered the words that she dreaded the most. "I understand if you want to see someone else." Each word felt like an ice pick to her heart.

He frowned. "I don't want to see anyone but you." He shifted closer to her and then took her hands in his, sending her pulse stampeding in her chest. "I will find a way to be with you, even though I make gazebos. I promise you, Kathryn, that we will be together. I won't stop trying."

She sniffed. *"Danki."*

"We will find a way. And God will help us." Then he leaned down and brushed his lips over her cheek. She closed her eyes and savored the sensation of his warm mouth against her skin.

Please, God, please find a way for us to be together.

Frustration and sadness rolled over Anthony as he and Kathryn walked back to find their friends. While she rejoined her girlfriends at the picnic bench, Anthony found Dwain standing near the volleyball nets.

"How did it go?" Dwain asked as they moved away from their friends.

"Her *daed* won't bend. He just doesn't approve of me."

Dwain frowned. "What are you going to do?"

Anthony leaned against a tree as anxiety coiled his muscles. "I will find a way to cherish her and take care of her for the rest of my life."

Dwain grinned. "You love her?"

Anthony nodded and looked over to where she sat with her friends. "I do. I love her, and I'm not going to give up. Somehow this will work out."

"With God's help," Dwain said.

"Absolutely," Anthony said as determination took hold of him.

Chapter Nine

Kathryn sipped her cup of white-chocolate-flavored coffee while she sat on a stool in the Coffee Corner on a Thursday, one month later. She rested her elbow on the table and her chin on her hand as she stared down at her uneaten cinnamon donut.

It had been a month since she'd last had a meaningful conversation with Anthony — a month since he'd touched her hand and kissed her cheek. The church services and youth group events had been hard to attend as she watched him talk to friends from afar. She longed to talk to him, laugh with him, and ride in his buggy with him. Instead, her father had made her promise to avoid him, and she'd done her best to obey his wishes. She and Anthony had only shared a quick hello before she spent the remainder of her time at the youth group with her girlfriends.

She had met Jeremiah once a couple of weeks ago. While he was a kind and soft-spoken man, she felt no spark with him. He was nothing like Anthony, who was the opposite of her father — funny, outgoing, thoughtful, and kind. When she was with Anthony, she felt as if he respected her and listened to her — unlike *Dat.* Anthony lit up the room with his smile, and he made her feel like she could speak her mind without being chastised. Poor Jeremiah could never compete with the feelings she already had for Anthony. He didn't stand a chance.

"Penny for your thoughts," Maria prompted with a smile.

Kathryn absently traced a heart on the tabletop with the tip of her finger. "I miss him."

"I know you do." Maria's smile flattened. "Don't give up hope."

"I won't." Kathryn sat up straight and cradled her coffee cup in her hand. "I know he still cares for me. I've seen him looking at me, and he always nods and waves to me. He said he wasn't going to give up, but I don't see how it can ever work out if *mei daed* won't bend."

Bethany walked over to their table while holding a cup of coffee. "Could I sit with you for a minute?"

"Of course." Kathryn gestured toward the stool beside her.

Bethany hopped up on the stool, and Kathryn could smell the caramel-flavored coffee in her cup. "It's quiet at the moment, so I thought I'd say hello." She turned to Kathryn. "How are you?"

Kathryn shrugged. "I'm okay."

"No, she's not," Maria chimed in. "She's devastated."

Kathryn shot her a look.

Maria gave her a palms up. "What? Why not be honest?"

Kathryn felt her shoulders sag as she turned to Bethany. "She's right. I miss Anthony so much that sometimes I feel like I'm going to crumble."

Bethany nodded. "He misses you too."

Warmth swirled in Kathryn's chest.

"Do you think there's a chance your *dat* will change his mind?" Bethany asked.

Kathryn shook her head. "He's stubborn and set in his ways."

A small smile took over Bethany's lips. "The *gut* news is that *mei bruder* is pretty stubborn too."

Hope took root in Kathryn's heart as she smiled at Bethany. "I'm glad to hear that."

"God's got this," Maria said.

Kathryn nodded. "I know." She just hoped God would find a way for them soon.

■ ■ ■ ■

Later that evening, Kathryn sat on the porch in her favorite rocking chair with Fred lounging by her side. She looked out over her father's pasture and barns as darkness crept in for the night. She rocked back and forth and held onto her mug of herbal tea, looking up at the dark clouds clogging the sky. The scent of rain filled the air around her.

"I think it's going to rain, Fred."

The dog looked at her and then peered upward as if considering the clouds.

Her mind revisited her talk with Bethany earlier in the day, along with Anthony's promise to not give up on her. And a question gripped her. "Do you think God answers our most fervent prayers?"

Fred tilted his head as he studied her.

"I do." She glanced over her shoulder at the screen door and held her breath, listening for voices in the kitchen. When it remained quiet, she turned back to her dog. "I feel in my heart I have to hold onto the hope that God will find a way for me and Anthony."

She leaned down toward Fred as his ears perked up. "Do me a favor, okay? Don't tell anyone I told you that, especially *Mamm* and *Dat.*" She sipped her tea and tried to evict thoughts of Anthony from her mind, but his handsome face and bright smile lingered there, insistent.

A light breeze drifted over her and a mist of rain cooled her face.

"I guess we need to go in." She stood and opened the screen door for Fred, who scampered into the kitchen.

She washed her mug and set it in the drainboard before walking into the family room, where her parents sat, both wearing reading glasses as they perused books.

"Gut nacht," she said.

They each nodded at her before she and Fred headed up the stairs for bed. The rain began to beat a steady cadence on the roof above her as she readied for a night of sleep. She glanced over at Fred settling on his dog bed and smiled.

"*Danki* for keeping my secret."

He tilted his head at her.

"*Gut nacht,* Fred." Then she climbed into bed.

As she settled into bed, she opened her heart up to God. "Lord," she whispered, "I know all things are possible with you. Please find a way for Anthony and me to be together. Please."

■ ■ ■ ■

Thunder roared in the distance as a flash of lightning lit up Kathryn's room later that night, jolting her awake. Rolling onto her side, Kathryn faced the wall as rain beat hard and loud on the roof above her.

Lightning again lit up her room like the afternoon sun and was followed by an immediate crash of thunder.

Fred rushed over to the window, pushed back the shade with his nose, and began to bark.

Kathryn popped up from her bed and rushed to the window beside him. She gasped as she spotted smoke billowing up from one of her father's barns. Then flames began to lick at the roof, moving quickly down the side.

Panic gripped her. *"Gut bu,* Fred. We have to get *Mamm* and *Dat."* Her heart pounded and her hands shook.

"Dat! Mamm!" she screamed as she grabbed her robe and dashed out of the bedroom toward their room down the hall. "*Dat!* Wake up! One of the barns is on fire!"

She banged on their door. "*Dat! Mamm!* The barn is on fire! I'm going to call nine-one-one."

"*Ach,* no! I'm coming!" *Dat* called.

Kathryn raced down the stairs, through the kitchen, and out the back door into the pouring rain, her feet sinking in the mud as she ran to the phone shanty to call 911. Her fingers shook as she picked up the receiver and dialed the number.

"Nine-one-one," a young woman said. "What's your emergency?"

"Lightning hit our barn, and it's on fire." Kathryn had to nearly yell over the sound of thunder rumbling above her as she gave the woman her address. "Please hurry! We have horses in that barn!"

She looked out toward the house and spotted her parents running toward the barn.

"Help is on the way, ma'am," the young woman said.

"Thank you." Kathryn hung up the phone and then ran toward the barn, where her parents were leading the horses out.

"Take the horses next door to Maria's farm," *Dat* said. Then he pointed to Kathryn's bare feet. "Go get your boots! I'll tie up the horses by the porch."

Kathryn sprinted into her house and up the stairs, where she threw on a dress and then tied a shawl over her wet hair. Then she pulled on her boots and grabbed a flashlight before hurrying back outside, where the rain had slowed slightly, but her father's barn was engulfed in flames. Sirens sounded in the distance as the stench of burning wood filled her lungs.

"Lord, please keep my family and our animals safe," she whispered as she led the horses toward the road.

With her flashlight guiding her way, she moved at a quick clip down the road to Maria's house. After tying the horses on their fence, she knocked on the back door.

Maria appeared in a few minutes, looking confused while dressed in her nightgown, her long, dark hair hanging to her waist. "Kathryn? What's going on?"

"One of our barns was struck by lightning." She pointed to the horses. "Could we please put our horses in with yours?"

"Of course. Just give me a minute."

"Maria?" her father called. "Who's here?"

Maria explained the situation, and after a few minutes, she and her parents appeared dressed and standing in the doorway. Her father stowed the horses in the barn before Kathryn, Maria, and Maria's parents walked back over to Kathryn's house. The rain had softened to a drizzle by the time they reached her house.

Three fire engines and an ambulance were

parked outside of the house, flooding the pasture with red and white light as teams of firefighters worked, all dressed in their uniforms and helmets, barking orders to each other. Fred sat on the porch, his ears up and alert as he looked on.

Kathryn, Maria, and Maria's parents stood on the porch with Kathryn's parents while they watched a team of firefighters fight the flames. Kathryn and Maria held onto each other as three different teams of firefighters sprayed the barn with hoses. While they worked, the lightning ceased and the thunder slowly faded into the distance.

By the time the flames were out, the steady mist had dissipated, and the sky was clear and full of twinkling stars — which seemed an ironic contrast to the barn now reduced to a smoky pile of ashes. The smell of burning wood filled the air and squeezed at Kathryn's lungs. Her eyes burned as she looked out over what was left of the barn. In the flash of a bolt of lightning, the barn had disappeared! How quickly life could change!

After the firefighters stowed their equipment, Kathryn and her parents thanked them. *Mamm* rushed inside the house and then back out, holding out a box of cookies and offering it to the weary firefighters. It was a poor show of gratitude for what the responders had done, but it was at least something.

"The Lord blessed us," *Dat* announced as the fire engines and ambulance motored away. "I lost my stable, but we saved our horses. And we didn't lose the dairy barn or any other animals. It could have been worse."

"That's true," Kathryn said.

Dat shook Maria's father's hand. "*Danki* for helping us. We appreciate you."

"Of course," Mel said. "You can keep the horses in our stable for as long as you need to."

"Let's get some sleep," *Mamm* said. "We'll figure out what to do next in the morning."

Kathryn hugged Maria and then headed into the house. "Thank you, Lord, for keeping us safe," she whispered as she climbed the steps to her bedroom.

"Did you hear the news?" Micah announced as he burst into Anthony's family's kitchen the following morning. "One of the Beilers' barns was hit by lightning last night. They lost their stable."

"*Ach,* no!" *Mamm* said as she set a platter of scrambled eggs on the table.

"Kathryn Beiler?" Anthony asked as worry

coursed through him.

"*Ya,* Kathryn Beiler," Micah said as he sat at the table beside Bethany. "I stopped at Dwain's hardware store on the way over here this morning, and he told me. He heard it from Maria."

Anthony dropped his fork. "Is she okay? Is her family okay?"

"Ya." Micah nodded before scooping a pile of eggs onto his plate. "Thankfully, it wasn't the dairy barn. They only kept their horses and supplies in the barn that was hit. They were able to get the horses out, but the barn burned to the ground."

Anthony looked at his father as an idea filled his mind. "Let's organize a barn raising."

Dat's dark eyebrows shot up. "What do you mean?"

"I want to organize the barn raising for them." Anthony sat up straight as the plan formed in his mind. "We can even donate the wood. We have a surplus, and we can get the remaining wood at a discount from our supplier. I'll pay for it personally."

"Wait a minute, Anthony." *Dat* held his hands up. "Do you know how much the wood will cost?"

Anthony nodded. "I do, but I want to do this for Kathryn."

Dat grimaced. "I know you want to prove to Nelson that you're worthy to date Kathryn, but this is a huge gesture. What if you spend all of this money and time, and then he still turns you down?"

Anthony shrugged. "I'll be okay. I just want to do this for Kathryn to show her how much I love her. No matter what happens, I'll always love her. I want her to know that much."

"I think it's a great idea." *Mamm* touched his hand. "Kathryn will appreciate it."

"I want to help too," Bethany said. "I'll call our cousins and ask them to help supply the food for the workers."

"Why don't we plan for next Thursday?" Micah suggested. "We should have the wood by then, and Nelson should also have the land cleared and ready for a new barn."

Anthony looked around the table as his family members smiled at him. Excitement filled him. "We'll order the wood today and start making calls. We can go see Nelson this afternoon."

"Let's do it," *Dat* said.

Anthony smiled as hope filled him. He prayed that he could not only help Kathryn's family but also show Kathryn that he would never stop loving her.

■ ■ ■ ■

Later that afternoon, Kathryn heard a knock at the door and rushed to answer it. She swallowed back her surprise when she found Anthony, his parents, and Micah standing on her porch.

She pushed the door open. "Hello."

Darlene, Anthony's mother, held up a casserole dish. "I brought you a hamburger casserole."

"Danki." Kathryn took the casserole dish, and then her eyes locked on Anthony's. "What are you doing here?"

"We'd like to speak to your parents," Anthony said.

Kathryn hesitated.

"Is your *dat* around?" Harvey asked.

"*Ya.* Please come in." Kathryn motioned for them to follow her into the kitchen, where her parents sat at the table looking at accounting books. "*Mamm. Dat.* We have company." She set down the casserole dish and then leaned against the counter as Anthony, Micah, and Anthony's parents came into the kitchen.

"Nelson." Harvey held his hand out for her father to shake. "How are you? We're so sorry to hear about the barn."

"We're grateful you're all okay," Darlene added.

Dat stood and stared at Harvey and then shook his hand. "*Danki.* Why are you here?"

"It was my idea to come and see you," Anthony said. When he glanced at Kathryn, she sucked in a breath before he turned his gaze back on her father. "I want to organize a barn raising for you."

Kathryn hugged her arms to her waist as gratitude and love for Anthony overwhelmed her. She looked over at *Mamm,* who gave her a stunned expression.

Dat blinked and then he stared at Anthony with suspicion. "Why would you want to do that?"

"Because you're part of this community, and it's our job to take care of each other," Anthony said as confidence filled his expression. "I've already bought all of the wood. I've contacted members of the community to come and help build the barn. *Mei schweschder* is working at her booth at the marketplace right now. I'm sure you've heard of the Coffee Corner. Anyway, she has contacted our cousins, and they are going to bring food to feed the workers. How does next Thursday sound? Will you have the land cleared by then?"

"Whoa." *Dat* held his hand up to silence

Anthony. "You want to not only organize the barn raising but also buy the wood." He gave a sarcastic snort. "Anthony, you can't buy *mei dochder* by giving me wood."

A muscle in Anthony's jaw flexed as his eyes narrowed. "I'm not trying to buy Kathryn. I just want to help you and your family."

"Why?" *Dat* challenged him. "You're not farmers. You have no idea what it means to lose precious barns when you depend on your animals and your land as a way to make a living and feed your family. This means nothing to you."

Kathryn's stomach twisted as she took in the resentment in her father's expression.

"Nelson," Anthony began slowly, "my family and I want to help you because we are part of the same community. That's what we do."

"Anthony is right," Harvey said, looking as if he were working to keep his tone even. "You seem to think that carpenters can't possibly understand how much a stable can mean to you. I think your determination to separate yourself as a farmer from those of us who are carpenters is making you prideful, which isn't a very Amish ideal. Besides, you know that we all have stables with horses that pull our buggies."

Dat blinked as he stared at Harvey.

"The truth is," Harvey continued, "that we completely understand. And we want to help you."

"We accept your help," *Mamm* chimed as she stood. "We weren't expecting to have to replace that barn this year, and the help is appreciated. You may or may not have heard that all of the farmers in our community are struggling right now. Our land value rose, which means our taxes have also gone up, and it's been a tough year. We graciously and humbly accept your offer." Then *Mamm* glared at *Dat.* "I think next Thursday will work. Won't it, Nelson?"

Kathryn cupped a hand to her mouth to stop her shocked gasp. Mamm *finally stood up to* Dat!

Dat nodded. *"Ya. Danki."*

"Okay. It's settled then." Anthony rubbed his hands together. *"Wunderbaar."*

Kathryn breathed a sigh of relief as *Dat* gave Anthony's hand a reluctant shake.

"Nelson, do you possibly have measurements for the barn that you lost?" Harvey asked as he and *Dat* started toward the door with Micah in tow.

"We can go look at it," *Dat* said before the three of them disappeared out the door.

"It's so *gut* to see you, Darlene," *Mamm*

told Anthony's *mamm* as they, too, walked out the door.

Once their parents and Micah were gone, Kathryn crossed the room, closing the distance between her and Anthony. "Why are you doing this?"

"Because I love you, and I want to help your family." He moved his fingers over her cheeks with a whisper of a touch as his smile shone like the sun.

Goosebumps chased each other down her neck as she looked up at him. Then her heart clenched as she took in his words.

"I love you too," she said, then shook her head. "But building the barn doesn't mean *mei dat* will let you date me."

"I know." He nodded. "But I meant it when I said I love you, and I'll do anything for you." He leaned down and rested his forehead against hers. "Don't give up on us. And don't give up on God."

"I won't." She felt a tingling in her chest. "I miss you."

"I miss you too." He took a step back, threading his fingers in hers. "We need to get outside before your *dat* suspects we're doing something inappropriate." He steered her toward the back door and then gave her hand a squeeze. "Have faith."

"I will." She smiled at him and looked out

toward where their parents and Micah stood by the pile of rubble that had once been the barn.

Thank you, God, for bringing our families together.

Chapter Ten

"This is just amazing," Kathryn said as she and Maria stood on her back porch the following Thursday afternoon and peered out toward where the new barn began to take shape.

Anthony, Harvey, Micah, and a large group of men from different church districts in the community had arrived early in the morning to begin working. They'd worked throughout the morning, only taking short breaks for water and a snack, which had been provided by Bethany, her cousins, and other women in the community. Fred sat near the barn, panting and watching the men work. As men walked past him, they'd stop and pat his head as he smiled up at them.

The late-August afternoon sun was bright and hot in the shimmering blue sky, but the men labored despite the unrelenting heat. Kathryn glanced toward the wooden skeleton beginning to look like a barn. The naked wood stretched toward heaven with an azure sky as its backdrop, and she counted at least twenty men lined up on the top of the structure hammering in the boards for the roof. Another thirty or so were on the ground cutting boards, building walls, and supervising the hard work.

Voices shouted over the noise as the men worked in unison with the hot sun beating down on them, and her heart swelled with gratitude for all the volunteers who had come out to help her family rebuild.

"Our community does take *gut* care of its members," Maria said.

"That's true."

Kathryn looked out to where Anthony stood by Micah as they hammered up sheets of wood for the barn walls. She smiled as she took in his handsome face, his long neck, and his broad shoulders.

He was sacrificing for her family. He had told her that he loved her. And she loved him. But how could they be together if her father disapproved? She felt her smile waver and then dissolve.

"You should bring him a bottle of water and thank him for all of this." Maria shoved a bottle of water at her. "Go. Talk to him. Tell him how much this means to you."

"But *mei dat* —"

"Just do it." Maria nodded toward the men working. "Talk to him while you have the chance."

Kathryn took the bottle of water and then descended the porch steps, passing the tables clogged with snacks and drinks for the workers. She nodded and smiled at men walking around the jobsite and made her way over to where Anthony and Micah worked.

She stood a few feet away from them, running her fingers through the condensation on the bottle as she tried to figure out what she would say to him. When Anthony glanced over his shoulder and saw her, a smile overtook his face.

He said something to Micah, set down his hammer, and then walked over to her. He pulled a handkerchief from his pocket and mopped up the sweat on his brow. "Hi."

"Hi. I thought you might need a drink." She held out the water.

"Danki." He shoved the handkerchief into his pocket and then opened the bottle and took a long drink. Then he replaced the cap.

"I wanted to thank you again." She pointed toward the barn. "I'm so overwhelmed by this. You've done so much for my family, and we can never repay you."

"I don't want to be repaid. I wanted to do this for you."

"Why did you spend your money on the wood for my family's barn?" She searched his eyes as her throat thickened.

He set the bottle of water on the ground and rested his hands on her shoulders. "Building this barn for your family is building a dream for us. I've told you that I love you, and I mean it, Kathryn. I want to help your family, and this was the right thing to do. *Mei dat*'s business is doing well, so I could afford to help you. Also, I'm not going to give up on us." Sincerity was etched in the lines of his eyes, his mouth, and his posture.

"And what you did is appreciated," a nearby voice said.

Kathryn and Anthony jumped apart as her father approached them.

"Nelson," Anthony said. "I didn't see you there."

"I know." *Dat* looked at Kathryn and then at Anthony. "I owe you an apology, Anthony. I misjudged you. Actually, I misjudged all carpenters like you." He gestured around at the barn. "I'm overwhelmed by the skill and craftsmanship here building this barn. Of course the talent comes from the Lord, and I had no right to believe that being a farmer was better. Your *dat* was right when he said that I was being prideful by thinking my profession is better than yours. I thought being a farmer was more godly, but what do I know about building barns? I was wrong about you and all of the other people here helping my family and me. I was so very, very wrong. And I sincerely apologize to you and all of the carpenters I insulted."

Anthony nodded and swallowed, his Adam's apple bobbing.

Kathryn's mind swam with confusion. She held her breath, awaiting her father's next words.

"Your skill as a carpenter is God's work," *Dat* continued. "And helping a member of the community is the best kind of work there is. I'm sorry for not seeing that sooner. I hope you can forgive me. I had been too proud to want to accept help from you, and being too proud is a sin and not an Amish ideal."

Kathryn let out a puff of air as she stared at her father.

"The truth is that it doesn't matter what you do for a living," *Dat* continued. "How you live and care for everyone in your community is what matters." He gestured around the barn that was taking shape. "You obviously care for your community. I also see now that you truly love *mei dochder.* And you make her *froh* as well, which is also important. It's not my place to choose whom she should love."

Kathryn cupped her hand to her mouth as her eyes stung with tears. Happiness exploded inside of her, making her feel dizzy.

"Nelson," Anthony began, his words and tone cautious, "are you saying that I'm permitted to date Kathryn?"

Dat looked at Kathryn and then back at Anthony. "*Ya,* you may date her." He glanced at Kathryn. "As long as she agrees, of course."

"Danki." Anthony shook his hand. "Thank you so much."

"No." *Dat* shook his head. "No, thank you for everything you've done for my family. We are grateful for you." He turned to Kathryn and touched her arm before heading toward the house. "You were right about him, Kathryn. I hope you can forgive me."

"Of course, *Dat,*" she said, her voice trembling.

Once he was gone, Anthony took Kathryn's hands in his. "Will you be my girlfriend?"

She gave a little laugh as she nodded. "I thought you'd never ask."

He chuckled and then squeezed her hand. *"Ich liebe dich."*

"Ich liebe dich," she whispered. "We'll talk more later."

"I look forward to it."

Then Kathryn started back toward the house, and she felt as if she were walking on a cloud.

Kathryn rested her head on Anthony's shoulder Sunday night as they sat on the glider on her porch and looked out toward the new barn. She breathed in the smell of moist earth as fireflies glittered by and cicadas serenaded them with their familiar song.

"I think the barn came out pretty well," Anthony said as he pushed the glider into motion with his foot.

"I think it's perfect." She looked up at him and admired his strong jaw. *"Danki."*

He smiled down at her. *"Gern gschehne."*

She sat up and looked at him. "Did you think that building the barn would convince *mei dat* to let you date me?"

He angled his body toward her. "When I told my family that I wanted to buy the wood and organize the barn raising, I honestly just wanted to help your family.

And I wanted you to see how much I love you."

"I'm so grateful to have you in my life." She touched his shoulder.

"I promise I will always cherish you."

His words were sweet music to her soul. He pulled her to him and brushed his lips over hers. The contact made her feel as if all the cells in her body were lit on fire and she was melting into a puddle.

When he broke the kiss, she leaned down and rested her head on his shoulder once again. "*Ich liebe dich,* Anthony."

"Ich liebe dich." He drew circles on her back with his fingertips, and she shivered at the contact. "I've never loved anyone as much as I love you."

Closing her eyes, Kathryn sent a silent prayer up to God, thanking him for convincing her father to give Anthony a chance. She couldn't wait to see what God had in store for them.

ACKNOWLEDGMENTS

As always, I'm grateful for my loving family, including my mother, Lola Goebelbecker; my husband, Joe; and my sons, Zac and Matt.

I'm also grateful for my special Amish friend who patiently answers my endless stream of questions. You're a blessing in my life.

Thank you to my wonderful church family at Morning Star Lutheran in Matthews, North Carolina, for your encouragement, prayers, love, and friendship. You all mean so much to my family and me.

Thank you to Zac Weikal and the fabulous members of my Bakery Bunch! I'm so grateful for your friendship and your excitement about my books. You all are awesome!

To my agent, Natasha Kern — I can't thank you enough for your guidance, advice, and friendship. You are a tremendous blessing in my life.

Thank you to my amazing editor, Jocelyn Bailey, for your friendship and guidance. I'm grateful to each and every person at HarperCollins Christian Publishing who helped make this book a reality.

Thank you to editor Becky Philpott for polishing the story and connecting the dots. I'm so grateful that we are working together again!

Thank you most of all to God — for giving me the inspiration and the words to glorify you. I'm grateful and humbled you've chosen this path for me.

DISCUSSION QUESTIONS

1. At the beginning of the story, Anthony has romantic feelings for Kathryn, but he's afraid she'll never see him as more than a friend. Why do you think he doubts her feelings for him?
2. Kathryn is devastated when her father won't allow her to date Anthony. What do you think about her father's reason for keeping them apart?
3. Maria tells Kathryn to not give up hope that her father will change his mind. She tells Kathryn to remember the verse from Proverbs 3:5. Do you find faith and hope in this verse?
4. Kathryn's mother refuses to help her convince her father to allow her to date Anthony. What is your opinion of the role of the submissive wife in the Amish community?
5. Which character can you identify with the most? Which character seemed to

carry the most emotional stake in the story? Was it Kathryn, Anthony, or someone else?

6. At the end of the story, Nelson agrees to give Anthony another chance. What do you think made him change his mind?
7. What role did the barn raising play in the relationships throughout the story?

To Raise a Home

KELLY IRVIN

To my son Nicholas, who gives me such joy and stories to tell.

And we know that in all things God works
for the good of those who love him,
who have been called according
to his purpose.

ROMANS 8:28

FEATURED FAMILIES FROM THE AMISH OF BIG SKY COUNTRY SERIES

BEN AND MELBA MAST

Delilah
Zeke
Martin
Mark
Abigail
Maisie

ANDY AND CHRISTINE (MAST) LAMBRIGHT

Matthew
Kaitlin

DEACON TOBIAS AND CECILIA EICHER

Mark
Seth
Elizabeth
Evan
Rachel
Atlee

Melinda
Nan
Robert

Menno and Mary Burkholder
John
Luke
Anna
Corinne
Justin
Eileen
Diane

Caleb and Mercy Hostetler
Matilda
Joseph

Levi and Nora Raber
Hope

Sam Parsons

Henry and Leesa Lufkin
Tommy (Adoptee)

Jack and Beatrice (Raber) Moser

Moser	**Raber**
Enoch	Levi
Diane	Mary
Joseph	Efraim
Charlie	Isaiah
Bobby	Hannah
Katie	Robert

CHAPTER ONE

Wham! The snowball sailed past Delilah Mast's head and smacked the barn. Chortling, she ducked and scooped up a handful of snow that glistened in the bright Montana sun. She packed it between hands clad in thick woolen mittens and shot a zinger at her little sister. Maisie returned fire.

It didn't matter that frigid mountain air so cold it made her lungs hurt nipped at Delilah's fingers and toes. What better way to celebrate their return to West Kootenai than with a snowball fight on top of a wedding? A year and a half of yearning for home had finally been relieved.

For you. Inhaling the fresh, clean scent of spruce she'd missed in Kansas, Delilah turned her back on the persnickety voice in her head determined to remind her that only she would be staying in West Kootenai. The rest of her family would return to Kansas now that their friends Henry and

Leesa Lufkin's wedding was over. Her parents would leave Delilah to the new start in her hometown she'd vehemently insisted she wanted.

Whack. An icy, hard-packed snowball smacked her in the ear. "Ouch!" She whirled. "Hey."

"That's what you get for daydreaming." A snowball in each hand, Evan Eicher taunted Delilah by brazenly taking his stand in the wide-open space between the Lufkins' new barn and the corral. Evan hadn't changed a bit in his black church clothes and hat. Solid, broad through the shoulders, blue eyes lit with laughter, the man stood before her in the flesh. "Welcome home."

"Danki." A shiver ran through Delilah that had nothing to do with the northern December wind. "It's *gut* to be here."

Heat spiraled through her, banishing the shivers. Did Evan recall the buggy rides they'd taken before the Caribou wildfires forced West Kootenai families to evacuate? Before Father decided to move the family back to Haven, Kansas? Did he remember the kiss — that single, breathless kiss — exchanged the last time he dropped her off on a warm late-August night? She could still feel the soft breeze on her face and hear the rustle of leaves on the tree branches overhead.

She could still smell the peppermint on his breath.

Her first and only — so far — kiss.

She'd promised to come back. He promised to wait. They both promised to write. For the first few months they had, once a week without fail. Then every two weeks. Then once a month. Then the letters petered out into nothingness.

Delilah was as much to blame as he was. It had become harder and harder to make that connection, to stoke the fire, when she had nothing new to write about. Life in Kansas had been as flat as the state's western landscape. Days on end of chores, baking, sewing, and the usual frolics.

She had wanted to return to Montana, to her home, to her friends, and yes, to Evan. Her parents kept saying no. How could she expect Evan to wait? It wasn't fair to him. Letting him go had seemed the right thing to do. Until now.

"Hey, no googly eyes during a snowball fight."

Delilah's brother hurled a snowball her direction. The other boys followed his lead. Snowballs rained down. Her breath pouring out in a steamy white cloud, she darted behind the corral gate and gathered more ammunition. Laughing that laugh that always made Delilah want to join him, Evan hunkered down behind a tree and fired back. A dozen other kids waiting for the wedding feast to begin joined in.

Joy warmed Delilah. The yoke of loneliness eased from her shoulders. Life would return to that sweet, peaceful keel that reigned in tiny Kootenai before the fire destroyed homes, drove away families, and divided couples. They could begin again.

She'd given up living with her family to come back home for this. Despite misgivings about her abilities, she'd agreed to take over teaching duties at the school now that Leesa was married. Being a lackluster pupil didn't mean she couldn't be a good teacher. She was determined to give it her very best.

Anything to return to her one true home.

"Coming through. I don't have a white flag." A high voice full of laughter floated over the raucous chatter. "Don't hit me. I'm defenseless!"

Delilah peered over the fence railing. Anna Burkholder stood on the porch. She held both arms over her head as she trotted down the steps. A single tendril of her ginger hair peeked bright from under the edges of her black woolen bonnet. Anna still had the smattering of freckles across her white nose and cheeks. She looked like a Raggedy Ann doll Delilah used to secretly covet at the Walmart in Eureka.

Evan shot across the yard toward Anna. "I'll be your shield."

"Danki. I appreciate it, kind sir." Anna laughed, a high breathless sound. They didn't touch. They didn't have to. Their faces said it all. "I need to get to my *schweschder*'s. I told her I wouldn't stay long. The *bopli* should be here soon. She's as nervous as a cat perched on the edge of a bathtub."

"Let me drive you." Evan towered over Anna, who had always been the runt in the gaggle of girls — including Delilah — who hung around together when they attended school. "My buggy is at the front of the line."

"Are you sure? Henry and Leesa are settling into the *eck.* Mercy and the others are serving the food. The cakes look yummy."

"I can always come back." Evan bowed and waved with a flourish. "After you. Does your *daed* know you're leaving?"

"*Jah. Mudder*'s already there."

Delilah straightened and watched them trot away, their boots crunching on the snow's crust.

Her hopes and dreams fizzled in her ears, the sound like air leaking from a balloon.

They had an easy way about their chatter. Like a couple who'd been together a long while.

A snowball smacked her in the nose. The painful impact brought tears to her eyes.

Not the sight of Evan putting his hands around Anna's tiny waist and lifting her into his buggy. Not the sight of their white puffs of breath mingling.

"*Gut* for you," she whispered. "Gut for you."

God moves in mysterious ways. Evan never really understood this maxim offered by his father in times of travail. To Evan's way of thinking God had a strange sense of humor. Stick Delilah and Evan in a buggy together. Allow a fire to threaten Kootenai. Send Delilah to Kansas. Then bring her back after Evan committed to another. He flicked the reins and urged Duke to pick up his pace. The horse snorted, his breath streaming white from his nostrils.

Evan had held out as long as he could. Winter in Montana was long, cold, and lonely. Everyone, especially his parents and the church elders, expected him to marry and start his own family.

"You're sure quiet." Anna tugged the fleece buggy robe tighter around her waist. "That snowball fight must've worn you out."

"*Nee,* I'm just enjoying the weather and the quiet after the big crowd at the wedding."

"Sorry, I'll hush."

Not for very long. The girl loved to talk. It didn't bother Evan. In fact, he welcomed it. That way the burden of making conversation hadn't fallen on him when they first started courting.

"That's not what I meant." Evan glanced her way, then back at the road. Her cheeks were flushed red from the cold. Her green eyes sparkled. She was a pretty girl. Plain folks didn't talk much about looks, but that didn't mean a man didn't notice. How could he help it? "Riding in a buggy with you is always a treat. I like your voice. It's just all those people talking at once starts to wear me down."

"You are a sweet talker. Riding in a buggy with you is the best treat." Anna tucked her hand under his elbow and leaned against his shoulder. "You're also warm. I like that."

"Wait until summer when I'm all sweaty. You won't like it so much then."

"I don't know about that." Her grip

tightened. "I reckon I'll like it even more . . ." Her voice trailed away. She cleared her throat. "I hope."

A hint. She'd been dropping them for a while now. Evan could be as dense as the next man when it came to matters of the heart, but he recognized her hints for what they were. They'd been courting for almost a year. He couldn't quite put his finger on how it happened. One minute their families were visiting over moose steaks for Sunday supper, and the next he'd been tangled up in her arms under a full harvest moon. Anna had smelled like lilacs, her lips were soft and her kisses fervent. She was kind, gentle, funny, smart, devout, and faithful.

He liked her a lot.

So why did the sight of Delilah Mast firing a snowball at him suck the air from his lungs and make his knees knock?

What did that say about him?

"Evan?"

He stared at the road ahead. The snow hid the deep ruts and steep turns. That's how he felt. Driving blind. "Jah."

"Are you . . . happy?"

"Of course I'm happy. I have a gut job at the Carriage Shop. I live in the most beautiful place in the world." Evan dug deep for the answer she wanted. "I have you. Things seem to be going well with us."

"*Seem* to be going well?" Her tone turned wry. Her hand dropped. "You don't sound too sure."

"I'm sure. I'm positive." He pulled into the yard at her sister's house and stopped. Taking his time, he slid around in the seat to face Anna. "I like taking it slow, making sure we're meant for each other, don't you?"

Her forehead wrinkled. She chewed her lower lip. "We've spent a year getting to know each other." She placed her mittens on his cold cheeks. "I hope you know by now my heart belongs to you."

Who could reject such a precious gift? Evan covered her hands with his. "You're a sweet girl. My heart isn't nearly as nice as yours, but you're welcome to it."

"You are such a goof." Her eyes bright with emotion, Anna glanced around. She stretched over and kissed him. Her lips warmed his. She let the kiss linger for a few seconds, then broke away. "Your heart suits me fine."

"You better go inside before your mudder looks out the window and sees you smooching on me." Evan nuzzled her cheek for a second. She smelled clean, like fresh soap — like innocence. "You brazen girl."

"She likes you." Anna chuckled. "She

keeps trying to get me to talk about you. She hems and haws and beats around the bush, wanting to know how things are coming."

How things are coming? Evan would've said good until a few minutes ago. He liked Anna's parents. He worked with her father at the Carriage Shop. Anna's father had an even temper and a kind streak a hundred miles long. Evan forced a smile. "They don't seem to mind me giving you a ride in broad daylight."

"Daed even suggested it." Anna pushed the robe aside. "Come inside. I'll make hot cocoa. You need to warm up before you drive back." She jumped down from the buggy and turned to look up at him. Her eyes were full of mischief. "I might find some other ways to warm you up as well."

"It is awfully chilly." A man didn't turn his back on a sweet, kind girl like Anna Burkholder. Hurting her would be the worst kind of sin. "Cocoa and you, a perfect recipe for a winter day."

Delilah Mast might be back in Kootenai, but her spot in Evan's life had been filled.

Chapter Two

The groan escaped despite Delilah's best effort to stifle it. She plopped onto the sofa across the fireplace in her sister's living room and grabbed the crocheted blanket that rested on its back. Winter in Kansas chilled fingers and noses, but a Montana winter turned the entire body to ice. After the snowball fight, she'd eaten too much turkey roast, mashed potatoes and gravy, green bean casserole, baked beans, rolls, and cake — two pieces — at the wedding. Try as she might, she couldn't fill the hole in her heart with food.

The newlyweds Henry and Leesa looked so happy. They were so busy holding hands under the tablecloth and staring at each other, they forgot to eat. Their soon-to-be-adopted son Tommy finally asked Leesa if she had a stomachache. Everyone laughed.

Delilah had the stomachache. She sighed. *Get over it.* If Evan had found happiness, she should thank God for that. She had a job to do in Kootenai, an important job, and she'd agreed to do it.

Of the few jobs permissible for a young, unmarried Plain woman, teaching would've been the last one Delilah picked. The irrefutable reason was simple. She would be terrible at it.

To say she'd been a mediocre student would be kind. Recess was her favorite subject. Baseball, her favorite sport. Followed by volleyball, kickball, basketball, and whatever other ball she could find.

Tough beans. Christine needed her. The school needed her. She'd made a commitment.

Another smaller groan escaped. Delilah slid her hand over her mouth. *Gott, I know I'm a silly goose. Forgive me for being so discontent. Help me be content.*

A tall order, even for God. Delilah cringed. *Sorry, Gott.*

"What are you moaning and groaning about? You're not the one who can no longer see her feet, let alone tie her own shoes." Christine plodded into the living room with mugs of hot tea in her hands. A short woman, her swollen belly preceded her. "This bopli isn't due for another six weeks, and I already stumble around like an expectant elephant."

"I ate too much. That's all." Delilah tucked her feet under the blanket and leaned back on Christine's hand-embroidered pillows. Having whispered conversations with her sister after everyone else went to bed had been one of the many things Delilah missed in Kansas. *Rumspringa,* boys, love, life — no topic had been off-limits. What she couldn't ask Mother, she could always ask Christine. "What does it feel like? Having a bopli inside you like that? It must be *wunderbarr.*"

"Don't get me wrong. It is special." Christine handed one of the mugs to Delilah. The fragrant scents of chamomile and lemon mingled with the aroma of burning wood. Christine settled into the rocking chair. "The first time I heard Matthew's heartbeat I cried. I pretended I had something in my eye, but I shed tears. The first time the bopli kicks you're filled with awe. It's a miracle. Of course, then the bopli gets bigger and sits on your bladder and your back hurts and you have heartburn all the time and you can't sleep at night. Then it doesn't feel like a miracle. You just want that bopli out of you. Then he's born and you love him so much the minute he's in your arms. We take giving life for granted because it's what we women do."

Most women did it. Not Delilah. Not yet. Or not ever?

"Don't worry. You'll know what it's like someday soon." Christine's big blue eyes saw too much. "I take it there wasn't anyone special in Haven?"

The catalog pages featuring Haven's small supply of young bachelors fanned out in Delilah's brain. Nice men. Mostly spoken for. Or not interested in the newcomer. Maybe she hadn't tried hard enough. "I went to singings. I sang. I ate cookies and drank sweet tea." She dunked the tea bag a few times, until her voice agreed to obey her demand that it not quiver. *Don't be a big baby.* "Everyone was nice. All the cousins were sweet. But everyone knew everyone. They've known each other since they were boplin. They have their inside jokes and their stories they've told a million times."

"You felt like an outsider."

"Pretty much. I could tell who liked who. Even if they weren't partnered up yet, they would be."

"I'm glad you talked Daed into letting you come home." Her expression absent, Christine rubbed her belly. "This is where you should be. Where the whole family should be."

Christine still refused to accept Father's decision to move back to Haven, where he could farm with his brothers the way he had growing up. He liked Montana fine as a place to hunt, camp, hike, and fish, but he no longer wanted to raise a family here.

"That's the thing. I wonder now if I've made a mistake." Delilah sipped the tea and let the hot liquid dissolve the lump in her throat. "I'll make an awful teacher. When the parents see how bad I am at it, they'll boot me out."

"First of all, that will never happen. Teachers are hard to come by. If you have rough spots, Leesa or Mercy or even I can help you figure out what to do." Christine rose and set her mug on the table. She moved to sit by Delilah. "In the second place, I need you here. To help me with the boplin and to keep me company. I've missed you, Schweschder."

Delilah scooched closer. Her sister's familiar scent of dish soap and lemon righted her world. "I've missed you too. But what if I do a bad job teaching? Those poor *kinner* won't know how to read and write."

"We'll ask Mercy to give you some lessons on teaching. We can meet her at the school and have a practice session. I reckon Leesa would be happy to help out too."

"I'm not asking a newlywed to come back to her old job. Surely there's someone else here who has a heart for teaching."

"No one at the moment. You wanted so badly to come home." Christine rubbed Delilah's shoulder the way a mother would comfort her child. "Tell me what's really going on."

"Why didn't you tell me Evan and Anna are courting?"

The rubbing stopped. Christine's eyebrows popped up. "I thought you knew. Mudder did. She and Anna's mudder write each other. They have ever since the fire."

"Mudder knew and she didn't tell me?"

"Anna's mom was just speculating. It's not like Anna came right out and told her. Maybe Mudder didn't want to make you feel bad over something that might only be a mother's intuition."

Anger mixed with embarrassment flooded through Delilah. Mother was the one who told her true love would withstand distance. Moving to Kansas didn't have to be the end of her fledgling courtship with Evan, if God meant them to be together. "She didn't think seeing them ogle each other in front of Gott and everyone would hurt?"

"You went on a few buggy rides when you were seventeen." Christine winced and shifted. She patted Delilah's shoulder, then let her hand drop. "It's not as if you were special friends. Maybe Mudder thought you'd forgotten about him or moved on."

In her homesickness had she made more of her time with Evan than it really was? Delilah plucked at a loose thread on the afghan. Aside from the kiss, what did she remember about their time together?

He had the capacity to surprise her. Evan never talked much before those buggy rides. She barely noticed him. In fact, she almost declined that first ride. What would they talk about?

It turned out he could talk, but he saved his thoughts for people he liked. People he cared about. Like her. He joked and told stories. He knew about wildlife and Montana history and he liked playing baseball.

"Do you really think I'm that fickle and foolish?" Delilah stopped and took a long breath. None of this was Christine's fault. "What if Andy found someone new when he went home to Lewistown while you were in St. Ignatius during the evacuation?"

Red crept up Christine's neck and across her cheeks. She fiddled with the bobby pins that held her *kapp* in her blonde hair. "A lot more went on during that time than you know." She stood, stuck one hand on her hip, and grimaced. "I have heartburn. Again. It's been a long day. Give me a hug and go to bed."

Christine could always be counted on for a good hug. Delilah stood and went to her.

"Tomorrow's another day," Christine whispered in her ear. "The sun will shine and things will look better. I promise."

"What happened between you and Andy?" Delilah hugged her sister's round body. "You never said a word."

"It's a long story, but basically Andy felt I got too close to a man named Raymond Old Fox during my time in St. Ignatius during the evacuation." Rubbing her belly, Christine plopped back on the couch. She tugged on Delilah's hand, forcing her to sit as well. "For his part, Andy failed to tell me something very important that happened to him before he and I courted. It wouldn't be fair to him to share it with you, but it colored the way he saw our relationship."

"You courted another man in St. Ignatius?" With a name like Old Fox, it didn't seem likely the man was Plain. Delilah's dilemma with Evan seemed staid in comparison. Suddenly her sluggishness disappeared. She was wide awake. "An *En-*

glischer? Did Mudder and Daed know? Is that why they raced back to St. Ignatius last year?"

"I didn't court Raymond. He's a Kootenai Native Indian. He taught me his tribe's history and about their beliefs." Christine's cheeks were radish-red now, but she didn't look away from Delilah. "For the first time, I had to defend our beliefs. It was hard. It is hard. To think someone as good and kind and smart and spiritual as Raymond doesn't believe in Jesus. That I won't see him in heaven."

"That does sound hard. I haven't ever spent time with anyone who doesn't believe in Jesus."

"That's because we distance ourselves from the world. I did a lot of soul searching. I wasn't sure I could come back here and pick up where I left off like none of it happened. *Onkel* Fergie called Daed. He and Mudder came back. It was a mess."

"Mudder wouldn't tell me why they were coming home." Their mother's explanation of the sudden decision to return to St. Ignatius had been vague and troubling. Delilah had been angry and disappointed when they didn't allow her to travel with them. "Daed looked ready to explode."

"I felt terrible about making them worry,

but I'll never be sorry I spent time with Raymond. He changed my way of looking at the world. I never liked being out in nature. I didn't appreciate it. Now I do. I sometimes wonder where he is and how his life is turning out."

Delilah studied her older sister. Christine's face was a kaleidoscope of emotions. Wistfulness. Sadness. Almost a tenderness. Yet contentment shone through it all. "But you're happy with Andy."

"So happy. We went through a time of trial and came through on the other side stronger and more united as a couple." Christine yawned widely and rubbed her eyes. She stood. "I really have to go to bed. Just know, Schweschder, now is your time."

"My time?"

"Sweet dreams." Christine yawned again and waddled away. "See you tomorrow."

Yes. Delilah's time. Time to make the best of it. Time to do her best.

God would use everything for her good. Scripture said so.

With or without one Evan Eicher.

Chapter Three

Teaching the teacher. Instead of a canning or quilting frolic, they were having a teaching frolic this sunny Friday afternoon. Delilah stood in the classroom, chalk in one hand, an English workbook in the other. Her students were a tad large — or too small — for the wooden desks that lined the room. Mercy Hostetler and her two little ones, Nora Raber with baby Hope sleeping in her arms, Leesa, and finally Christine, who sang softly to Matthew, who'd rather be crawling around on the dusty floor. An occasional fit of laughter marred an otherwise sedate practice run through a typical day in a Plain one-room school.

"Okay, you've read Scripture and recited the Lord's Prayer. You've let two scholars pick three hymns and lead the singing." Mercy, who had grown rounder with each of her babies, shifted little Joseph to her other arm. He squawked in protest and tried to climb down. "Now you can have the older students work on their arithmetic problems while you hear the first and second graders do their English reading."

"You haven't been out of school that long," Leesa, who looked bright eyed and rosy cheeked after one day of marriage, chimed in. "You remember how it goes. Besides, if you don't do it exactly like the teacher before you, it doesn't matter. You'll establish your own routines."

Easy for her to say. Delilah's memories of learning at school were hazy. What she did remember was the neck-breaking race around second base headed for third on the school's baseball diamond, a slide headfirst into home, and the accompanying rips in her apron. The dirt on her dress and her face. It didn't make Mother happy, but Delilah still smiled at a run scored and a game won.

She had, on occasion, been accused of being overly competitive.

"Delilah!" Christine clapped. "Pay attention. If you don't, your students won't. Too much downtime and they'll find other things to do."

"Isn't it recess time yet?"

Delilah's pretend scholars laughed.

"Or lunchtime?"

More chuckles.

"I don't remember school being so much fun." The deep voice booming from the back of the room ended the frivolity in a split second.

Every pretend scholar swiveled to stare at Bishop Noah Duncan. He stamped snow from his boots and clapped his gloved hands together as if to warm them.

Beside him stood Anna Burkholder.

White heat spread across Delilah's cheeks. Her mind went blank. "We were just . . . just . . ."

"Preparing for the new school semester." Mercy popped up and shifted her baby to her hip. "We'll do some cleaning too. What brings you here, Noah?"

Delilah turned to lay the chalk on the chalkboard ledge. It slid from her hand and hit the floor. In three pieces. She knelt to pick them up. Her head collided with the desk. "Ouch!"

Hand rubbing her temple, she stood. Anna still hadn't moved or spoken, but unmistakable humor flashed in her green eyes.

Not funny. So not funny.

"I came by to tell you the school board had an impromptu meeting this afternoon." Stripping off his gloves, Noah moved toward the wood-burning stove where he warmed his hands. "We decided to try something new. We've asked Anna to team teach with Delilah for this next semester. She's agreed."

After a second Delilah remembered to close her mouth. The parents who served on the board must have their reasons. Maybe they remembered Delilah's school years. Anna had been a good student. She often helped with the younger scholars. She liked to read. Everyone wanted her on their team for spelling bees.

"That is gut." Delilah managed a smile. "Two minds are better than one."

"We seem to go through a lot of teachers here." Noah flashed her a smile in return. "Love is in the air in Montana, it seems. This way we'll have a backup teacher prepared and ready to go should the need arise."

His diplomatic way of saying should one of them marry. Leesa and Mercy were both former teachers, now married. That's the way it worked. Did he know Anna was the one most likely to stand before him to take her wedding vows in the not-too-distant future?

Why pick Delilah? Options for single women of age in their district were limited. That's why they'd agreed to bring Delilah back. So why the decision now to add a second teacher? Why not have Anna do it to begin with? All questions Delilah didn't dare pose. She waved at Anna. "Come up front. We're doing a run-through of the entire day."

Grinning from ear to ear, Anna brushed past Noah and trotted to the front. "I'm so excited. It's such a joy to be asked to teach. I loved school, didn't you?"

Ignoring Christine's snort of laughter, Delilah nodded. "I liked parts of it." Lunch. Recess. Passing notes. Singing. "We can divide the students up by age, or do you think it's better to do it by subject?"

Anna patted a stack of magazines clutched in one arm. "I've been reading up on the *Blackboard Bulletin.* I have lots of ideas. We can get together for a planning session, if you want."

Of course Delilah wanted to do a good job. Be a good teacher. Even if that meant spending every day with Evan's special friend. "Jah, we can do that after we get done with the run-through."

"Very gut." Noah beamed. "The board members will be happy to know our scholars are in gut hands again this year."

With that he strolled out the door. Delilah faced her pretend scholars. "The first, second, and third graders will start with their reading assignment on pages 15 through 18 in the workbook. Fourth through eighth grades will do lesson 14 in the math book. When you're done, seventh and eighth graders will exchange papers and grade them before grading everyone else's papers."

"Don't you think when we have actual students, I should review their work?" Anna's forehead had a tiny wrinkle that traveled between her eyebrows. "Math was my best subject. I want to make sure they work the problems out correctly."

Her tone was eager and her smile no doubt genuine. Delilah scrambled to match it. "If we're spending our time going over work with the students, we won't have time to teach all the subjects in a day —"

"In the *Blackboard Bulletin* it says the older children can help the middle grades with their work — that makes it a review for them as well. But we don't want to turn the scholars into teachers, do we?" Anna tapped the stack of magazines lying on the desk. "The important thing is to make sure every student is learning during every period throughout the day."

Her forehead throbbing, Delilah moved toward the chair behind the teacher's desk.

Anna did the same. Their hands touched it at the same time. Delilah drew back. "Oh, you go ahead."

"No, you go ahead."

Neither moved.

"It sounds like you two will work well together. Having two teachers will be so helpful." Mercy stood and tugged Joseph's coat onto his chubby body. "Write the lessons on the board for each subject and grade. Divide up the duties and you'll be fine. Remember, your scholars know what to do. If you get overwhelmed, give them an essay to write and take a few minutes to regroup."

Sage advice from a woman who'd taught school in a garage in Eureka during the Caribou Fire evacuation. If only Delilah had her presence of mind. "We haven't finished the run-through."

"I have a schedule all written out." Anna held up a spiral notebook. She plopped into the teacher's chair and flipped over the cover. "Every minute is accounted for."

Delilah shot a beseeching glance at Christine. Her sister offered her an encouraging smile. "You two will do fine. We'll get a ride with Mercy. I'll leave the buggy for you."

In seconds the room cleared, leaving Delilah to sink into a desk on the front row as if she were the scholar and Anna her teacher.

Anna rose and went to the blackboard where she began to write the subjects across the top and grades down the side. "School starts at eight thirty, so we should get here at least thirty minutes before to get the fire going and warm up the place. At least on Monday. After that we can assign the older boys to come in early and get the fire going. I have a chore list ready to go unless you can think of other chores besides bringing in firewood, sweeping, cleaning the chalkboards, emptying the trash cans —"

"How long have you known they wanted you to teach?"

Anna stopped with the piece of chalk suspended in the air. She swiveled. "Noah came to the house last week to talk to Mudder and Daed and me. They thought it was best we pray about it. So we did that. Then this afternoon, we got together and I made the commitment. But truth be told, I knew as soon as he asked that I would say jah if Mudder and Daed agreed."

"It's just that it was never mentioned, and we've been here for over a week." Delilah drew circles in the chalk dust her hands had deposited on the desktop. "It came as a surprise. What made them think a second teacher was needed?"

"Just what Noah said — it's a backup plan." Anna's cheeks turned pink. Her upper lip twitched. "What other reason would there be?"

"Maybe they had second thoughts about having me teach. That's all."

"I'm sure that's not it." Anna turned back to the board and started writing out sentences in Pennsylvania Dutch and English. High German would be reserved for the older children once they had a better grasp of English. Learning to read and write two new languages was a tall order. "Evan did say he was surprised that you would be teaching. He and I both remember how much you daydreamed in class, and you never could remember your division tables. You hated writing essays —"

"You and Evan were talking about me? Why?" Delilah swallowed the snarky retort that threatened to escape. "I can't believe you remember that much about my school days."

"They were my school days too." This time Anna dropped the chalk onto the tray and turned around. She brushed her hands together. "I always secretly wished . . . I could be more like you."

"Me?" Delilah's voice squeaked with astonishment. "You were a gut student. You always knew the answer when teacher called on you. Your essays never had black eraser blotches all over them."

"Everybody liked you. Everyone wanted to be on your team at recess. I was always the last one picked."

Because she was small and afraid of the ball.

But boys outgrew the stage where their only thought was who could hit the ball the hardest. One day they decided they liked the prettiest girl who baked the best pie and would make a good wife.

That was Anna.

"It was a long time ago."

"Let's not get sidetracked. We should look through the bulletins." Anna grabbed the stack from the teacher's desk and brought them to Delilah. "This one on top has an article written by a teacher who shares her tips for helping students who fall behind in their reading. Also one on memorization tricks for multiplication and division tables. They have a lot of ideas for how to decorate the room too. Don't you think that will be fun?"

So far the room had laminated placards with the names of the months in English across the top of the blackboard. And the alphabet in cursive. After the scholars did art projects, they could display their drawings on the walls. Nothing else was needed. Delilah took half the stack of bulletins and dutifully opened the first one. "Jah, definitely."

Anna hadn't answered her question. Why had Evan been talking to Anna about Delilah?

Did Anna know about her special friend's short but sweet courtship with Delilah?

Courting was private. She didn't know Anna well enough to ask her any of the questions that pestered her like overgrown horseflies.

"The chore chart Leesa used is just like mine. I can transfer the names to mine since it's fresh." Anna flipped through the pages of her bulletin. "No sense in reinventing the wheel. Leesa didn't want to teach, either, when she first started. She was down in the dumps and needed something to do. It turns out she was good at it. She even helped Henry's foster son settle down and learn. If she can do it, you can do it."

Another example of how the fires turned lives upside down. Leesa's first special friend had taken the opportunity to dump her during the wildfire evacuation. "What makes you think I don't want to teach?"

"When I walked in with Noah you looked

petrified. I can understand that. Starting something new, especially standing up and talking in front of people — even kinner — is a little scary."

"I'm not afraid." Delilah wiggled in her chair. Not much, anyway. "It's just something new."

"We'll make it an adventure." Laughing, Anna clapped. "That's what Evan calls everything. No matter what it is, he loves trying new things. I really like that about him."

The perfect opening. "How long have you been courting?"

"About a year. We'd seen each other around, of course, but we never connected until after the rebuilding was finished and life got back to normal in Kootenai. It seemed like everyone from school was getting married and starting families. Except Evan and me . . ." Her cheeks pink and her eyes shiny, Anna's voice trailed away. She had left the building and flown back to the memories of those days when life should have returned to normal but never quite did.

"I think we both felt silly going to the singings. We were the oldest ones there. One night we started laughing about it and one thing led to another. He walked up to me after the singing, big as you please, and asked if I wanted a ride. It's funny how a person can be right in front of you all that time and you never really notice them. Until the time is right."

Big as you please. A year after his last buggy ride with Delilah, Evan had strolled into Anna's life.

Delilah forced herself to ignore the pain that seized her heart. Evan had moved on. So should she. "We'll use the schedule you wrote on the board tomorrow. I should get going. I need to help Christine with supper. Mudder and Daed are headed back to Kansas on Monday, so we only have a few more days together."

Anna patted Delilah's hand. "I know how I'd miss my family if it were me. But you'll be so busy teaching, you won't have time to think about it. And you'll have me to talk to."

How could a person be ugly in the face of such kindness? "Danki. I'm so happy to be back in West Kootenai. I know it'll be just fine. Do you need a ride home?"

"That's sweet of you. Daed is coming for me." Anna made a shooing motion. "Go on. I'll close up. Get a gut night's sleep. The fun begins on Monday."

As much as she wanted to be surly, Delilah couldn't help but smile as she trotted out to the buggy and set out for Christine's house. No wonder Evan liked Anna. She exuded sunshine and goodwill. And she was pretty. And smart.

Okay, okay, no need to pile it on.

Delilah did what she always did when her thoughts stank. She sang. First "How Great Thou Art," followed by "Bringing in the Sheaves." When that didn't do it, she proceeded with every single verse of "Amazing Grace."

Paddy nickered and shook his head.

Delilah didn't have the best singing voice in the world. "Everybody's a critic."

"Sounds pretty gut to me." A Plain man riding a creamy butterscotch gelding pulled alongside Delilah's buggy. "Quite the concert you're giving. I've been enjoying it for more than a mile now."

"I didn't know I had an audience." Heat singed Delilah's cheeks. She sideswiped the stranger with a glance, then turned her attention back to the road. He was massive. Long legs hung down past his horse's belly. Broad shoulders strained against his black coat. No beard. Tufts of pale-blond hair stuck out from under his straw hat. Delilah snapped the reins and picked up her pace. "A person ought to make himself known."

"I'm Sam Parsons. You must be new

around here." Sam had a raspy voice like sandpaper on wood. He looked to be around Delilah's age, but he had an old man's voice. "I'm sure I've met everyone in my six months in Kootenai."

He was the new person. He'd figure that out on his own, eventually. Delilah snapped the reins again. "Not everyone, I reckon." She pulled ahead and made a right turn toward Christine and Andy's fifteen-acre plot.

"At least tell me your name." His laughter-filled voice followed her.

What was so funny?

Chapter Four

If faith followed by family came first in Plain communities, food wasn't far behind.

Delilah skipped up the back porch steps into Christine's kitchen. She hung up her coat and squeezed between her sister and mother to wash her hands. The scent of roast beef floated on air warmed by the propane oven. Fresh baked rolls bloomed in their pans on the counter. Potatoes boiled on the stove next to a pot of green beans seasoned with chunks of bacon and onion. Two apple pies cooled on the prep table.

"What a feast." Delilah dried her hands and exchanged her apron for a clean one. "How can I help?"

"You can mash the potatoes." Mother opened the oven door. Another wave of mouth-watering aroma flooded the kitchen. "The roast will be done in about ten minutes."

"I know there's a lot of us, but this seems

like a mountain of food." Delilah grabbed hot pads and manhandled the huge pot to the sink. She shrank back from the hot steam as she drained the water from the potatoes. "Are we having company?"

Christine handed a stack of plates to little sister Abigail, who handed half of them to Maisie. "We are."

Something in her dry tone warned Delilah. "Who?"

"Ask Mudder. She did the inviting."

"You make it sound like I did something awful." Mother used her apron to wipe steam from her dark-rimmed glasses. "I just want to see all my friends before we leave on Monday."

"Uh-huh." Christine brushed Maisie's hand from a plate of chocolate chip chocolate fudge cookies nestled on a plate next to the pies. "You'll ruin your appetite, Schweschder."

"Who did she invite?"

"Go see for yourself." Christine held out an enormous pitcher filled with water. "Fill the glasses while you're at it."

Three long strides into the open space that served as dining room and living room told Delilah everything she needed to know. Andy Lambright squatted next to the fireplace adding wood to a blazing fire. Father sat on the sofa next to Tobias Eicher. The deacon's younger sons played Life on the Farm with Delilah's brothers. That left the rocking chair.

Evan occupied it.

Delilah did an about-face and scurried back to the kitchen. "Why would you do that, Mudder?"

Mother had the audacity to look puzzled. "Do what?"

"Don't pretend to be innocent. How could you invite the Eichers over here? You knew about me and Evan," Delilah whispered even though the raucous game of Life on the Farm assured that no one in the living room could hear themselves think, let alone hear a conversation in the kitchen. "Why didn't you tell me about Anna?"

"I didn't know anything for certain." Mother's chin jutted. "It's none of my business."

"We all know how fast gossip travels around here." Delilah added milk and butter to the potatoes, snatched up the potato masher, and went to work — the poor potatoes didn't stand a chance. "You and Daed let Christine stay in St. Ignatius so she could be close to Andy, but you said I was too young. I had to go to Kansas, even though it meant being apart from Evan. You said if it was meant to be, we would survive the separation."

"All very true. You were seventeen. If Gott's plan for you included Evan, He would make a way. He still will. Cecilia doesn't know anything for certain." Mother dumped the rolls in a basket and sashayed toward the door. "She only said Evan moped around forever after we moved to Kansas. One day he picked himself up, dusted himself off, straightened his hat, and started smiling again."

Good for him. Delilah mashed so hard the potatoes whipped into high peaks. Really. No one should have to pine forever. No one should be lonely forever. Life went on. "Where is Cecilia? Why isn't she here?"

If Evan's mother had come with her family, she'd be in the kitchen cooking up a storm. When it came to feeding people, she couldn't sit idly by.

"At home. She has a cold."

No picking her brain about Evan's decision to dump Delilah. She mashed harder.

Christine laid her hand on Delilah's. "I believe those are the fluffiest mashed potatoes I've ever seen. You can stop now."

"Fine." Delilah dumped the potatoes into a bowl and scraped the bottom of the pan until every last morsel of potato surrendered. "Just fine."

"Your face is flushed. You look pretty." Christine chuckled. "I'm sure he'll notice. He'll know what he's been missing."

"Anna is a nice girl. I like her. I'm glad for her." Potatoes in hand, Delilah marched from the room. "Flushed, indeed."

She arrived in the dining room just as Andy closed the front door. "Welcome, welcome. Glad you could make it."

"Danki for the invite. I stopped at the cabin to feed my *hunds* and change my clothes after work." Sam Parsons stomped his snowy boots on the rug and grinned. "But I never miss a chance for a home-cooked meal."

He looked directly at Delilah. "Or the chance for another serenade."

A serenade? Evan rose from the rocking chair and stuck his hands behind his back, as if warming them on the fire. Delilah must've sneaked in the back door. He'd been waiting for her to show up since he and his family arrived at Andy's house. Not that he would dare admit that. He only wanted to talk to her. He wanted to know why she stopped writing. Why hadn't she returned home sooner? Had she really come home because Kootenai needed a teacher or was it because of Evan? Or both?

And how did she know Sam? Sam who showed up one day in Kootenai looking for a bed and a job. The Ohioan never met a person he didn't like, and he never lacked for a story to tell.

Plus he was a crackerjack craftsman who could make harnesses and other gear for horses and buggies with his eyes closed. He snapped up a job at the Carriage Shop and moved into one of the vacant cabins. A person could hardly remember when he hadn't been a part of the Kootenai community.

Sam acted like he knew Delilah too. How could he? She'd only been back a week. Sam had attended Henry and Leesa's wedding. But what did that have to do with singing?

Either way, it was none of Evan's business. He traipsed forward. "I didn't know you were coming. Did you have a gut holiday?"

"I finagled an invitation after the wedding." Sam wiggled from his coat and hung it on a hook by the door. He was an imposing figure. Evan stood six one and weighed 170 pounds. Sam was at least two inches taller and 15 pounds heavier. He should've been a lumberjack.

"I invited him." Delilah's mother, Melba,

bustled to the table, bearing a bowl of green beans. "The more the merrier."

True.

Christine followed, bearing a pan of tasty-looking roast. "Sit, everyone, sit."

The men had stuck two long tables and benches together. Plus they placed a smaller table nearby for the children. Laughter and a low murmur of anticipation filled the room as more than a dozen people jockeyed for position, women to one side and men to the other.

In the meantime Christine, Delilah, and their mother continued to bring food to the table and fill water glasses. Determined not to stare, Evan fixed his gaze on the bowl of green beans. He began to count the beans. One, two, three . . .

Delilah's dad cleared his throat. Conversation ceased. Heads bowed. After a few moments of silence, Ben said amen and everyone talked at once.

"I hope you like roast beef, Sam." Delilah leaned between Evan and the other man with a mammoth bowl of potatoes. Her arm brushed against his. Accidentally, no doubt. "Help yourself before the boys take it all. It's every man for himself around here."

It certainly was. She obviously didn't plan to acknowledge Evan's presence. He grabbed a roll from the basket and picked up his butter knife. "I didn't know you two had met."

"We haven't." Sam stabbed a healthy slab of meat and deposited it on his plate. "Our paths crossed on the road earlier this evening, but she didn't bother to tell me her name."

Delilah slid onto the bench directly across from Sam. Her dimpled cheeks were flushed. A strand of blonde hair spiraled from under her kapp. The familiar blue of her eyes captured Evan. Her expression, however, said something different. She smiled at Sam. "It's Delilah. Christine is my sister."

She went on to explain why she had left Kootenai and why she had returned. No mention of Evan, of course. She wanted to be with Christine. She wanted to teach. Sam nodded, smiled, and chewed. Evan might as well have been in Missoula. He slathered butter on his roll and stuffed half of it in his mouth to keep from saying something he shouldn't.

"I know I'll love teaching. I loved school."

Evan inhaled bread. It caught in his throat and he coughed. Sam slapped him on the back, hard. "Are you okay? You're supposed to chew before you swallow."

Her eyebrows lifted, Delilah stared but said nothing.

Evan gulped water and wiped his face with his napkin. The girl he knew couldn't wait for the school bell to ring so she could be set free. "I'm fine. It went down the wrong pipe."

"What's going on down there?" Ben Mast hollered from the other end of the table. "Sounds like someone is dying."

"We're gut. I was just telling them how much I like my new home." Sam raised his water glass. "This is mighty fine food. I haven't had a good roast like this since I left home."

He launched into a story about his father's farm back in Ohio. Evan had known the man for six months, and it seemed he'd already heard every story twice. Sam liked to talk. He also seemed to like the sound of his own voice.

So did Delilah, apparently. She listened with rapt attention, the food on her plate barely touched.

"Aren't you hungry?" Evan kept his voice down. Still, she glanced his direction. He nodded at her plate. "You haven't eaten."

"I lost my appetite."

Evan glanced at the others. Everyone seemed entranced with Sam's story about bear meat and a pot of stone soup. "Why?"

She shook her head. "Mudder and Daed are leaving soon. I'll be here . . . alone."

"Not alone."

Delilah's nose wrinkled. She slid from the bench and picked up her plate. "More green beans? Mashed potatoes?"

"Nee."

"I better get the pies ready." She whirled and strode away.

A definite chill in the air. He deserved that and more. In his defense, her letters had become more and more infrequent. She prattled on about singings and frolics and fishing. She sounded happy and settled. Then the letters petered out until they stopped.

She never wrote to say she was returning. She simply showed up two days before Christmas. A wonderful Christmas present — except it wasn't for him.

The meal dragged on. Delilah didn't return to her seat. Instead she and the other women cleared the tables and brought out pie. Or cookies for those who had a hankering for chocolate.

Evan slid from the bench and went to stand by the fire. It also gave him a view of the door to the kitchen. Sure enough, after a bit Delilah slipped from the kitchen, wearing her coat. She added her gloves and wool bonnet at the front door and disappeared through it.

Glancing around, Evan grabbed his coat from the hook and followed. Delilah had a head start, but he followed her boot prints in the foot-deep snow until he found her standing at the corral fence, staring up at the star-filled sky. A three-quarter moon cast a bright light on her dark figure.

"It's too cold for stargazing."

Delilah jumped and whirled. "The house was too crowded." She turned back to the fence. "Now it's crowded out here."

Evan stopped within arm's reach. He inhaled. The cold air seared his lungs. "Why didn't you write to tell me you were coming back?"

"That's not a question you should be asking, not now." Delilah edged away. "How's Anna doing?"

"Anna's a sweet girl."

"Why are you standing here talking to me then?"

"You don't understand what it was like."

"I don't?" Bitterness mingled with hurt in her soft laugh. "I'm the one who moved to a new place, away from the home I grew up in. Sure, I had family but not friends. Not even Christine. You were still here. You had

Kootenai and your family and all your old friends. You didn't have to move. You didn't change jobs."

She was right. Nothing had changed, yet everything had been different. Some of his earliest memories included Delilah. Their families fished together at Lake Koocanusa. They camped in the Cabinet Mountains. They hunted for moose, deer, and elk. Delilah was always there. He and her brothers played pranks on the girls. Christine and Delilah returned the favor. They had fun. It wasn't until eighth grade and the end of school that he realized how much he looked forward to seeing her every day.

The memory of his sweaty hands and his big feet tripping over the steps the night he first asked her to take a ride in his buggy floated in his mind. She seemed surprised at first. Then pleased. At least he thought so. That fleeting grin gave him the courage to ask her again.

Then came the fire.

"I'm sorry it was so hard for you." He gripped the railing with both hands, searching for the right words. "I thought about you all the time."

"At first." Delilah ducked her head and sighed. "Me too. I thought of you. It was so hard. I kept asking to come home, but Daed said nee. It seemed wrong to prolong the agony. It seemed like we would never be together again. Writing letters only made me want to be here even more. Still, it was wrong to just stop writing. I should've written to you about how I was feeling."

"It's okay. I know exactly what you mean." The hard reality of life had intruded for Evan as well. "Did you know *Daadi* and *Mammi* died over the summer?"

"Nee." Her voice softened. She turned to face him. "I'm sorry."

His father's parents had lived with Evan and his seven brothers and sisters for as long as he could remember. Grandma cooked, cleaned, baked, sewed, sang, and laughed until the day she died peacefully in her sleep. One month later Grandpa followed her to Glory. He had no problem with her going ahead. After fifty-five years of marriage, he simply couldn't bear to be left behind.

"They lived gut lives. They were humble, obedient servants." That's what Evan's father had said. That should make him feel better, but it didn't. Evan still went to the *dawdy haus* at night to sit at their tiny kitchen table and breathe their smell of peanut butter cookies and coffee. "It made me think, though."

"The fire and the evacuation — everything about last year made me think." Delilah cocked her head and pointed at the sky. "It's hard to believe you and I stared at the same stars in Kansas and up here, practically in Canada."

"I'm sorry I stopped writing. I'm not making excuses. Daadi and Mammi were the first people I ever lost. I shut down. I couldn't put into words what it was like. The last thing I wanted to do was write a letter about it." He gripped the wooden railing and searched for words in the glittering snow. "To me, it seemed like everything was changing. You were always here when we were growing up. Then you were gone. Daadi and Mammi were gone. My mudder and daed acted like we should be happy for them, and we should be. But I didn't feel happy."

Out of breath, he stopped. All those words. They'd been stewing inside of him for months. He had a hole where his grandparents had been. A hole where Delilah had been. A man didn't put words to such foolishness. He couldn't tell anyone. Yet here he stood baring his soul to Delilah. He'd known her his entire life. If anyone would understand she would.

With her he had a closeness he'd never

felt with another living soul.

Did she feel it too?

"I wish I could've been here for you. Like you were here for me when Mammi died. You listened to all my stories about her, even though you knew most of them already. You didn't mind when I wet your shirt with my tears."

"It's okay. You didn't have a choice. You had to go to Kansas." The memory of Delilah's tear-streaked face washed over him. The desire to reach for her hand followed. Nee. Nee. He wasn't that kind of man. "It's getting late. I should go in."

"You should."

"It's cold. Your feet must be frozen."

"That's okay. I'd rather not feel anything right now."

The crippling ache in Evan's chest made it hard to breathe. He shared her desire to be numb. "I'm sorry, Delilah. I'm so sorry." He gritted his teeth and backed away from her. "I should've let you know. I never meant for you to be hurt."

"It's fine, Evan. Don't worry about it."

"It's not fine."

She sighed. "I'll be okay."

"I'm so sorry. I didn't think you were coming back."

"Neither did I."

"Now you're here and I —"

"And you have a special friend." She swiveled and smiled up at him. "Go on. I reckon she's waiting for you right this minute. Anna's a gut girl. Don't keep her waiting."

Evan whirled and tramped toward the house.

Her sweet voice trailed away on the coldest north wind to ever blow across the Montana mountains. "Be happy, Evan."

Chapter Five

Peanut M&M's wouldn't assuage the pain in the vicinity of Delilah's heart. But they wouldn't hurt either. Bag of candy in one hand, she stood in the middle of the aisle in the Kootenai General Store and debated. Her mission as assigned by Mother was to buy snacks for her brothers and sisters to enjoy on the long trip home to Kansas.

As if Kansas was home.

"One for me, one for you." She dropped the bag into her red hand-held basket and grabbed another one. "It seems only fair."

Delilah might not be making the trip physically, but emotionally her heart would be squeezed into the middle row of the van with Maisie, Abigail, and their smelly dogs Socks and Shoes. *Don't think about it. Think about treats.* Store-bought snacks were a special treat. Maisie and Abigail wanted Baby Ruth and Snickers candy bars. Mother had suggested breakfast bars. Rice Krispies

Treats qualified as breakfast bars, didn't they? "One for me, one for you."

And one more for good measure.

Mother would think twice about giving Delilah free rein with her money in the future.

"You sing to yourself. Now you're talking to yourself."

Not again. The familiar voice held laughter — again. Delilah took a long breath and let it out. Smile firmly affixed to her face, she turned to gaze up at Sam. He slid his straw hat back, letting a shock of unruly blond hair escape. "It looks like you have quite the sweet tooth."

"Hi. What are you doing here?"

Heat billowed through her. *Silly question, you ninny.* Like her, he had a basket hanging from one arm. It held a loaf of bread, peanut butter, jam, a quart of milk, and a bag of chips.

No fruit or vegetables.

Bachelor cooking.

He didn't seem to notice her discomfort. "A person can get away with singing alone but talking is different. Someone might think you've gone round the bend."

"I only talk to myself when I'm upset." Now why had she blurted that out? "I mean, there's so many choices of candy.

How is a person supposed to know what to choose?"

Even sillier. *Gott, let me melt into a puddle of pudding and seep through the cracks in the pine plank floor. Please.*

God wasn't in the mood for answering silly prayers it seemed.

"I reckon there are worse things in the world than having too many choices in the candy aisle. Personally, I like the combination of peanut butter and chocolate." He held up a package of Reese's Peanut Butter Cups. "You can always claim it's good for you. It has peanut butter in it."

"I like the way you think."

He grinned and held out the bag. She smiled and accepted it.

"Don't you want one for you?" His thick blond eyebrows rose over pale-blue eyes. "It was one for you and one for me wasn't it, or did I hear wrong?"

Delilah groaned and studied her shoes. "No one was supposed to hear that. I was just feeling sorry for myself."

"Because your family is going home and leaving you here?"

"Kootenai *is* home." No sense in taking it out on him. Delilah softened her tone. "Yes, because they're leaving and I'm staying. But

I'm a grown woman. Plus I chose to stay here."

"I chose to leave my family and home in Ohio to come here." Sam reached past her and scooped up two packages of jelly beans from the shelf. He added them to her basket instead of his own. "I'm a grown man out on my own. That doesn't mean I don't miss them. It doesn't mean I don't sometimes wonder if I did the right thing."

"So you get homesick."

"Sure I do. I went from living with ten other people to living alone in a two-bedroom cabin in a town where I've only known people a few months. They've got history with each other. I don't. You have your sister and your friends. Everyone here knows you."

"You're right. I'm just having a big ole pity party." Delilah stuck one of the jelly bean bags in Sam's basket. "I don't need a stomachache on top of a heartache."

Now why had she said that? Because Sam had warm eyes and an easy smile that said "You're not alone. I'm here"?

"We're two grown-ups feeling at loose ends." Sam shrugged and shot her a lop-sided grin. "Why don't we try keeping each other company?"

"Us?" Delilah's mind went blank. There

had to be a reason they couldn't do that. None came to mind. "When?"

"Tonight?" Sam motioned for her to move away from the middle of the aisle. The pastor from the Kootenai Community Church rolled his overflowing basket past them. He waved. They waved in return. "I can't."

"*Ach.* I didn't mean to make you feel awkward." He clutched his basket closer and made as if to turn away.

"I can't tonight because I only have two nights left with my family."

He turned back. "Right, right. What about Monday night then? You can tell me about your first day of school."

"How do you know it's my first day of school?"

"I listen." He touched the straw hat's brim. "I'll swing by after dark."

Because that's what Plain men did when they went courting.

They weren't courting. They hadn't even met until the previous evening.

Delilah opened her mouth.

But Sam was already at the counter paying.

He looked back, held up the jelly beans, and gave her a big thumbs-up.

What just happened?

Chapter Six

The smell of sawdust had a calming effect. At least it did for a wheelwright like Evan. It probably made other folks sneeze. He tied on his leather apron and picked up a handful of spokes made from hickory. His friend Levi Raber needed new wooden wheels for his buggy. Truth be told, Levi needed a new buggy, but those were too expensive. Repairing buggies, wagons, and carriages kept Kootenai's Carriage Shop in business and Evan employed.

The sound of the propane-fueled auger in use by his boss, Declan Huston, provided background music for the methodical work of tapping in each spoke to the hub using a mallet. Evan leaned in so he could hear the solid sound when the spoke hit the hub's core. Once the spokes were attached, he could add the felloes. Simply followed the plan.

At least his work life remained orderly.

"*Guder mariye,* my friend."

Evan glanced up from his work. Sam had arrived. Five minutes late. It might as well be an hour. Declan valued punctuality. He didn't ask much, but eight thirty meant eight thirty. Plenty of time for folks to have breakfast and do chores before heading to work or school.

School. Anna and Delilah together all day long. That couldn't be good.

Evan paused long enough to acknowledge Sam's greeting. "Welcome to Monday."

"It's a gut day, is it not?" Sam tucked his coat onto the rack next to the door. He went to the counter, where he opened a thermos and poured a steaming hot cup of coffee. Another aroma that calmed a restless soul. *"Kaffi?"*

"Nee." The smell might calm but the caffeine did not. Evan needed a steady hand for his work. "But danki."

"It's colder than the Arctic out there." Sam sipped his coffee as if he had all the time in the world. "But the sun is shining. It might even warm up enough to start melting the snow."

Evan picked up the spoke cone. He needed to shape the spokes before adding the felloes to them. Talking about the weather wasted time and breath. Weather in

December in Montana could be summed up in one word: cold.

"Why so glum?"

"I'm not. Just busy working."

"Ach. I get it. I'm late." Sam tied on his apron. His work consisted primarily of repairing leather tack, but sometimes he filled in with other tasks. "Sorry about that. I stopped by Andy's to see the Masts off. I'm praying for a safe trip. The roads could be icy in some stretches between here and the Kansas state line."

Sam was a thoughtful man. Evan had considered stopping by as well. It seemed more thoughtful not to subject Delilah to his presence. An even more pointy thought made the muscle under his eye twitch. Maybe Sam stopped by to see Delilah specifically. He'd let her refill his coffee cup twice and eaten both apple pie and fudge cookies on Friday night. For a skinny guy he seemed to have endless room for food — maybe a hollow leg.

Every time Evan looked her way — which was far too often — they were talking or smiling at each other. *None of your business. Get over it.* "That was nice of you. And you don't have to apologize to me. I'm not your boss."

"No, but you take ownership in this place.

You work hard. You expect everyone to do the same."

"It's not my place to judge."

"True, but it surely is human."

Whistling a breathy tune, Sam examined a work order for Levi's horse and buggy tack. Like his buggy, it had seen better days even though it was apparent the man had taken good care of it for as long as possible. Evan went back to work shaping the spokes. The hum of the auger soothed him.

The whistling stopped. "I have a question for you."

Evan paused and looked up. His face ruddy, Sam loomed over him. He had an awl in one hand and a ball of number ten shoe linen thread in the other. Evan nodded. "What's on your mind?"

"I've been here six months."

"Jah."

"I was surprised to find there's not many . . . available women here."

Evan glanced around the room. Declan had disappeared into the warehouse. There was no escaping this conversation. "It's a small district."

"You've lived here your whole life."

Get to the point. Please get to the point. "I have."

"What do you think of Delilah?" Sam

pivoted toward the counter, where he laid the awl down and began to untwist five feet of thread in preparation for waxing it. "She seems nice and she's been gone awhile so I'm thinking she's not . . . attached."

"Are you asking me if she's courting?" People didn't do that. Everyone minded their own business. On the other hand, how was a guy like Sam supposed to know? Who was Evan to stand in the way? "Or do you want to know if something's wrong with her?"

"Both I guess."

Nothing was wrong with Delilah. She loved the outdoors. She hunted with the best of the men. She adored horses. She thought s'mores made a great breakfast food and hot dogs grilled over a campfire should be loaded with cheese, mustard, catsup, relish, and onion — an opinion with which Evan wholeheartedly agreed. "Delilah is nice."

"Any particular reason she hasn't married?"

Because she moved to Kansas and her special friend didn't wait for her. "Not a question I can answer for her."

"It's funny. I thought I saw you follow her out the door the other night at Andy's."

"I needed some air. I ate too much. We

happened to be outside at the same time." *Gott, forgive me. It's the truth, You know, but You also know it's not the whole truth.* "She said it was too warm in the kitchen with all those girls washing dishes and cleaning up."

"I reckon you've known her your whole life."

"My daed and hers are friends. They went to school together. Our families spend a lot of time together." *We spent a lot of time together.* Evan pushed away the thought and the memories that came with it. Their friendship was special and private. "Us kids are all about the same age. We grew up playing together."

"It's hard sometimes to fit in when everyone has known each other for generations."

"We don't mean to be standoffish."

"You're not. I found a place to live and a job. Everyone at church has been kind. The *fraas* invite me for supper. I can't complain."

Where was this going? "People are getting to know you. Before you know it, you'll be the old-timer welcoming a new family from Jamesport or Nappanee."

"I like Delilah. She's funny." Sam leaned against the counter and fiddled with the thread. "I asked her to take a ride with me tonight."

Evan dropped the spoke cone. He leaned over to pick it up and smacked his head on the wagon wheel. "Ouch." Rubbing his head, he stood. "You better get moving. Levi's coming over after work to see where we are on his stuff. And we have orders backed up. Everyone gets their repairs done during the winter."

As if Sam didn't know that.

A puzzled look on his face, Sam nodded. "Sure. Just making conversation."

"Courting is private."

"I know. I'm still learning my way around here." His laugh held a note of wistfulness. "I know folks move here all the time, thinking it's beautiful and they can hunt, fish, and hike, and it's like a vacation year-round. But I knew better. My onkel Jake lived here years ago, when the district was new. He came back with stories about how hard it was to make a living. The winters in Ohio are cold but not like here. Anyway, I came here with eyes open."

"So why did you come?"

"Daed would call it wanderlust. But I've got five brothers back home. There's not enough farmland to go around. Some folks are moving to Indiana to work in the RV factories. I can't see myself doing that, but I wanted to make my own way."

"And you are."

Sam ducked his head and picked up a leather punch. "I've never lived alone before. I have eleven siblings — seven of them still at home. Plus Daadi and Mammi. Daed and Mudder. The talking and laughing and storytelling never stops. It's like living in the middle of a circus. Here it's so quiet at night I can hear the snow melting and dripping off the tree branches. I hear the owls hoot. Every time the wind blows, the branches scratch on the roof and it sounds like someone begging to come in."

"You need to get a *hund.*"

The melancholy gone from his face, Sam laughed. "Gut advice. But I think what we really need are fraas and a passel of kinner. Don't you?"

"Are we talking about you or me? Because I have *bruders* and schweschders coming out my ears too. My daadi and mammi passed last summer, but the house is always full. Two of my bruders and one of my schweschders are married and have kinner. When they visit, there isn't an open chair or a bite of leftover food to be had."

"I saw you leaving with Anna Burkholder after the wedding."

A man didn't discuss his special friend with others. "I thought we were talking about you."

"I'm just saying that's why I asked about Delilah. I'm not trying to be gossipy like a bunch of old women at a quilting frolic."

Sam needed friends. Evan wanted to be his friend. How could he fault the new guy for liking Delilah? Evan should be happy for him. And her. "Mudder sent a pan of enchiladas for lunch. Enough for everyone. Let me know when you get hungry."

Sam's face lit up. "You know me. I'm always up for a homecooked meal." He scooped up Levi's harness and applied himself to the task. "Enchiladas! That's so much better than a PB and J."

Fighting the urge to shake his head, Evan went back to work. Best to keep his hands and his mind occupied. That way he wouldn't think about Sam and Delilah.

Or that kiss.

"But I think I *will* get a hund."

Sam always had to have the last word.

Maybe Evan should take his own advice and get one too. Maybe then he'd stop thinking about the wrong woman.

Chapter Seven

The hands of the battery-operated clock sitting on the teacher's desk refused to budge. Delilah forced her gaze back to Charlie Moser. *"Don't let his angelic face fool you."* Those were Leesa's last words of advice before she left church the previous day.

The second grader grinned and offered her the picture he'd drawn of a horse and buggy on a dirt road, with mountains in the distance. A dog sat on the buggy seat. In fact, he might be driving the buggy. The child had artistic talent, no doubt about it.

"That's my dog Gussy." Charlie scratched his nose covered with a sprinkling of freckles. He had curly brown hair and eyes like his half brother Levi. "One of them. She had a litter of puppies during the wildfires. I got to keep one. His name is Dodger."

"Very nice." Delilah forced a stern tone. "But you were supposed to be working on your English vocabulary."

"I learned English last year. Enough English." His tone suggested this was not new information. "I'm never going to write anything in English. Why would I? I'll live in Kootenai my whole life. I want to build furniture with my bruder Levi."

"Many of Levi's customers are *Englisch.*" Delilah handed the drawing back to Charlie. "Write your vocabulary words ten times each. You're behind now. The others are practicing their penmanship. Do you want to stay after school to finish?"

"Nee." Charlie face squished up in comic horror. "We're building a snow fort after school — as soon as our chores are done."

"Then I expect you better get busy." Delilah moved over to the third and fourth graders who were studying their spelling words in preparation for a spelling test. Anna had the fifth and sixth graders. The older children had exchanged history papers and were grading them.

This wasn't so hard. What had she been worried about?

Tick-tock. Tick-tock.

Her stomach rumbled. Watching the van carrying her family drive away this morning had filled her with sadness. At first she'd been happy to think of something else — like teaching. Then the nerves set in.

And then there was Sam. He'd shown up to see her family off. Or so he said. Mostly he stood close to her as if offering silent but firm support. He was nice. When he left, he waited until the others were headed into the house to whisper, "See you tonight."

Between his words and the thought of teaching, she hadn't been able to eat a scrap of the waffles Christine had made.

Her stomach rumbled so loud one of the first graders looked up and grinned.

Come on. Come on.

Ding-ding-ding.

Finally.

"Lunchtime." Prepared to dash toward the stove where she'd left her metal lunch box to keep her goulash warm, Delilah pivoted and smacked into Anna. "Oops, sorry."

Anna's eyebrows rose. They'd been getting a workout all morning. "Scholars, line up by age. You need to wash your hands, get your lunch boxes, and sit back down. Then I'll set the timer for twenty minutes. No one goes outside to play until the timer goes off."

Anna and her egg timer. Delilah sighed. Anna shook her finger. "Otherwise they wolf their food down so fast it's a wonder they don't choke. That's what Mercy told me."

Delilah ducked past her co-teacher and snagged her lunch box. The children wouldn't be the only ones wolfing down their food.

"We should go over the afternoon curriculum while the kinner play." Anna's sedate pace toward the stove put Delilah to shame. "The eighth graders are behind on their science reading."

That's because they knew they would have little use for science once they graduated in April and embarked on what the Englishers liked to call vocational training. In other words, working.

"Isn't it important for us to get some fresh air too?" Delilah shooed the whine from her voice. "We've been cooped up all morning too. I need a brisk walk around the yard."

"You were as much a wiggle worm this morning as the first graders." Anna opened her lunch box and produced a ham-and-cheese sandwich, followed by an apple and a chocolate chip cookie. "You're the teacher now. Time to set the example."

"Our teachers played with us at recess. Remember Martha?" Delilah dug into the goulash. She savored the zesty tomato sauce, chewed, and swallowed. "She played baseball with us and volleyball."

"And she fell and broke her arm when she

climbed a tree to get Hannah's cat down."

"She couldn't leave the kitty up there."

"One of the boys could've climbed up there just as easy — easier."

"You're no fun."

Anna took a bite of her apple. Juice trickled down her chin. She dabbed at it with her napkin and smiled. "I don't know about that. There's a time and place for fun. This just isn't it. Besides, Evan thinks I'm fun."

Evan would know. He always seemed like the quiet boy in school. But he had the heart of a joker. He rarely took credit for pranks, but he often prompted the other boys. On their buggy rides he told funny stories about customers who'd come into the Carriage Shop or the latest joke told by his boss, Declan.

Delilah dropped her buttered roll into her lunch box and sat back. She took a long swig of water from her bottle. The goulash settled down. "I'm going outside. If I don't get some fresh air, I'll nod off during lessons."

The egg timer dinged. To their credit the children were better behaved than Delilah. They returned their lunch boxes to their shelves, grabbed their coats, and lined up to go outside. "You may —"

They were gone. Delilah longed to follow. Anna laughed and made shooing motions. "Go on. You know you want to."

"I'll sit still this afternoon. I promise." Delilah followed them. With a foot of snow on the ground, they couldn't play baseball, but the net was still up for volleyball. Why not? "Who wants to play volleyball?"

"It's too cold to hit the ball with my hands." Charlie wiped his runny nose with his coat sleeve. The seven-year-old was too short to be a good volleyball teammate. "Let's play hide-and-seek."

The log cabin–style school sat on a wooded plot of land donated for this purpose by the Plank family when they first moved to West Kootenai twenty years earlier. Hide-and-seek wasn't a bad idea. It didn't involve a ball, but it would do. "Who wants to be it?"

"You, Teacher, you be it."

The children made their choice loud and clear. Delilah trudged through calf-high snow to the building, where she put her gloved hands over her eyes, leaned against the wall, and counted to twenty. "Ready or not, here I come."

She turned to find the playground empty. Her steamy breath white against the blue sky, she giggled like a third grader. "Here I come."

The older boys and girls had chosen not to play. The girls were busy *botching,* the clapping and laughing loud in the quiet of winter, while the boys hung around discussing plans to go ice skating later in the week. That left sixteen little ones to be found. Humming, Delilah started with the outhouses. Two girls screamed and laughed when she found them snuggled behind the door out of the wind. Their job now was to help Delilah find the others. "Let's stick together."

They both nodded and smiled, showing off matching gaps where their two front teeth had once been.

From there the game sped up. In a matter of minutes she had followed a meandering path through the playground, around the picnic tables, past the boys' outhouse, and into the outlying woods. Each spot produced another giggling child. Delilah's feet were no longer cold. Her cheeks tingled. The sun warmed her face. She was wide awake for the first time all day.

"Okay, is that everybody?" She pivoted so she could see the line of children following her. She lifted her finger and pointed. "Fifteen? That's not right. It should be sixteen, right?"

"I want to be it now." First grader Lori Shrock offered. "Can I be it now?"

"Who's missing?"

A fourth grader raised her hand. "Teacher, where's Charlie?"

Everyone turned to stare at Tommy Lufkin. The two were like peanut butter and jelly, always together. "Jah, Tommy, where is Charlie?"

"I don't know." Tommy shrugged and waved toward the tall Douglas fir and spruce trees. "We split up to make it harder for you to find us. I went north. He went south."

Directions weren't Delilah's strong point. "Left or right?"

Tommy jerked his thumb left.

"Let's find him —"

The school bell *ding-donged.*

Uh-oh.

"Teacher, we have to go in." The kinner scattered in the opposite direction. "We can't be late."

That was the rule. Being late after recess meant minutes would be removed from the next recess. Nobody wanted that. Least of all Delilah. "Charlie? Charlie! Come on. It's time to go in." She spun around in a widening circle. "You don't want to be late, do you?"

No answer.

"Charlie! You'll have to stay after school and write fifty times 'I will not be late.' "

No answer.

Delilah glanced back. The children lined up outside the school door and tromped inside. Anna would wonder what Delilah was doing. An innocent game of hide-and-seek. How could that go wrong?

Tromping from tree to tree deeper into the thickening woods, Delilah sped up. An animal scurried across her path. A mouse? A vole? The cold seeped through her coat. Her nose went numb and her voice turned hoarse.

"Charlie Moser, answer me this instant."

"Delilah, did you find him?"

At the sound of Anna's voice, Delilah did an about-face and retraced her steps toward the opening to the grassy area where the playground began. Anna stood, arms folded, waiting. "The kinner said you couldn't find Charlie."

"He isn't answering." Delilah's stomach rocked. Her palms were wet with sweat despite the cold. "We were playing hide-and-seek. We used to play it all the time."

"The kinner aren't supposed to go into

the woods."

"They never mentioned that."

"Of course they didn't. They followed your lead. They wanted to have fun with the fun teacher."

"That's not fair."

"Stay with the kinner. I'll take my buggy and go get Jack Moser. Charlie's his *suh.* He'll want to search for him. He'll get some men to go with him."

"I want to look for Charlie."

"You've done enough. Your job is to take care of the kinner, not play with them."

Anna had less than a day on the job. But she was right.

"I can't just leave him out here. What if he's hurt? What if he fell in the creek?"

Anna's face blanched. "Don't borrow trouble. The men will find him."

"The older girls will supervise the younger ones." Delilah backed away. "I lost him. I'll find him. You go for help."

How far could a seven-year-old go? Why would Charlie do this? Because he had a mind of his own. Not a sterling quality in a Plain boy, but one Delilah admired. Charlie reminded her of someone. Her.

She rushed deeper into the stand of firs, larch, oaks, and maple trees. "Charlie. Charlie! Please answer me."

She threaded her way through the dense thickets of bushes that gave way to more larch and pines. The sound of rushing water froze her blood. *Please, Gott, keep Charlie safe. Don't let him fall in the water.*

A few short minutes and hypothermia would set in. Did Charlie know how to swim?

Delilah squeezed between a fallen Douglas fir and a dark, leafless maple tree. The creek ran deep in the winter as snow fell, melted, and then more followed. She spun left, then right, and picked her way through rocky outcrops, careful not to slip on icy ground. *Please, Gott, please.*

"Charlie!"

"Help! Over here . . ." The high little boy voice trailed away.

Delilah's heart resumed beating. "Charlie, it's me. Delilah. Where are you?"

"Over here."

"Keep talking." Delilah cut away from the creek. She stumbled through skeletal bushes of chokeberry, sagebrush, and silverberry.

Charlie sat on the ground with his hands around his ankle. His cocoa eyes bright with tears, he huffed a sob. "I think I hid too gut."

Chapter Eight

For a little fellow Charlie weighed a lot. Delilah tried hefting him into her arms, but that didn't work. His legs were too long. They settled on having him put his arm around her waist and lean on her. That way he could hop alongside her on his good leg. In his haste to find the perfect hiding place, he'd caught his boot under a gnarly tree trunk, tripped, and fell. He seemed to have sprained or broken his ankle.

"Did you know you weren't supposed to go into the woods?" Delilah didn't mean the words to sound accusatory. "You didn't mention it when you suggested we play hide-and-seek."

"I didn't really want to play hide-and-seek." Despite the pain, Charlie managed a cheeky grin. "I just like to go into the woods to search for animals. I look for chipmunks, wood rats, and voles. But there could be foxes, wolverines, or mule deer. Even black bears or grizzly bears."

The child had quite the imagination. At least Delilah hoped he did. No wonder the school board didn't want the children playing in the woods. Then again, surely the bears were hibernating. "It was wrong of you to go off like that."

"I know, but I only go to school because Daed says I have to."

"What do you think he'll say about what you did today?"

"I reckon it'll be a trip to the woodshed."

Charlie still managed to sound amazingly cheerful.

The woodshed would be the least of Delilah's problems.

They were about to find out. Several buggies were parked by the hitching post in front of the school's porch. A group of men stood in a circle, talking. Probably organizing the search party. Surely they would be happy to see no search was necessary. Delilah raised her hand and waved. "I found him."

Jack Moser whirled and marched toward them. He was a tall, lean man. Imposing. Delilah braced herself. As he came closer his expression behind dark-rimmed glasses became clearer. Relief, exasperation, disbelief, uncertainty, and yes, anger. "There you are. Are you all right, Suh?" His long strides ate up the snow-covered ground. "Where were you? What happened?"

"We were playing hide-and-seek —"

"I know what you were doing." His tone icier than the December north wind, Jack shook his head. "I want to know where my suh was."

"I meant to hide, but I fell and hurt my ankle." Charlie frowned and took Delilah's hand. "I wasn't lost. I knew where I was. I just couldn't get back."

Jack dropped to one knee and examined the boy over from head to toe. His frown eased. "Let's get you into the school, get you warmed up. I'll take a look at your ankle. It's probably just a sprain. Mudder will put an ice pack on it."

Jack picked up Charlie with the ease of a big man built to do hard labor daily. He didn't look at Delilah. Not wanting to remind him of her presence, she trod a few steps behind him.

"He's found. He's fine," Jack hollered to the other men. A few came forward to commiserate with him and check on Charlie. Lucas Zimmerman, the minister, had some medical training. He poked at Charlie's ankle and pronounced it a sprain. Together, they tromped into the school.

No one gazed Delilah's way. What had she expected? Thanks? She did find him, after all. Of course, she'd been the one to lose him.

She made it as far as the porch steps. There, Noah Duncan and Tobias Eicher stood side by side, their faces stony. Fearful her voice would quiver, Delilah settled for a nod. Noah smiled, but his expression remained troubled. "What happened?"

"We were playing."

"We know that. You're the teacher. Your job is to oversee and keep the kinner safe." Noah didn't raise his voice, but disappointment drenched his words. He stroked his beard. "You showed poor judgment today."

"He wasn't lost. He hurt his ankle —"

"You not only lost him, you allowed him to wander into a situation where he got hurt. You proved us right today." Anyone with eyes could see where Evan got his dark hair and blue eyes. He was the spitting image of Tobias. Right now, Tobias looked spitting mad. "It was suggested that you were too immature to be the teacher. You are."

"It was one mistake —"

"That could have cost a child his life. We can't take chances with our kinner. They are gifts from Gott."

His voice still gentle, Noah interceded.

"We think it's best that Anna continue as the sole teacher. Christine can use your help at home."

Hot shame coursed through Delilah. She could do better. She would do better. "But —"

"Your service is no longer needed here." Tobias slapped his black winter hat on his head and stomped into the school. "Go home."

One day. Delilah hadn't made it through one day as a teacher.

Chapter Nine

Whoever said a buggy ride on a snowy moonlit night was romantic hadn't actually experienced one. Evan kept that thought to himself. He gathered the reins in one hand and used the other to tuck the fleecy robe tighter around his left thigh. The bitter cold air kept seeping under it. His legs were freezing. So was his nose.

Thirty minutes of winding back roads of Kootenai and he longed to call it a night. A full day of repairing old wheels and making new ones had left his back and shoulders aching. Usually those aches and pains faded when he slid onto the seat next to Anna, but not tonight.

Tonight a strange, restless malaise followed him directly from the shop to Anna's house, where she'd been sitting by the window sewing, the lamp throwing a soft light on her pensive face. What had she been thinking about before he tapped on the glass to get her attention?

The familiar smile that spread across her face reminded him of a sunrise on a cloudless spring day. So why hadn't he smiled back? He was tired, that was all. Everyone had off days. "Are you warm enough?" Evan scooted closer to Anna. Their thighs touched. She didn't edge away. "I can take you home."

"But it's a beautiful night." She slid her hands ensconced in thick woolen mittens under the robe. She wore a gray knitted scarf wrapped around her shoulders, neck, and lower face. It muffled her words. "The moon's out. The snow is sparkling. The company is gut."

"You must be tired after teaching your first day of school." If he was tired, she had to be as well. The thought of twenty-four children in one room requiring full attention for an entire day made a person tired just to think of it. And Anna would take her responsibility to teach them well seriously. "You haven't said how it went."

"I'm surprised your daed didn't tell you."

"I worked late tonight. I came to your house directly from the shop."

"Ach, it was a mess. She meant well, but Delilah made a big mess of everything." Anna tut-tutted. She sounded like Evan's mother when she did that. "On the other hand, it's a day the scholars will remember for a long time."

If Evan's father was involved in his capacity as deacon, it couldn't be good. "What did she do? What was my daed doing there? Checking up on you?"

"Not on me." Anna proceeded to tell the entire story. To her credit she didn't embellish or lay blame. She didn't need to.

Evan slowed the buggy. Duke whinnied in protest. He didn't like the cold either. *Sorry, buddy.* He pulled over to the side of the road. "She didn't purposely lose Charlie. In fact, Charlie purposely lost himself. Everyone knows he's a handful."

"I have no doubt Charlie received his just punishment when Jack got him home, but he's seven. He's expected to make errors in judgment and learn from them. Delilah is a grown woman. What was she thinking? Playing hide-and-seek like a little girl? Letting the smallest kinner traipse into the woods alone?"

"Most of them walk to school on their own."

"On clearly marked roads."

"Delilah meant no harm. She has a gut heart."

"Why are you defending her?" Anna's

voice crept up for the first time. She moved away from Evan. Cold air invaded the space between them. "She even refused to go back inside and supervise the children while I went for help. She insisted on searching for him on her own. She's stubborn, willful, and full of herself."

"That's harsh. You don't know her very well if that's what you think of her."

"But you do, which is why you're mad at me for criticizing her. You like her."

A dark pit opened in front of Evan. He took a breath and leaped to fill the silence before she drew the wrong conclusion from it. "I'm not mad at you. I hate to see a person unfairly judged."

"Delilah, you mean."

"Anybody. People make mistakes. I'm sure she realizes the mistake and won't make it again."

"Nee, she won't. She's been dismissed. Your father and Noah sent her home. They said she was too irresponsible to be the teacher. It seems someone had suggested this when her name came up for the position. That's why they decided to have me co-teach with her. She proved them right the very first day."

Evan tried to hide his wince. Delilah would be devastated. She always wanted to do her best. She liked children. She liked being helpful. Teaching might not be the right fit for her, but she would do her best to make sure the children received a good education. "That doesn't seem fair. Everyone deserves a second chance."

"Delilah deserves a second chance, you mean."

"Why do you keep saying that?"

"Because you've been different since the wedding last week. I saw you having that snowball fight with her. Lots of kids were out there, but you and Delilah were throwing balls at each other like it was just the two of you."

"That's not true."

"Why are you so cranky, then?"

"I'm not."

"I'm not a silly little girl, Evan. Your families are close. You and Delilah grew up playing together. I've heard the gossip. Did you two court before she left for Kansas?"

How did they get from hide-and-seek to courting in a few scant seconds?

Anna grabbed the flashlight he kept under the buggy seat and turned it on. Evan threw his arm across his forehead to shield his eyes. "What are you doing?"

"I want to see your face. You're an honest man. Your face shows everything. Did you and Delilah court?"

"Turn that off. Yes. For a very short time. Right before the fires."

Anna flipped the switch. The night went dark.

They sat in silence for several moments.

"Do you love her?"

"I'm here with you now."

"That's not an answer."

"She went away before we had a chance to know what we had." Evan longed for words that could convey the uncertainty of their situation, magnified by the fire, by the evacuation, by the prospect of being fifteen hundred miles apart, not knowing if or when they would see each other again. "It was only a few buggy rides. It didn't have time to be more."

"But it could've been."

"But it's not. Instead I found you." Evan reached for her hand. She allowed him to take it. "You're sweet and kind and funny and smart. You're everything a man would want in a fraa."

"That's not love." Anna's voice quivered. "You should've been honest with me. When she's around, you have eyes for her only."

"When you came outside the day of the wedding, I had eyes for you only. I took you home, remember?" Evan scooted closer and put his arm around her. She leaned her head against his chest. He hugged her tight. "What we have is the start of love. Give me time."

"Are you sure?" Anna unwrapped the scarf from her neck and shoulders. She let it drop to her lap. Tears wet her cheeks. "I can't afford to risk my heart on someone who isn't willing to do the same."

"I wouldn't be here now if I wasn't sure." A man didn't back out of a commitment because someone else came along. It didn't work that way. "I want to get to know you better. I want this to work."

Anna raised her face to his. He kissed her gently.

The *clip-clop* of horse's hooves sounded nearby.

Not now. Evan raised his head and peered into the darkness. Who else could be out on this back road in the cold after dark?

A buggy came into view. Sam drove it. Delilah sat next to him, a chunk of space between them.

Evan moved one direction, Anna, the other.

God did indeed have a sense of humor.

Of all the dark, back roads of Kootenai, how had Delilah and Sam ended up on the same one as Evan and Anna? Where bitter cold had nipped only seconds earlier, sudden heat roasted Delilah from head to toe. She glanced around, praying for escape. His expression placid, Sam slowed the buggy as if preparing to stop.

"Keep going, keep going!" The words escaped before Delilah could haul them back in. The heat rose a hundred degrees. "I mean, they're . . . you know . . . they're —"

"Doing the same thing we are, I reckon." Sam's smile widened. "We're bound to run into other couples on these roads. Kootenai is a small place."

They were not doing the same thing. Evan and Anna had been kissing. They shot apart like two guilty kids. Sam and Delilah were simply taking a buggy ride. Kissing would not be involved.

Not tonight or any time soon. She'd learned her lesson with Evan.

Sam pulled even with Evan's buggy and stopped. "Howdy, neighbor. It's a gut night for a drive, isn't it?"

"It is." Nodding, Evan wrapped the reins around his hands. "It's a bit nippy though."

"I think it's perfect." Anna waved a mittened hand. Her high voice sounded funny. Like she was getting a cold. The frigid air might not be good for Kootenai's one and only teacher. "I like the way the moonlight sparkles on the snow. Don't you, Delilah?"

Obviously she wanted to see if Delilah harbored ill will toward her. Anna couldn't be blamed for anything. In fact, she'd been the voice of reason Delilah chose to ignore. She pasted a smile on her face. "I do. It's a pretty night for a drive."

"Well, we better get going. It's getting late and we have work tomorrow." Evan guided his buggy past Sam's. He picked up speed. The creak of the wooden wheels and *clip-clop* of hooves quickly receded into the darkness.

"I guess he was embarrassed too." Sam snapped the reins. The buggy jolted forward. "I don't know why. There's no shame in courting."

"It's private." Delilah scooted farther from him. "We're not a couple. We hardly know each other."

"I'd like to change that." Sam's hand came out. He tugged at the fleece robe so it climbed higher toward Delilah's waist. "Not to get ahead of myself, but I think you're nice."

"Danki." Another wave of heat engulfed Delilah. She pushed the robe back down. "It's nice of you to say."

"I'm just speculating, but you must think I'm nice or you wouldn't have said jah to a buggy ride."

How could she explain to this stranger the twists and turns in her life that careened into a dead end when she saw Evan and Anna together at Henry's wedding? "I'm turning over a new leaf."

"I see." His tone suggested he didn't see at all. "I turned over a new leaf when I came to Kootenai. It can be a tricky thing. Do you think Anna was crying because of your old leaf?"

Sam was far more astute than most men Delilah had known. "I don't know what you mean."

"I couldn't help but notice the way Evan's gaze followed you the other night at dinner. Plus, I saw him follow you outside after supper. You seemed upset when you came back in the house. I mentioned it at work today, and he said it was pure coincidence — you two being outside at the same time. Evan shouldn't lie. He's too honest. It shows in his face."

"No one should lie."

"So tell me the truth."

"We courted for a short time before the Caribou Fire. Then I moved to Kansas." Delilah stripped off her gloves and stuck her cold hands to her warm cheeks. The words tumbled out. "That was the end of it. Evan and Anna are courting. I'm here to help my sister with her new bopli when he — or she — arrives."

Sam clucked and gently shook the reins. His horse sauntered onto the road with an approving whinny. "And teach."

"I got fired today."

"You're having quite the day." The darkness hid his expression, but Sam's tone was kind. "I'm sorry if I made it worse by insisting you take a ride with me."

"It's gut for me to get out of the house. No sense in crying over spilled milk." She plucked at a loose thread on her glove. "Don't you want to know why I was fired?"

"I won't make you relive it. Unless you would like to vent."

So Delilah vented. She'd already told Christine the entire story. Her sister had nodded and agreed in all the right places. It was more embarrassing to tell Sam. He didn't know her well enough to overlook her obvious character flaws. "The elders were worried that I'm too irresponsible to be the teacher. I got fired on my first day of teaching."

"I'm sorry to hear that. Sometimes a person needs time to lick her wounds." He sighed a warm, understanding sound. "Maybe some medicinal singing would help."

The memory of how she first met Sam floated to the surface. He was perceptive. "What do you mean?"

"Isn't that why you were singing that day?"

"I don't know many men who understand these things." Delilah smiled for the first time since the day began. "Singing reminds me Gott is still here. He sees us and hears us even when we feel alone."

"What shall we sing?"

" 'Amazing Grace'?"

"Too hard. I'm a terrible singer. You'll see." He shoved his black church hat back and scratched his forehead. "How about 'This Little Light of Mine.' "

A sweet, easy children's song. "Perfect."

Sam was right. He couldn't carry a tune in a bucket, but that made their impromptu chorus that much more fun. They sang every verse. Then Sam made up verses. Not to be outdone, Delilah made up her own. They were so awful, they laughed aloud, the noise causing the horse to shake his head and whinny.

Hand on her chest, Delilah gasped for breath. "You're right."

"I'm a terrible singer?"

"Singing makes you feel better."

"Laughter is the best medicine."

"Danki."

Sam halted the buggy in front of Andy's house and hopped down. "What for?"

"For being kind and listening and not passing judgment."

"Do unto others as you would have them do unto you." He wrapped the reins around the hitching post and came around to her side of the buggy. "I don't suppose I could talk you into a cup of hot cocoa before I find my way home."

Delilah hesitated.

"It's okay. I'm sure you're tired and I have work —"

"Please come in. Christine made some cinnamon rolls that are perfect with cocoa."

"A woman after my heart — Christine, I mean." An apologetic look on his ruddy face, Sam offered his hand. "I promise to make no demands on yours."

"You're too nice." She allowed him to help her down. "I'm surprised a woman back in Ohio didn't offer you her heart."

"I don't think it's possible to be too nice." Sam let go of her hand and led the way up the steps. "Being nice has its own rewards. It comes back to a person a hundredfold."

Let him be right, Gott. If anyone deserves to

be rewarded for a godly attitude, it's this man.

Delilah could learn a thing or two from Sam, and it looked as if he planned to stick around while she did it. She didn't deserve his niceness, which made it all the more a gift.

Chapter Ten

Maybe the heart could be won by sheer persistence. The days after Delilah's first buggy ride with Sam turned into weeks. The snow melted. More fell. January became February. Montana winter refused to give up. So did Sam. He came around two or three times a week. He kept his promise not to make demands on Delilah. Instead he told stories about his family back in Ohio and quizzed her about life growing up in Kootenai. He never once brought up Evan or the debacle at the school. Delilah avoided Evan and Anna, buried herself in housework, and spent quiet evenings sewing crib quilts and nightgowns for Christine's baby.

Life was peaceful.

Just like it had been in Kansas.

Why couldn't she be content with a peaceful existence? That question pestered her — while she baked, while she washed clothes, while she mopped, and while she sewed. A nice man liked her enough to keep courting her even when she still sat at the far end of the buggy seat. Her sister said she liked Delilah's company. If Andy minded having a third wheel around the house, he kept it to himself. By the grace of God her parents had agreed to let her stay even though she no longer taught. Returning to Kansas in disgrace would have heaped misery upon misery.

Delilah had no reason to complain. So she did her best to zip her lips and turn her restlessness into elbow grease. The first day of March rolled around and Christine's baby still hadn't made an appearance. The midwife simply shrugged and suggested Christine had miscalculated the due date. Which sent Christine into a pity party the likes of which Delilah had never seen before.

Once her sister calmed down, she threw herself into cleaning the house top to bottom. This worked out well since it was the Lambrights' turn to host the church service on Sunday. That meant the windows, walls, and furniture had to be washed down by hand. They also mopped the floors, laundered curtains, and dusted every nook and cranny while Andy cleaned the barn and the other outbuildings.

Delilah gave the benches crammed into

the living room and dining room one last swipe with a dust rag early Sunday morning and went to the kitchen to make *schmeir* from peanut butter, corn syrup, and marshmallow fluff. The ten loaves of bread baked by their women friends earlier in the week had already been sliced. The kitchen still smelled like the ten dozen ranger cookies Delilah made on Saturday. She left the egg salad, pickled beets, and cheese spread in the refrigerator until after the service. Mercy, Leesa, and Nora were bringing pies and cookies. Vats of coffee took up every burner on the stove. It smelled like a family reunion.

By the time Delilah returned to the living room, the women were trickling in. The men would chat outside until the last minute. Christine looked miserable even though she tried to smile as she chatted with Mercy's mother.

Please, Gott, let that bopli come soon.

Anna strolled into the room with her mother and three sisters. They accepted their holy kisses from Noah's wife with bright smiles. Delilah took a deep breath. She hadn't spoken to Anna since that night in Sam's buggy on a dark road. This was silly. She edged between the benches until she reached the spot where the women had seated themselves. "It's gut to see you. How are you?"

"Gut. Looking forward to spring." Anna removed her mittens and tucked them into her bag. Her niece crawled into her lap and snuggled against her chest. Anna patted her shoulder. "I didn't see you at the quilting frolic yesterday. I thought maybe you were sick."

Not sick. Avoiding the knowing eyes of all the women who'd been whispering among themselves for weeks over her dismissal as teacher. "I've been keeping busy." *Come on, come on, you can do it.* "How are your scholars doing? Are you enjoying teaching?"

Said without a hitch in her voice. Delilah mentally patted herself on the back.

"Very well. I really love it." Her head bent, Anna smoothed her niece's kapp. "I'm glad to be of service. I like being useful."

As another single Plain woman, Delilah knew exactly what Anna meant. "Me too. I enjoy helping Christine. I'm looking forward to helping her with the bopli. It seems a better fit for me."

Not that her dismissal didn't still rankle, but Delilah understood the elders' decision to put the safety of the children first. A second chance for her could not be more important than them.

"Having a bopli must be wunderbarr." A wistful look flitted across Anna's face. She hugged her niece closer. "I can't wait. Can you?"

They had so much in common. How could they not be friends? "I can't. Our day will come."

A furtive wave caught her gaze over Anna's shoulder. Sam winked and sat down next to Evan, who seemed fascinated with his black church boots. Delilah smiled. Her expression puzzled, Anna glanced back. "Ah. Jah."

Let Anna think what she wanted. Delilah and Sam had not progressed beyond an occasional touch on the hand or arm. However, certain facts could not be ignored. Sam wanted to be her special friend. Delilah simply needed to let go and allow him in.

What kept her from opening herself up to the possibility? "I better go sit with Christine and Mercy. I help entertain the little ones."

Anna nodded but her expression was knowing.

Delilah settled in next to Christine and took Matthew from her. The singing — Delilah's favorite part of the service — began. Low and slow but a sweet, sweet sound in God's ear.

Christine clutched her belly and groaned. For a second Delilah couldn't be sure she wasn't singing. No. Her sister grabbed Delilah's arm and leaned in. "I need to get up."

"Are you . . . ?"

"I am. Now." Christine's grip tightened painfully. "Right now."

Delilah whispered in Mercy's ear. Nodding, she handed her little one to Nora and took Matthew. "We'll pass the word to Phoebe," she whispered.

Fortunately the midwife sat only a few rows away. Delilah helped Christine stand. Her dress's blue material was dark and wet in the back. Delilah moved closer to shield her from view.

It seemed everyone followed their progress. Delilah waited until they reached the end of the row to glance back in search of Andy. His worried gaze collided with hers. She nodded. He rose and edged his way toward the hall.

In the hallway Christine groaned again. Andy put his arm around her. "How long have you been having contractions?"

"Since last night."

"Why didn't you say something?"

"It was our turn. The benches were already here. All the food was made." Christine doubled over, both hands on her belly.

"Ach. I need to walk."

So they walked up and down the hall for another half hour. The sound of Lucas's sermon followed them. Jesus's instruction that they store up treasures in heaven, not on earth, resounded.

Finally they convinced Christine to change so she could lay down and rest for a while. Tobias read the Scripture. Noah began the main sermon on hypocrisy. Another hour passed. Christine groaned into her quilt. Delilah rubbed her back. "You're so strong."

"Nee, it would be embarrassing for them to hear me." Christine's face had turned radish red. Sweat soaked her nightgown. "I can't believe this is happening right now."

"They don't care." Delilah patted her face with a cool, wet cloth. "They're praying for a healthy bopli. They will be so happy when you and Andy are blessed with this new life. Just think, a bruder or schweschder for Matthew. Any minute we'll know which."

It took another two hours. Little Kaitlin Lambright decided to take her time making an appearance. Her cheeks were pink and pudgy. She had a head of dark hair like her father and all ten fingers and toes.

Delilah was number four behind Phoebe, Andy, and Christine to whisper sweet nothings in the ear of the family's newest member. "Can I show her to Mercy and Nora?"

Christine leaned back against a stack of pillows and closed her eyes. "Please do. When you come back, bring Matthew. He'll want to make sure I'm okay."

Her tiny niece wrapped in a crib quilt she'd made, Delilah trotted into the living room. The service had ended. Food had been served. People were leaving. How could life go on when something so momentous was happening? It seemed impossible.

Evan bent over the last bench and picked it up. When he saw Delilah, he let the bench settle back on the floor. "The bopli is here, then."

"She is. Gott's gift has arrived." Delilah couldn't contain the joy. It needed to be spread across the world. Such a miracle. So perfect and so innocent. "Would you like to meet her?"

His expression diffident, Evan slid his black hat back on his head and nodded.

Delilah moved closer. So did he. Together, they gazed down at the sleeping baby. Kaitlin sucked on one tiny fisted hand. "I think she looks like Andy, don't you?"

"Jah, but I can see Christine in the shape of her face and her nose." Evan touched the quilt. His hand was as big as the baby's head. He smiled. "What is it about bopli that turns us into big piles of mush?"

"They're miracles in the flesh." The memory of how his hand felt around hers warmed Delilah. Such big hands to have such a tender touch. She brushed the thought away. "You look at a bopli and what you see is love."

"You're so smart." His somber gaze went from Kaitlin's face to Delilah's. "And wise."

Tears simmered near the surface. "You're the only one who thinks so. I didn't last one day as a teacher."

"It's not my place to second-guess our elders, but I can see both sides of the situation. Everyone makes mistakes. No one is perfect. Noah would be the first to admit that." Evan shook his head. "Just know that you've been forgiven for your mistake. It's only their concern for the kinner that keeps them from reinstating you. It's been discussed. They've prayed over it. You had your own misgivings about being a teacher. I know you did."

"You're right. It's likely my pride that keeps me wanting to try again," Delilah whispered. "I don't want to be a failure. I want to prove I can be the responsible adult. Not the right reasons for allowing me back in the schoolhouse."

"You're not a failure. And everyone deserves a second chance."

Did that apply to love? "I wish we . . ."

"Me too." Evan backed away. He hoisted the bench under one arm. "I better get this bench out to the wagon. They're waiting on me."

"Evan."

He looked back.

No words big enough existed to sum up the enormity of Delilah's longing in that moment.

Sadness etched on his face, Evan nodded. "I know."

Delilah watched him lug the bench through the front door. When he was gone, she sighed and turned.

Mercy stood in the doorway to the hall.

"Were you eavesdropping?"

"I went to Christine's room to see if the bopli had arrived. She said she'd sent you out to show her off to everyone so I came looking for you." She made a beeline across the room and held out her arms. Reluctantly Delilah handed over the baby. Her dimples on full display, Mercy chortled with delight. "She's beautiful."

"She is."

"Can I give you some advice?"

As if there was any stopping Christine's best friend. With an exaggerated sigh, Delilah nodded. "Please do."

Mercy drew herself up to her full height. A tall woman, she could be formidable when on a mission. "Marriage is for life. You don't want to be yoked to the wrong person. Don't lead a man on if you have feelings for another — and he has feelings for you."

"Evan wants to do what's right. He's made that clear." Plain women didn't pursue men. They were expected to sit demurely, waiting for the Plain man to make up his mind. "There's nothing I can do — that I'm allowed to do. Besides, it's too late."

"You're allowed to pray." Mercy's admonition was soft but an admonition nevertheless. Her brown eyes were somber. "Seek Gott's will and then submit to it. If He wants you and Evan to be together, you will."

And if He didn't, she'd have to live with it. "I know. I just can't imagine how it would be possible without anyone getting hurt."

"I'm glad you see that and have a kind heart yourself." Kaitlin fussed and Mercy gently rocked her. "But people will be hurt much more if they aren't truthful with each other."

"Did you have that problem with Caleb?"

"You're not the only one whose life was

changed by the Caribou Fire. Me, Nora, Christine — we all encountered obstacles we never expected. Caleb and I were at cross-purposes during the evacuation and even afterward. There was an English smoke jumper and Caleb misunderstood . . . Anyway, we had to work our way through it. We didn't give up. We persevered."

"It's different for me. By the time I came back from Kansas, things had changed. It was beyond my control then, and it's beyond my control now. My feelings don't matter."

"I don't know." Mercy brushed back a tendril of chestnut hair that had escaped her kapp. "It didn't look that changed to me."

"Evan is a gut man. He wants to take the high road." Delilah moved toward the kitchen. She should help with the cleanup instead of standing here moaning and groaning over something she had no right to want. "I wouldn't ask him to do otherwise. I respect his honorable nature."

"I do too. That's why praying is the only option that makes sense." Mercy followed her to the hallway, then took a right. "This bopli needs her mudder. Ask Christine about what she and Andy went through —"

"She told me. I understand that sometimes relationships are honed by trial. But you all have the benefit of hindsight. I don't. I'm in the middle of it." Delilah fought the urge to put her hands over her ears and sing *la-la-la-la.*

God's will would prevail whether Delilah liked it or not. A hard truth.

Another hard truth: She'd set Sam up to be hurt. Regardless of what happened with Evan, she would never be in love with Sam. She hadn't led him on, but she hadn't refused his attention either.

She was stuck. They all were.

Chapter Eleven

Thy will be done. The words danced in a circle inside Delilah's head. It had been two weeks since Kaitlin's birth. Every day she prayed for God's guidance and for the taming of her rebellious spirit that refused to submit.

The sun warmed the earth. Soon it would be time to plant their spring flower and vegetable gardens. Sam hadn't driven his buggy up to the hitching post in front of Andy's house in all that time. No explanation. Relief mixed with a tinge of regret. Delilah enjoyed Sam's company. He made her laugh. After nearly three months, though, the thought of his presence didn't send a shiver through her. Mercy was right. Even if Delilah couldn't be with Evan, she shouldn't keep stringing Sam along, hoping something more would bloom.

She settled into the rocking chair and picked up her latest sewing project. She was teaching herself to knit with the hope she could create sweaters, scarves, mittens, socks, and blankets to serve as Christmas presents later in the year. Andy and Christine had gone to bed. Having a new baby who wanted to eat every few hours all night long took its toll.

Delilah usually didn't mind having the living room to herself. Tonight she missed her noisy bunch of brothers and sisters playing dominoes or card games. Her dad would be snoozing in his chair, his seed catalog forgotten on his lap. Mother would have her basket of darning within reach and a cup of apple-cinnamon-spice tea on the table next to her.

Everyone would talk at once.

Stop feeling sorry for yourself. You wanted Kootenai. You got it. Make the best of it.

Sorely lacking as a pep talk.

A rap on the front door sent Delilah lurching to her feet. She peeked out the window. Sam stood on the front porch. She opened the door and motioned him inside. "They're asleep."

"I'll be quiet." He wiped his boots on the mat and shed his coat. "How's the bopli doing?"

That wasn't the purpose of his visit, but Delilah obliged. "Gut. Growing like a weed already. She's a gut eater but not a gut sleeper."

"Like most boplin."

How much did Sam know about boplin? "Would you like some tea or hot chocolate?"

"Cocoa would be nice."

He followed her into the kitchen, where Delilah assembled the ingredients and heated the milk. "It's been a while since you stopped by." She stirred the concoction without looking his direction. "I thought maybe you changed your mind about . . ."

What exactly were they doing?

Sam didn't respond. Delilah swiveled to look at him. His gaze dropped to the floor and his dirty work boots. Delilah tried to ferret out the emotions mingling on his handsome face. A touch of belligerence. A bit of sadness. A smidgen of resignation. A sliver of uncertainty. "Sam?"

His gaze rebounded to a spot over her shoulder. His fair skin turned scarlet. Determination overtook the emotions on his face. He stood and strode toward her.

"Sam?"

His hands grasped her shoulders. His gaze traced her features. Then he leaned down and his lips found hers. A soft kiss at first, then deeper, searching, seeking.

Her heart pounding in a painful *rat-a-tat-*

tat, Delilah jerked away.

Disappointment replaced uncertainty. He let go of her shoulders and moved a step back. "That's what I thought."

Delilah took stock. Still no shiver of delight. No longing to throw herself against his big frame and find his lips again. *Gott, why? Why can't I give him what he wants? It would be so easy. He's a nice man. A kind man.*

No answer.

God probably thought she should be able to figure this out on her own. "You just surprised me. That's all."

His lips curled in a sardonic smile. "It's kind of you to try to let me down easy. You're a nice girl."

They were both nice. Such a lukewarm word.

"Maybe it's too soon. Give me time. I'll get there."

"You have no idea how I wish that were true." Sam wheeled around and planted himself on a chair at the prep table — as far away from Delilah as possible in this roomy kitchen. "The day of the church service here, I was helping with the benches. I started to come back in to help Evan carry out that last bench. But I saw you and Evan . . ."

The tableau appeared in Delilah's head as it had so many times in the past two weeks. She and Evan stood so close together she could've touched his face or stretched on tiptoes to kiss him. Together they stared at the baby and imagined what it would be like if she were their baby. How that would feel. The joy of it. Their own gift from God.

What must that have seemed like to Sam?

"I was showing the baby to everyone, not just Evan."

"But only Evan made you look like that." Pain flitted across Sam's face. He shuttered it and smiled. "I'd have to be blind not to see it."

Delilah trudged to the table and sat across from him. If only there were a way to comfort him without adding salt to the wound. "I never wanted to hurt you."

"I've always known."

"How could you?"

"I work with Evan. I saw how he changed after you returned to Kootenai. He moped around the shop. He stopped cracking jokes. He tries to make the best of it, but it's obvious something is eating at him."

"If you suspected this, why did you keep coming around?"

"Hubris, I reckon." Sam drew imaginary lines on the pine planks of the table. He didn't meet her gaze. "I thought I could win you over. In fact, I was sure of it. But you never gave me any sign that you wanted more. You didn't inch closer on the buggy seat. You didn't reach for my hand. You laughed at my jokes — that's about it. When I dropped you off, you hopped from the buggy, waved, and ran into the house like a cougar was chasing you. I had to ask to be invited in."

A litany of obvious signs.

"I'm sorry. I really am."

"No need to be sorry. You can't tell your heart what to do. I wasn't going to come back here. But it seemed wrong to stop coming without an explanation. Plus, I needed to know for certain."

"The kiss."

"Jah." He chuckled, a dry, sparse sound. "You acted like I had a deadly, contagious virus."

"I did not."

"Did too." He stood. "I should go."

"Stay. Have the hot chocolate."

"Why?"

"Because I enjoy your company." Words to express her longing scattered. She had to run around picking them up like an overturned basket of apples. "You're my friend and I could use a friend right now. I get lonely."

"I can't be your substitute special friend." His voice turned hoarse. "It hurts."

An admission not easy for a man to make. "Right. I shouldn't ask you to. Men and women can't be friends."

"Maybe out in the world, but not Plain men and women. It's not our way."

Delilah followed him down the hall to the front door. He put on his coat and turned to face her. "Be kind and tell me you weren't thinking of Evan the entire time we rode around in my buggy."

"I wasn't. I promise. I do my best not to think of him." Sam didn't need to know how often Delilah failed in this endeavor. She schooled her voice to be sweetly neutral. "He's with another. I don't expect that to change. I wanted us — you and me — to have something special. I tried. I really did."

"I believe you." Sam pulled the door open and stepped out into the crisp night air. "Danki for that. Take care of yourself. I wish you the best with Evan."

"There is no Evan and me."

"There is." He doffed his hat to her. "Believe me. There is."

Chapter Twelve

Schoolkids didn't know how good they had it. Evan folded his arms and leaned against the cabin-style school so he could watch Anna's scholars compete in a noisy, lighthearted baseball game. They probably thought the end-of-school picnic the third week in April was the best day of the school year. No more learning until September rolled around again.

Learning was a good thing. They might be surprised to know how much he used math, English, and reading for his job. The same was true for farming, making furniture, or building cabin kits. Learning didn't cease when school ended, but for him, it had been harder. Being a wheelwright had a big learning curve. Declan's apprenticeship had been a blessing.

They'd find out soon enough. Fun was good too. With a few parents who wanted to relive their younger days, they had enough for two full teams of nine each. Evan, too, enjoyed a good game of baseball, but today he felt more like the tortoise than the hare. That wouldn't be fair to the other players. He only came because Anna wanted him here. His boss had closed up shop for the day. They had three children at the school.

Charlie smacked a line drive that bounced over the tiny first baseman and landed in right field. Did he have any regrets that his actions led to Delilah's dismissal? He'd probably already forgotten about it.

The next batter approached the makeshift home plate. Grinning like a third grader, Delilah swished the bat back and forth and then let it rest on her shoulder.

Charlie hopped up and down. He yelled encouragement. Delilah faked a huge grimace and pointed the bat toward center field. No hard feelings there.

The fact that she wanted to participate in the game came as no surprise. Her presence at the picnic had. She had no children at the school. Neither did Andy or Christine. Evan straightened. His favorite school memories of Delilah all involved sports. She hit better than most of the boys. She loved a good hot box between the shortstop and the third baseman. Sliding into a base made her laugh. She could shag the highest, farthest fly ball. She stepped in front of hard-hit line drives without hesitation.

Her love of the game didn't dissipate as she grew older. During their brief courtship, he'd bought her a new glove for her birthday. The grin on her face suggested she might kiss him. Only the presence of her family kept it from happening.

The kiss. Their one kiss had been sweet, deliberate, and yet dizzying. The memory kept him awake the first few months after she'd left for Kansas.

It still appeared in his dreams.

Anna's didn't. In fact, he tended to avoid those moments of intimacy. The hurt in her eyes haunted him.

He stifled a groan and turned his back on the game. Anna stood behind one of the picnic tables set up for the feast, talking to Mercy. Her children weren't old enough to be in school. Maybe Anna invited the entire *Gmay*. The more the merrier.

Hand on his hat to keep it from blowing away in a brisk, balmy wind, Evan approached the table and picked up a large Styrofoam plate. Potato salad, coleslaw, chips, dip, barbecue beans, a ham sandwich. He heaped his plate high even though his stomach had hung out a CLOSED FOR BUSINESS sign.

"Have a brownie. I made them. Andy and Noah are making homemade ice cream." Smiling, Anna broke away from Mercy and rushed to the table. She put her hand on his plate. "Let me get it for you."

"I'll come back for dessert." Evan didn't relinquish his plate. "I think my eyes may be bigger than my stomach."

Her smile faded. She let go. "I'm glad you decided to come."

"It seems as if everyone in the Gmay is here."

"I thought it would be nice to have a community picnic. Don't you?" Her expression uncertain, she rearranged the rocks they were using to keep the tablecloth from blowing away. "It's fun, and everyone supports our scholars and our school, not just the parents."

"I know. I just didn't expect it."

"Didn't expect to see Delilah, you mean." Anna's voice dropped to a whisper. "I don't think you should expect to avoid her for the rest of your life."

"I'm not avoiding anyone. I'm still here, aren't I?" His words sounded begrudging in his own ears. At this rate he would never have children of his own playing baseball at an end-of-school-year picnic. "I wanted to be here to support you, so I came."

"If you have something you'd rather be doing, by all means, you should do it."

"Nee, nee, I'm just out of sorts because I didn't sleep good."

"You're out of sorts a lot lately." Her head down, Anna brushed chip crumbs from the vinyl red-checked tablecloth. "It seems like you never sleep well. Maybe you should go to the doctor in Eureka. Maybe you're sick."

Sick at heart. "I'm fine. Really, I am. I'm sorry I've been so grouchy. I'll be back in a bit for dessert."

Anna nodded, but she didn't look convinced. He could feel her gaze following him to the lawn chair next to the third base line, where he settled down and shoveled potato salad into his mouth. Mind over matter.

By now Delilah had scored a run and stood chatting with the other players behind the screen at home plate. Her laugh floated on the air. She might be a grown woman, but she took a childlike joy in simple things. The more she laughed, the more he shoveled food in his mouth and chewed, determined to fill that hole near his heart.

The other team finally managed a third out. Instead of taking the field with her team, Delilah walked over to where Christine sat with Andy, who was feeding ice cream to Matthew. Words were exchanged.

Christine handed over Kaitlin and headed to the food tables. Delilah went the opposite direction, toward the school.

Don't do it. Stay. Ignore it. His brain offered good advice. His heart raised its voice in argument. *Go. Talk to her. Just for a minute. Talking isn't wrong.*

He'd been so careful, so good. They hadn't talked since the day Kaitlin was born.

His body had a mind of its own. He stood, strode to the trash can next to the porch, threw away his plate, and segued right into the building.

Delilah looked up immediately at the sound of his boots on the pine planks. "Are you lost?"

"Nee. I saw you come inside. I wondered if something was wrong."

"You wondered if I needed help changing a leaky diaper? Kaitlin filled her diaper and then some. You won't want to get too close. It reeks to high heaven." Her smile took the sting from her words. "I need to clean her up and change her clothes. I thought it better to do it inside, out of the wind."

"How have you been?"

"Keeping busy. You?"

"Same."

"Christine lets me take care of Kaitlin during the day. Between that and helping around the house, I keep plenty busy. I'm looking forward to planting the vegetable garden soon." She offered him a tremulous smile. "It's gut. But sometimes I wonder if I'll ever have my own boplin, a house I share with my *mann,* and a garden to feed my family."

"I wonder the same thing."

"Things aren't going well with Anna?"

"They're fine. Gut." He couldn't tell Delilah the truth. It might give her hope where there was none. "It takes time to get to know a person well enough to consider a lifetime with her. Don't you find that to be true with Sam?"

A shadow passed over her face. Her dimples disappeared. She turned back to the teacher's desk and went to work changing Kaitlin's dress. "I'm not courting with Sam anymore. He realized my heart wasn't in it. We agreed it was best that we not see each other anymore."

"Your heart wasn't in it? Why?"

"You know the answer to that question. My feelings for you haven't changed since that last buggy ride. Not one iota." She glanced back at him and kept talking, her voice soft and husky. "You're the only one I've ever kissed. It looks like you're the only one I ever will."

Such a sweet declaration. If only he was in a position to tell her how he truly felt as well. "Delilah —"

"You should go. You shouldn't be in here, alone with a woman who isn't your special friend. Go on. You know better."

"I know. I'm sorry."

"Me too. Go on."

"I can't throw Anna away like clothes that don't fit me anymore."

"I wouldn't want you to." Delilah didn't look up. "I hope you two are happy."

She might have a childlike delight in living, but Delilah was the grown-up when it came to doing the right thing. Evan allowed himself a few more seconds watching her dress Kaitlin. His imagination didn't need much encouragement to see her diapering their baby in their home.

Gott, what do I do? Please help me. Either take this love from my heart or show me the way to my heart's desire. Please.

Evan stumbled out the door and went to find Anna. Time to eat a brownie and enjoy it — whether he liked it or not.

Chapter Thirteen

Who didn't love the smell of fresh-cut wood in the morning?

The tools attached to his tool belt banging on his hips, Evan picked his way across the field where Levi Raber had decided to build his new barn. Piles of lumber, equipment, the crane provided by a construction company that employed several Plain men in Eureka, and sundry tools made the walk an obstacle course. If he veered too close to the build site, he could trip over the concrete foundation he and several others had helped Levi lay three days earlier. That didn't stop Evan from sucking in a deep breath and enjoying the cool air.

Most everyone had arrived before five in the morning. The earlier the better for a full day's work. By afternoon the workers at the barn raising would feel the May heat, a harbinger of summer poised on the horizon. But for now it still felt like lingering spring.

Working next to his friends and family was a treat. Raising the frame and trusses on the first day of a twelve-day build was hard work, but he welcomed the camaraderie that always came with these events. Families from as far away as Libby and St. Ignatius had arrived the previous night in order to be ready for the predawn start today. News had been exchanged. Babies kissed. Exclamations made over how tall the children had grown. It was almost as good as a holiday visiting.

"Ready to hoist."

The barn-raising manager and Mercy's father, Jonah Yoder, sang out the command. At least fifty men grabbed sturdy poles and leaned into the task of pushing one timber frame upright until the end timbers slid into the holes prepared for that purpose. Muscles working, men grunted, heaved, and panted.

The wall stood upright. Caleb and his coworkers at the Montana Furniture Store rushed to prop it up with beams.

"One down, three to go." Caleb Hostetler clapped Evan on the back. "That's some good-looking pine."

"You would say that since it came from that stand of ponderosa pine on your property." Evan settled into place for the raising of the second wall frame. Caleb squeezed in next to him. Mercy's husband was a hard worker who could easily run the barn-raising. One day he probably would. Evan rubbed his aching back muscles and smiled. "The hard work was done at Andy's sawmill and you know it."

"It's not like Andy turned the logs into timbers by hand." Grinning, Caleb wiped sweat from his forehead. "The machines do the work for him."

Not so with the mortises and tenon joints. Levi, Andy, Evan, and Caleb had spent hours cutting the mortises and joints before drilling holes so the timbers would be ready for pegs.

All the walls would be constructed in post and beam. However, Levi had decided to make the rafters out of prefab trusses — thus the need for the crane. They were too heavy for the men to lift.

"Here comes frame number two."

Evan grabbed the next beam and together they heaved it into position. His muscles twinged and sweat dripped into his eyes. Caleb grunted. Someone yelled out, "Gut job. You got it."

Another half hour and all four wall frames were in place. Now the work of placing the joists between the beams could begin. But first Evan needed a long drink of water.

He hopped down from the concrete pad and hotfooted it across the grassy field to the tables where a dozen water Igloos had been arranged at a water station. Four or five boys too young to be allowed on the build clustered around the Igloo on the end. They mostly carried tools or moved pallets of wood, and they were excited to be allowed to do that much.

Evan threaded his way through them to the Igloo. He tugged his water bottle from his tool belt and reached for the spigot.

"I think I was here first."

A shiver ran through Evan. He forced his gaze from the spigot to Delilah. Her tone had been apologetic, but she managed a smile.

They hadn't talked since the school picnic. He'd been so careful to make sure of that.

She glanced at the boys, who'd moved off to the side to allow Evan to get his water. "There's no sin in saying hello, you know."

"I know. The truth is, I'm still figuring out how to act like it's no big deal to be around you." Evan flipped the spigot. Water flowed into the bottle. "I try to act casual, but I can't."

"I know it's hard, but we should be able to treat each other like people who've known each other since childhood." Delilah shifted Kaitlin to her other arm and picked up the plastic cup she'd filled with water. "Maybe I should go back to Kansas. That would make it easier for you, wouldn't it?"

"I don't want you to have to do that. You deserve to be happy. If being in Kootenai makes you happy, you should be here. I'm trying to do the right thing." Even when it meant being miserable. Was that God's plan, or had Evan muddled things up all on his own? "You are too."

"Your water bottle is overflowing."

Evan looked down. Sure enough. Water flowed over his hand, onto the table, and splashed on the ground. He flipped off the spigot and put the lid on the bottle. "I know how you feel . . ." He glanced around. She was halfway across the yard, headed toward Nora and Levi's house.

Gott, there must be a way. It's wrong to marry a woman I don't love. I believe that, but how do I know I'm not just thinking that so I can have what I truly want? A life with Delilah. How do I do this without hurting Anna? Help me, Lord, please help me.

Would God see this as a selfish prayer?

Help me discern what is proper and right in this circumstance, Gott. Thy will be done. If Delilah and I aren't meant to be together, please change our hearts according to Thy will.

His heart ached far more than his shoulders and back muscles.

CHAPTER FOURTEEN

Was taking care of her sister's baby a blessing or a form of torture? A little of both. Delilah dumped the dirty cloth diaper into a plastic garbage bag and proceeded to pin a clean one on Kaitlin. It might be good practice for when she had her own baby, or it might be a consolation prize.

What if she never had one of her own?

Every time she saw Evan, she had to rebury this question. It wasn't her place to question God's plan. If she never had more than she had now, so be it. God knew what was best for her.

Please, Gott. Tame my rebellious spirit. Bend me to Your will. You know what is best for me. Thy will be done.

"Gott is smarter than we are." Delilah tugged a fresh dress on Kaitlin. "Don't ever forget that. Your *aenti* does and it gets her into trouble every time. My job right now is to be your aenti, and I plan to be the best one ever. You will be blessed by me and I by you."

Her eyes bright with interest, Kaitlin stared up at Delilah and cooed. They'd become best buddies in the two months since her birth. Delilah had her days — except for feedings — while Christine took the nights. Oftentimes, Delilah could've taken nights. She had that much trouble sleeping.

All because of Evan. She tried so hard to bend to God's will, yet she couldn't curb her desire for more. She was caught in that baseball hot box between what she wanted and what she could have. Which would win out?

Delilah laid Kaitlin on a blanket she'd spread on the grass for that purpose. Using water from her water bottle, she washed her hands. Kaitlin squawked and batted her tiny fists in the air.

"I know, I know. You think I'm a silly girl who wants something because she can't have it." Delilah knelt on the blanket and picked up the baby. Her assigned duties had mostly been supervising the toddlers while their mothers helped with serving the food. "If I could change how I feel, I would. Gott knows what's in my heart. He sees me. He hears me. But He knows what is best for me. Someday I'll be able to see what He sees and He'll say, 'I told you so, *Dochder.*' "

In the meantime she would work so hard she would fall asleep at night out of exhaustion.

"It's you and me, squirt," she whispered to Kaitlin. "We can organize a singing with the little ones. How about that?"

Kaitlin responded with a faint snore. Delilah peeked at her charge. She slumbered in peace. How did babies do it? Awake one minute, asleep the next. What a gift. "Fine. Be that way."

She laid Kaitlin back on the blanket, making sure she reclined in the shade of the maple tree. Hands now free, Delilah stretched her legs out in front of her and leaned back on her palms. The barn was coming along. The raw wood of the wall frames glowed yellow against the serene blue sky. Men crawled like worker bees amassed on the cement pad. Others sat on beams higher up, pounding in pegs that would adhere the joists to the beams.

She put her hand to her forehead and squinted. Evan stood on top of the frame. He balanced like a tightrope walker as he slipped across the joist from one beam to the next. A tape measure in one hand and a mallet in the other, he nimbly negotiated a turn and stopped on the closest wall, facing her.

Delilah held her breath. The barn rafters would be two stories high when they were attached. His relaxed posture said he had no fear. Delilah had enough for them both. The urge to call to him grew. *Be careful, Evan, be careful.*

Someone called his name. Mallet lifted, he turned.

It happened so fast Delilah couldn't be sure she hadn't dreamed it.

One second Evan balanced on the beam. The next he disappeared from her sight.

Followed by an ugly, sickening thump.

"Evan? Evan!" Delilah scrambled to her feet. Her arms and legs didn't want to work. Her feet stumbled. Her arms flailed. Her heart careened in circles inside her chest, banging against her rib cage, trying to escape.

Sound seeped away. Time forgot its familiar forward thrust.

She raced past others who had stopped to stare, their mouths agape. A hard knot of fear lodged in the back of her throat. She pushed her way through the men who crowded around Evan's prone figure. "Evan!"

Jonah Yoder squatted next to Evan. His

eyebrows raised, he looked up at her as if to say, "What are you doing here?"

"Is he all right?"

Jonah's hand went to Evan's chest. "He's breathing."

"I called 911." One of the Englishers held up his phone. "The volunteer fire department in Eureka will send someone out."

They would take too long. Far too long.

"I have paramedic training from when I was a volunteer firefighter back in Ohio." Sam broke away from the cluster of men who towered over Delilah. "Let me take a look."

He squatted next to Jonah and examined Evan. He seemed to know what he was doing. It no longer mattered what anyone thought. Delilah knelt across from the two men. Evan had landed sprawled on his face in the mix of sand, gravel, and rocky soil a hairsbreadth from the barn's concrete foundation. Any closer and his head would have banged against the rock-hard concrete.

One arm was underneath his body, the other flung out. His legs spread in opposite directions.

"His pulse is strong." Sam's hands traveled along Evan's legs, his spine, and his free arm. "Doesn't feel like he has any broken bones."

"Praise Gott," Jonah murmured. "What about his head? Did he hit it?"

Sam gently touched Evan's neck, then moved on to his head, which he lifted an inch or two. Evan's nose was squashed and bleeding.

He moaned.

"He's coming around." Sam eased Evan's head to the ground. "Evan, Evan, talk to me. Where does it hurt?"

Evan groaned a second time. He rolled over onto his side and curled up into a ball. The arm underneath him came up. He cradled it against his chest. He coughed. "What happened?"

"You fell." Delilah reached toward him. The sudden acute realization that nearly every resident in her Gmay stood watching — along with many others from Libby and St. Ignatius — forced her to stop. "You're hurt."

"I'm okay. I'm fine." Evan struggled to sit up. "My arm hurts and my nose, but not bad."

"You should probably wait for the folks from the fire department to examine you." Sam nudged him back to the ground. "You're gonna have a humdinger of a headache. That arm looks like it might be broken."

"Sam, can you and Levi stay with Evan? Andy, get the first-aid kit Melba keeps handy. And get him some ice for that bump on his forehead." Jonah rose. "Help will be here soon. No sense in losing the rest of the day's light. Let's get back to work."

Just like that. A near catastrophe was over. Her legs almost too weak to carry her, Delilah struggled to stand. The crowd dispersed, the men back to work placing the beams, the women to the food tables.

Kaitlin.

Delilah staggered between piles of lumber. The men talked among themselves. Somehow it felt as if they were talking about her — the woman who made a spectacle of herself in front of everyone over a man who wasn't her special friend.

She sped back to the trees where she'd spread the blanket. The women serving food murmured. They glanced at Delilah and then away, their faces knowing or wondering or both.

Anna stood in the shade, Kaitlin in her arms. "She was wailing."

Delilah slowed. She stopped at the edge of the blanket. "Danki for picking her up."

"She's so sweet."

Neither spoke for a second.

Why hadn't Anna run to her special friend

when he fell? Wasn't she concerned for Evan's well-being?

Maybe someone else arrived first.

Delilah fought the urge to cover her face with her apron. Everyone knew now. Anna knew. "I'm sorry —"

"I've known for a while."

"Known what?"

Anna swayed, her dress's skirt fluttering in the afternoon breeze. "Don't do that. You two have been pretending for long enough. I reckon Sam figured it out before I did. Maybe because I didn't want to believe it."

"Neither of us wanted to cause pain or hurt."

"I know. My mudder says a heart wants what a heart wants."

"Does yours want Evan?"

Anna moved closer. She held out Kaitlin. Delilah took her. Anna touched the sleeping baby's cheek. "I thought I did. But when he never sought to grow closer, I began to wonder if he simply didn't have the ability to go deeper. Then you showed up and he withdrew even more. I realized it wasn't him. It was me. He didn't care for me — not in the way I wanted him to."

"He does care for you."

A wan smile appeared. "Like you care for Sam. Like a bruder and schweschder."

"Like a friend."

"That should be a gut thing, yet it hurts." Anna's gaze shifted to the straggly grass at her feet. "Yet it's possible my pride is hurt more than my heart. When Evan failed to give his all, I began to backpedal. To protect myself."

"I'm sorry —"

"Don't keep apologizing. It only makes it worse." Anna dabbed at her cheeks with her apron. "Tell Evan I wish him well."

"You don't want to talk to him yourself?"

"No reason. The whole of Kootenai — all of northwest Montana — knows how you feel about Evan now. I'm sure they've figured out how he feels about me simply by the length of our courting. I kept wondering why he didn't pop the question. I knew the answer. I just didn't want to admit it. Now I have no choice. At least I still have teaching."

Delilah chewed her lower lip to keep from apologizing yet again. Her expression resigned, Anna brushed past her and headed toward the long lines of buggies on the road in front of Levi's house. Delilah wanted to say something to make her feel better.

Such words didn't exist. Delilah knew better than most the truth of that statement. In order for the door of hope to open for Delilah, another door had to close for Anna. It didn't seem fair.

"Life isn't fair." Father's voice thundered in Delilah's head. No matter how many times he said it, she still wanted it to be fair. For Anna's sake as much as her own.

Now they would each look for that way forward down a different path.

CHAPTER FIFTEEN

Fresh, damp dirt smelled of spring, new beginnings, and hope. Delilah stood and brushed dirt from her hands. She inhaled and surveyed the orderly rows of her vegetable garden. Leaf lettuce, cucumbers, tomatoes, carrots, green beans, green peppers, and cabbage. It had taken all day to plant this cornucopia of goodness. Working outside by herself felt good.

Christine had said nothing of the barn-raising accident earlier in the week other than to remark that she hoped Evan took the time to recover properly before going back to work. Her lips turned up in a small smile and her eyes twinkled, but she didn't elaborate. Andy simply took another bite of lasagna and chewed. He was too tired from day number five on the project to talk.

Delilah toted her basket of seed packets and planting tools back to the porch and sat next to a tall glass of cold tea. The sun dipped beyond the horizon. Dusk made an appearance. She'd finished just in time.

She would have to wait until Sunday — two more days — to know how Evan was recovering. Mercy had shared the news that his wrist was broken. They'd put a cast on it. That would make it hard for him to work on buggies, so missing work might not be avoidable.

What about his nose? Mercy didn't say and Delilah didn't want to ask. She'd already made a spectacle of herself.

Did he know yet of Anna's decision to end their courtship? Surely he'd spoken to her shortly after his accident. Would he feel honor bound to win Anna back? Delilah had to prepare herself for the possibility. She didn't want to be so selfish as to assume he would come back to her if Anna no longer wanted to pursue their courting. He might need some time to decide. Anything was possible.

A long swallow of tea didn't dissolve the sudden lump in her throat.

The *clip-clop* of a horse's hooves sounded in the distance. Delilah squinted into the sun. The buggy meandered along the dirt road, throwing up puffs of dust behind it.

Evan's cinnamon gelding led the way. Delilah stood. She was about to find out.

The buggy stopped at the hitching post. Evan dragged himself from it and stood next to the narrow sidewalk. He seemed stuck. Delilah took her time looking at him. His nose was swollen and bruised. He had two black eyes and a bruised forehead. A snow-white cast adorned his arm cradled in a black bandana sling. At least it was the left one.

"You're here."

What a silly thing to say. She always managed to state the obvious.

"I am." Evan did the same. "I thought we should talk."

"Here?"

He glanced around. "I'm sore. Driving a buggy doesn't feel great."

Her heart thrumming, Delilah moved her basket to the porch floor and patted the spot next to her. "Andy turned in early. Christine is putting the kinner down for the night. Have a seat."

Evan made his way toward her with a slight limp. With a grunt, he used the porch handrail to lower himself to the step.

"You're moving slow." More stating of the obvious. Delilah closed her eyes, then opened them. "How are you feeling?"

"I have a headache and my nose throbs." He touched his noggin. "But the doctor who looked at my arm says I'm blessed that nothing worse happened. Landing on the dirt instead of the concrete probably saved my life."

A shiver ran through Delilah. Her stomach churned. Thinking about what might have happened only made it worse. "I'm so glad you didn't die. I know we're supposed to be okay with it, but I'm not ready for you to go."

"Me neither." He rubbed his knee with one hand. "I'm not ready to go or for you to go."

That was a good start.

"Sam told me what happened." He switched to his other knee. "He said everyone saw. Including Anna."

"I'm sorry if I embarrassed you. I saw you fall and I didn't think. I ran."

"Don't apologize." Echoes of Anna's words. Evan's fingers slipped from his knee to Delilah's hand. He squeezed. The pressure felt good. "I just came from Anna's house."

"You talked to her then?"

"We had a gut talk. At first she said it wasn't necessary. I could simply go about my business without worrying about her. I couldn't do that. We've spent a lot of time together in the last sixteen months."

"She and I talked. The day you fell."

"She told me. She was very calm. She said she'd had time to think about it. She didn't want to be yoked with someone who didn't truly love her, mann to fraa."

"I pray she finds that person." Delilah concentrated on the feel of Evan's hand on hers. Like a long-lost friend. "She deserves to have that in her life."

"After I worked so hard not to hurt her, she broke up with me."

"And Sam broke up with me."

"Does that mean they are braver than we are?" His forehead wrinkled. He shook his head. "Or just more discerning?"

"Both, I reckon." Delilah peered at the sky through the gathering dusk. It seemed as if they had been at cross-purposes for far too long. They thought they were doing what was best and honorable, but they were only postponing what seemed inevitable to those closest to them. "Anna said she held back in committing her whole heart because she knew you weren't giving your all. That's discerning."

"Gott has a better plan for her. I believe that." Evan chuckled softly. "I wonder what He has in store for Sam."

Delilah studied his face and its sudden mischievous expression. "Evan? You're not thinking about doing a little matchmaking, are you?"

"It can't hurt to nudge him in that direction, could it? If it's Gott's will, gut things will come of it. If not, we tried."

"You mean *you* tried."

Evan grinned. "Come on. I just want them to have a second chance the way we do." He leaned closer. "You smell like earth and plants. You smell nice."

His proximity sent a volley of mingled emotions through Delilah. After waiting and denying for so long, it didn't seem real. She stretched toward him. "I've missed everything about you."

His dark-blue eyes traced her face. "I'm sorry I didn't wait."

"Let's not dwell on the past."

"There's something I've wanted to do since that day I saw you standing in front of Andy's house with a snowball in each hand."

"What's that?"

He swiveled and tugged her close with his uninjured arm. His lips found hers.

All the angst fell away. The hurt. The bewilderment. Delilah slid her arms around his neck and gave herself up to the emotions she'd held locked away for so long. Her heart found its old rhythm. The bars that held it captive fell away.

Danki, Gott, danki.

His lips were even sweeter than she remembered. She drew back and touched his face, his neck, and ran her hands across his broad shoulders. "I keep thinking this is a dream. I'm afraid I'll wake up and you'll be gone and I'll be alone —"

"It's not a dream. I'm real. I'm here and I'm not going anywhere." Evan nuzzled her neck, kissed her cheeks and her forehead. "I've waited two years for this moment. I'm never letting you go."

Before she could respond, he bent his head and kissed her again, a kiss that made promises that couldn't be broken. Broken dreams rearranged and became whole again. After a long while, he pulled away. His gaze full of emotion, he cupped her cheek with one hand and stared. "I love you," he whispered.

"I love you." Delilah's response came with no hesitation. She ran toward her second chance, knowing she didn't deserve it, knowing she'd been given a gift she would never take for granted. "I've always loved you. I will never stop loving you."

"Will you marry me?"

"In a heartbeat."

They didn't talk anymore. No more words were needed. They made up for lost time with kisses that sealed a future that would be spent building a life together.

Delilah was home for good.

DISCUSSION QUESTIONS

1. Delilah's mother told her not to worry about her relationship with Evan. If the relationship was meant to be, it would survive long distance. How do you feel about long-distance relationships? Do you think she was right? Why or why not?
2. After several months, Delilah and Evan stopped writing each other. What role do you think lack of communication had in the events that transpired when Delilah returned to West Kootenai? How could they have handled their separation and her return differently?
3. Evan believes it would be wrong to break up with Anna because Delilah has returned to West Kootenai. Do you think he's right? Do you think he should've talked to Anna about what he was feeling? Why or why not?
4. Delilah comes to realize that she doesn't have feelings for Sam, not the way she

does for Evan. Yet Sam is the one who confronts her about her feelings and ends the relationship. Have you ever stayed in a relationship in order to avoid being alone? How does choosing to continue that relationship impact the other person? What do you think is the right thing to do in these circumstances?

5. Delilah decides to play with the children during recess. Their game leads to Charlie's disappearance. How do you feel about how Delilah handled the situation, in particular refusing to return to the classroom but instead looking for Charlie until she finds him? Did she do the right thing? Were Noah and Tobias correct in dismissing her from her teaching position? Why or why not?
6. Delilah agrees that Evan should honor his relationship with Anna. She agrees to buggy rides — tantamount to courting — with Sam because she hopes she'll forget her feelings for Evan. Should she have begun courting with Sam under those circumstances? Was it fair to him? Why or why not?
7. Scripture says in all things God works for our good. How do you think this verse in Romans applies to Evan and Delilah's situation? How does it apply to the out-

come experienced by Sam and Anna?

8. Mercy tells Delilah to pray and then accept God's will for her future, with or without Evan. Have you ever prayed for God's will in a situation in your life and not received the answer you wanted? How did you handle it?

Love's Solid Foundation

Kathleen Fuller

To James. I love you.

Prologue

April

Dear Nettie,

We figured out you've been writing to both of us and that you tried to pursue a relationship with one of us and then the other. We don't know why you did this — it makes no sense — but it doesn't really matter. Whatever the reason, we feel sorry for you.

But we've also forgiven you. Please, for your sake, straighten out your life. Go to the Lord. We're not bishops or ministers or anything close, but even we can see that you might not find your way back if you keep going down this path.

Sincerely,
Zeb and Zeke Bontrager

Nettie Miller folded the letter, her heart filled with unexpected shame. This wasn't the first time she'd read the letter the Bontrager twins sent her. At that time she'd been incensed. How dare they feel sorry for her? She'd been so offended that she nearly tore the letter into pieces. But instead of tossing it, she'd stashed the thing in her nightstand drawer and stewed in her anger.

Then, for some reason she couldn't fathom, she started wondering if the brothers were right about the path she was on, a path she'd started down last fall. After briefly seeing them at a wedding — and as bored with her life as she'd ever been — she'd formed a plan. It hadn't been difficult to obtain their mailing address in Birch Creek, where they'd moved years ago. She started writing them to amuse herself, changing her handwriting between the two sets of letters, insisting the brothers keep their correspondence a secret from each other. Which twin could she attract first? Which one would return to Fredericktown for the chance to date Nettie Miller, the prettiest girl in the district and from the best and most well-off family? In her mind, she'd offered them both the opportunity of a lifetime.

Not that she'd had any real interest in either of them. She was just having a good time, never caring if they got hurt. She'd toyed with men before, hadn't she? And the Bontrager twins were such easy targets. When they were all still in school, Zeb had a crush on her, and Zeke was a flirt. They'd moved to Birch Creek before they were old enough to date, or she might have found some way to amuse herself with the boys then.

She opened the letter again, the last sentence sending a chill down her spine. Now she was afraid she might not find her way back from the selfishness and cruelty she'd let creep into her heart more and more with each passing year. Zeb and Zeke were right. She needed to change. But she didn't think she could, not on her own.

She stilled as another realization dawned. The brothers had also pointed her back to her faith. Back to the One who could change her.

Alone in her bedroom, she fell to her knees, closed her eyes, and prayed.

Lord, help me . . .

CHAPTER ONE

Devon Bontrager halted in front of old Man Elmer's house, standing in the very Ohio town he'd vowed to never be in again.

Nine years ago, Devon and his large family, including nine of his ten siblings, had left Fredericktown for a better life in Birch Creek, their current home in Ohio. His only sister, Phoebe, had already moved there. He'd never imagined leaving Birch Creek for any reason, but God had a funny way of changing well-laid plans.

He adjusted his duffel bag's strap on his shoulder and headed up the rundown home's driveway. The property's front yard was a mess. Both the grass and the bushes were overgrown, as was the patch of land to the side that had once been a garden. Then his gaze lifted to the top of the house, something he couldn't help doing whenever he saw a structure with a roof.

Rather than making farming his life's

work, like his father had, he'd trained in all forms of construction. But his favorite job was roofing. Some of his coworkers thought he was crazy since roofing was difficult work. But he found satisfaction in laying a new roof. In some ways, it was the most important part of a building. A roof destroyed or in disrepair had to be dealt with immediately, before the entire structure was ruined.

Now that he saw this roof, though, he wondered if coming here meant biting off more than he could chew. Many of the shingles had peeled off, and some had fallen to the ground, leaving behind the black tar paper that wouldn't keep the elements at bay for long. And if the outside of the house looked like this, what did the inside look like?

And what would Old Man Elmer think of him just showing up out of blue? It was bad enough that he'd fibbed when he told his family he had a construction job here, not wanting them to know the real reason he was returning. But what would he tell Elmer?

He shook his head as he finally strode to the front porch, then knocked on the door despite the dread he felt. When he didn't get a response, he knocked again, then mashed his finger against the doorbell even though he knew the old man would hate the shrill, steady ring. Devon's family had been the victim of ring-and-dash pranks when they lived here, sad to say from some local *English* kids, and he wouldn't have been surprised if Elmer had disconnected the thing.

"I'm coming. I'm coming." The old man's cantankerous voice came muffled from the other side of the door.

Devon tapped his foot against the chipped concrete step until the door slowly opened. Elmer was more stooped than Devon remembered, his face more wrinkled and craggier. His skin tone was sallow. "Hey, Elmer."

Elmer coughed, then brought a wrinkled, old, and stained handkerchief to his mouth and wiped his lips. "Who are you?"

"Devon," he said, the question throwing him for a second. But he'd been fifteen when he moved away. Maybe he'd changed more than he thought he had. Or maybe Elmer needed new glasses. "Devon Bontrager."

Peering at him, Elmer nodded, but his grumpy expression remained. "Why are you here?"

"I heard you were sick." As Devon said

the words, Elmer coughed again. He considered revealing how his mother had mentioned Elmer's ongoing illness after she received a letter from Wilma Yoder, the one person she was still in contact with from this community. Wilma had lamented that the old man wouldn't let anyone help him, at least as far as she knew. Devon decided against telling him that, though, sure Elmer would hate the Amish — or anyone else — knowing his business.

"So?" Elmer spat.

"I came to help you." The knot in Devon's stomach tightened. He didn't know how to nurse anyone back to health, much less an old *English* man who seemed to hate people.

"Don't need no help."

Elmer started to shut him out, but Devon wrapped his fingers around the edge of the door and held it steady so he couldn't slam it. "Looks like you do to me."

Elmer tried to shove the door closed, but he made no progress in his weakened state. Finally, he stepped back. "Whatever," he said, then turned and shuffled back into the house.

Devon paused. He'd never been inside, and he had no idea what he would find. But he was here to help Elmer. He owed the man that much.

■ ■ ■ ■

Four Weeks Later

Nettie had just finished packing her picnic basket when her mother entered the kitchen. "What are you doing?"

"Getting ready to take some food to Old Man Elmer."

Mamm placed her hand on Nettie's back, almost as if to push her aside. But she didn't.

"Again?" She grimaced. "I've told you. It's *gut* that you want to help a neighbor. God calls us to do that." She pursed her lips. "But this isn't the right time, and he's not the right neighbor."

Nettie stayed silent as she closed the basket's lid. She was disappointed in her mother's words — and not for the first time lately. Yes, this *was* a challenging time for her family to be giving away food, but her mother was wrong when she said Elmer wasn't the "right" neighbor. True, he was surly and off-putting, and growing up, Nettie had been as terrified of him as the other Amish children in their community were. But her feelings toward him had changed in the last few weeks. *She'd* changed. And she refused to let her mother stop her from helping someone who was sick, regardless of what *kind* of neighbor she'd determined him to be.

But she'd have to tell *Mamm* something, hoping she could pacify her somehow. "This time I bought food and ingredients with *mei* own money."

Mamm stepped back, her eyes narrowed. "*Yer* money? Did you forget our agreement? Any income from *yer* job goes into our *familye* account. And now you're telling me you're holding money back?" Her words were pointed, but what she didn't say made Nettie not only more disappointed but ashamed. *After all we've done for you, this is how you treat us.*

As the only child of the wealthiest family in a small Amish district, Nettie had always had her way — as long as it was within the Ordinance of the community . . . at least as far as the bishop knew. Whatever Nettie wanted, she got.

But she'd taken that self-centered attitude a step too far by toying with the Bontrager twins. Thankfully, though, the letter the brothers wrote saying they'd found her out, yet had forgiven her, became the catalyst for her asking God to change her. And he had. She was grateful for what the twins had done, and she'd finally worked up the courage to write them one last time only a few days ago, apologizing. She just hoped they'd accept her apology.

She withdrew a short stack of cash from her apron pocket, the rest of the money she'd earned that week working at the little mercantile in town. Her parents had never wanted her to work — which had been fine by her — but when her father's lumber business started its downslide, they'd had no choice but to let her. Her father had stopped taking a salary so he could pay the few employees he had left. Then he became ill with double pneumonia as well. Even if her mother could work outside the home, that wasn't possible with a sick spouse. *Daed* needed her. And although Nettie pitched in as much as she could, *Mamm* had to help care for their animals after they had to let their hired man go. Her father was still too weak to do it himself.

She handed the money to her mother. "Here's the rest. I was going to give it to you when I got back."

Mamm snatched the bills out of Nettie's hand with a fierceness that stunned her. "Next time, give me all of it." Then she stalked out of the kitchen.

Nettie stilled. This was the most agitated she'd seen *Mamm,* but at least she hadn't demanded the food be put away for their own family's use. She'd never considered her mother — or her father — greedy. Now that they were in financial trouble, though, she'd seen that trait clearly in *Mamm,* a side of her she didn't like. She'd also recognized that same greedy streak in herself, but she'd asked God to change her in that area too.

She'd also asked God to change her mother's attitude, not only about money but toward people she deemed somehow beneath her, like Elmer. She'd even hoped *Mamm* would see the change in her own daughter when Nettie discovered Elmer was sick and began taking him food. But so far, neither prayer had been answered.

After lifting the basket from the counter — its contents a little heavier than usual — she slipped on her coat in the mudroom, then began her half-mile walk to Elmer's house. It was May, but yesterday she'd heard a customer at work say a rare cold front was due to move in last night. Sure enough, it had, bringing the smattering of snow beneath her feet.

As she neared Elmer's place, her heart started beating faster — but not from fear. After visiting him several times, she'd realized he was just a lonely, cranky old man who'd pushed away everyone around him.

No, Elmer wasn't the reason her heart thumped wildly. That was because she might see Devon Bontrager.

As she neared the small home, she spotted the object of her affection shoveling the thin layer of snow off the driveway. Although Devon had been here helping Elmer since early April — she still didn't know why — she hadn't interacted with him much. He'd kept to himself, even at church. Just as well, she'd thought. Best to avoid any Bontrager after what she did to Zeb and Zeke. But when she started visiting Elmer, she found herself drawn to Devon. She shouldn't be surprised. She'd always been attracted to men with dark hair, and Devon's was nearly black. His eyes were bright blue, and he possessed a wiry, but athletic body. She'd have to be out of her mind not to notice his handsomeness.

His looks were only part of the reason she couldn't stop noticing him. As she observed everything he was doing for the old man, she'd developed actual feelings for him — and in such a short time. Fortunately, if Devon knew what she'd done to his brothers, he didn't seem to have told anyone in her district. She knew one thing, though. Only a kind man would move in with a grouchy old thing like Elmer, nurse him back to health, and get his rundown property into shape. How could she not be interested in a man like that?

But that was just wrong. After her awful behavior with his brothers, she shouldn't even be *thinking* about a Bontrager man. She shouldn't be thinking about any man, period. She had much more penance to pay before she'd deserve a real relationship. Until then, she'd make sure she had as little interaction with Devon as possible.

Devon pushed the snow off Elmer's driveway with a bent, rusty snow shovel. The light accumulation had fallen overnight, and removing it wasn't hard. Nor was it a necessary chore considering the flakes would surely melt away by noon. On top of that, he'd discovered the old man hadn't driven his car for months, so he was sure Elmer didn't care if his driveway wasn't in good shape. But Devon had to get out of the house for some fresh air.

Even though Elmer had neglected his car, Devon had sneaked out to the garage several times to start the engine. He'd gathered enough knowledge over the years to know a car's battery would die if the vehicle sat idle for too long. The last thing he needed was to worry about whether Elmer's car would start in an emergency. Thank goodness he'd spotted the keys on a hook by the back door, because he was positive Elmer wouldn't have handed them over without a fuss. He was also grateful the man could sleep through anything, including the opening and closing of the garage door.

He shoveled the last bit of snow, then looked up to see Nettie Miller coming toward him, looking as beautiful as ever. She was petite, with fair skin that went perfectly with her pale-blue eyes and corn-silk-colored hair, and he fought to keep from staring at her. His stomach turned, disgusted that he could be attracted to the shallow woman who'd played his brothers for fools in such a heartless way. When he'd told Zeb and Zeke he was returning to Fredericktown, they'd revealed what Nettie had done, mostly as a warning to be wary of her — though they also said they'd written her, advising her to change her ways.

Devon hadn't been shocked by what they told him. He remembered Nettie — and particularly her rich parents. They'd had more money than anyone would know what to do with while his father struggled to put a meal on the table for their family of thirteen. Worse, even when bringing them food — merely out of obligation to their

Amish faith, he was sure — Nettie and her mother had treated them almost as lesser beings. Although his parents had tried to hide it, he'd seen their hurt expressions after Sarah Miller and her snotty daughter left.

Despite all that, he couldn't deny that Nettie was a beautiful woman. *On the outside.*

As Nettie neared, though, he thought about how hard it was to reconcile this woman carrying another basket of food for Elmer with the haughty brat he'd known and the scheming woman who'd deceived his brothers. He had no idea if she'd changed, and he'd rather not talk to her, but he wasn't about to run away whenever she showed up.

He leaned on the handle of the shovel and looked directly at her. "Nettie," he said impassively. He made sure to keep his expressions distant and his thoughts closed when she was around. If she wondered if he knew about the trick she'd played on Zeb and Zeke, let her wonder.

She met his gaze. "Devon," she replied, her tone equally impassive. "I brought a few more things for Elmer."

"He's up. You can take them inside."

She nodded, then walked past him and disappeared around the side of the house.

He shook his head, unable to understand why he thought Nettie Miller was the most stunning woman he'd ever seen despite the probability she was the same person she'd always been. Helping Elmer so often could be another pretense, this time to play *him* for a fool. But he wouldn't be a sucker. He wasn't about to fall for Nettie Miller or her schemes.

Nettie knocked on the back door three times before stepping inside, relieved that her pulse had slowed once Devon was out of sight. She took off her coat in the mudroom, then set her basket on the counter in the kitchen. Elmer sat hunched over his small, splintery table. "Good morning. How are you feeling today?"

He set his coffee mug on the table with a clatter. "What's it to you?" he grumbled.

"Nice to see you too." She smiled and moved closer. "Would you like more coffee?"

He nodded and held out his mug.

She took it, then poured the still-hot brew from his fancy coffee maker. It was an electric appliance, but it did make coffee faster than her mother's percolator did — the best percolator money could buy, of course.

Nettie had no idea how old Elmer was, but he had to be well over seventy. His knuckles were swollen and gnarled, probably from whatever job he'd had before he moved to Fredericktown fifteen years ago. She couldn't fathom why an *English* man would relocate to a tiny Amish town, especially one where the people kept to themselves — so much so that community membership had never regained its former numbers after the Bontragers left. Rare was the Sunday when they had visitors at church, and everyone seemed to like it that way.

She set the steaming coffee in front of Elmer. "Did you have something to eat?"

He grunted and gave her a nod. "That lousy kid won't leave me alone in the mornings. Nags me until I eat the eggs and toast he makes." Even though the coffee was piping hot, he took a healthy swig and set it down on the table. "Big pest, that's what he is. Needs to go back where he came from. I told him I don't need his help."

In the past, she would have tried to learn why Devon was there helping Elmer, unable to keep her nose out of his business. She would have used sneaky tactics or directly asked him. The method she used to gain insight into other people's business never mattered, just the information. If she wanted to know something, she'd find out.

But she was learning she didn't have the right to be nosy — and that the world didn't revolve around her. Whatever Devon's reasons for being here, she was glad Elmer had someone to help him in ways she couldn't, someone who could do more than bring him food. She didn't think she'd ever seen any other visitors at Elmer's house.

She could relate to that. Her own attitude and behavior had cost her the few friends she'd had. The lack of companionship was another part of her life she wanted to change, but she was apprehensive about approaching any of the young women in the community. So soon after she overheard Wilma Yoder saying Elmer was sick, she'd knocked on his door one day and simply breezed past him before he could reject her and her food basket. She was sure he needed a friend, and she was determined to be one.

"It's a good thing he's a pest." She wiped breakfast crumbs off the kitchen table with the only clean cloth she could find. "You look better than you have in weeks."

Ignoring her comment, Elmer took another drink. "You missed a spot," he said, pointing to a single crumb at the edge of the table.

Nettie wiped it away, then shook the cloth in the sink. While it was clear Devon's attention to Elmer had improved his health — and the outside of the house and yard had certainly improved as well — neither man seemed capable of keeping a neat home. Last week she'd decided to tackle each room, one at a time. Fortunately, Elmer's house was small. Unfortunately, it was full of junk. "Today's the day," she said, turning on the tap, then pouring a small amount of dish detergent into the sink.

"What day is that?"

Nettie lifted her gaze and stared out the window. Now Devon was splitting firewood. She frowned. Elmer didn't have a fireplace or woodstove. Who was he cutting firewood for?

"Girl? Did you hear me?"

She bristled and turned off the tap, tempted to whirl around and give him a piece of her mind, just like she would have in the past. How dare he talk to her like that? But just because Elmer was rude didn't mean he didn't need a friend. Taking in a deep breath, she turned and smiled. "I'm cleaning your living room today."

He peered at her over his crooked, thick-lens glasses. "What?"

"Remember? Last week I told you your house needs a good cleaning." A real good cleaning, one she intended to provide. She knew how to care for a house. Cleaning, cooking, and laundry were chores her mother — not as prone to spoil her as her father was — had insisted she learn. Last week she'd been surprised to discover cleaning supplies in an old cabinet in Elmer's mudroom. She had been sure he didn't own any. Of course, she didn't find a supply of clean dust cloths to work with, so this morning she'd placed several from home in the bottom of her picnic basket.

"I remember. And I remember telling you my house is fine." He averted his gaze. "But I guess I can't stop you," he added, his tone softer.

In moments like these — becoming more frequent — she knew he was grateful for her help. "You can supervise me if you want, and I think you'll be happy when I'm done."

He slowly rose from the table without comment. Although he didn't use a cane, he couldn't stretch to his full height, and he wasn't that tall to begin with. His gray hair was combed back, revealing deep lines across his forehead. He shuffled over and handed her the mug. "I'll be in my chair."

"Okay. I'll be in after I wash the dishes."

He gave her a backhand wave and left the kitchen.

The water in the sink wasn't warm enough, so Nettie added a touch of hot water to the bubbles, determined not to look out the window again. But she couldn't stop herself. Devon was still chopping wood, and having taken off his jacket, he was working in just a light-blue, short-sleeved shirt, broadfall pants, and dirt-scuffed boots. Even at this distance she could see how muscular his forearms were, and she marveled at the ease with which he cleanly split the wood.

"I ain't got all day, girl," Elmer shouted from the living room.

She rolled her eyes and finished washing the dishes as quickly as she could, giving Elmer only enough time to complain about her slowness once more. Then she took another look at the attractive man outside. *Lord, if only things were different, maybe Devon and I would have a chance.*

But they weren't different . . . and she had only herself to blame.

Chapter Two

Devon saw Nettie finally leave a little after noon. As he'd tried to ignore his growing hunger, he'd wondered what was taking her so long. To kill some more time, he'd piled the stack of firewood he'd chopped next to Elmer's garage. Elmer didn't have a fireplace or woodstove, but before he'd realized that — used to Amish houses with no other source of heat — he'd purchased an unsplit cord. At least the sweaty work had helped him take his mind off the fact that, somewhere inside of himself, he didn't really want Nettie to go.

That confused him. Why would he want her here if his goal was to ultimately avoid her? The only upside to her visits was that Elmer was always in a little better mood when Nettie was here. But Elmer's moods didn't have any bearing on why Devon had moved in.

He shoved the woman out of his mind as

he made his way through the back door, famished. He'd have to make lunch for himself. Whatever Nellie brought was for Elmer.

But then he spotted an extra place setting on the kitchen table, surrounded by what looked like several turkey and tomato sandwiches, plus a bowl with a good amount of macaroni salad and a large bag of potato chips. He almost drooled when he saw a plate of homemade oatmeal raisin cookies.

Elmer was munching on one of those and reading the newspaper as Devon stepped to the sink to wash his hands. When he finished, he sat down and bowed for a silent prayer of thanks. *Thank you, too, Nettie.* But her generosity toward him was confusing as well.

"Cookies ain't bad." Elmer turned a page while Devon piled his plate with food. "You Amish know how to bake, that's for sure."

"You should taste my mother's cookies."

"Maybe." He paused, never looking up. "Your family doing all right?"

Devon frowned. Elmer hadn't asked about them since he arrived. He assumed that was because he didn't care — if he knew anything about his family at all. He was probably just being nosy. Still, he felt the need to answer his question. "They couldn't be better."

The old man didn't respond; he just continued reading as Devon ate his lunch, thinking about another recent family revelation. Not long before Devon left for Fredericktown, his father shared new details about his struggles when they lived here. The bishop had blamed his father's supposed lack of faith for their farm failing and for his family's impoverishment. His father admitted pride — but not faith — had been a problem for him, but given that Bishop Weaver had already sent Devon's only sister, Phoebe, and her son, Malachi, away, it hadn't taken much for his father to move the family to Birch Creek, where the man Phoebe eventually married was from.

Bishop Weaver hadn't spoken to Devon other than a brisk hello at church. That was fine. Not only was he avoiding interaction with anyone in the district, usually a staid community anyway, but he had very little to say to the man who had treated his family so unjustly.

He finished his lunch, then hoping Elmer would stow away the leftovers on his own, he placed his dishes in the sink and headed for the spare bedroom to get his hat. He'd need it now that the sun was out. Then he walked into the living room to leave by the front door. He had some weeds to attend to.

He halted. The room was spotless. The stacks of books and magazines littering the old coffee table and some of the floor had been placed neatly on the built-in shelves on the opposite side of the room. The furniture had been dusted, the flattened couch pillows fluffed, the window panes cleaned to a shine. The curtains were pulled back, and bright sunshine filtered into the room.

So this is what Nettie was doing here so long.

"Not bad."

Devon turned to see Elmer shuffling in. He wasn't smiling, but Devon could see a spark of humanity in the old man's eyes. "Not bad at all," he replied.

"Still needs vacuuming." Elmer crossed his bony arms over his chest. "Said she couldn't use my vacuum because it's electric, but she'll bring her carpet sweeper next time she comes." He huffed. "As if my vacuum isn't good enough."

"Do you even know where it is?"

"In this house. Somewhere." Elmer lifted his chin, then looked over the room before glaring at Devon. "You better not make a mess, boy."

Chuckling, Devon said, "Don't worry. I won't."

Elmer nodded, then made his way to his favorite seat, an old tufted chair. He scooted a matching stool out from under it, then sat down, propped up his feet, and closed his eyes.

For the first time ever, Devon saw Elmer's expression relax. He looked around the room again. He could have cleaned it himself, but he'd been focused on the outside of the house and the yard, determined to spruce up and repair all the areas subjected to years of Elmer's neglect. He'd already spent most of his savings to fix the roof, paint the house, repair the stoops, and do a little landscaping. He'd have to get a construction job for real before he ran out of money. But he didn't regret spending a single dime. And he'd stay until he was sure Elmer was all right.

Soft snores came from the chair, and Devon quietly left. He was confused again. Nettie — one of the most self-absorbed people he'd ever known — had worked hard in a short amount of time, going well beyond bringing an old, sick man some food and washing a few dishes. Even without the vacuuming, he was certain Elmer hadn't lived in a room this clean in all the years he'd lived in Fredericktown.

Maybe Nettie *had* changed.

Nettie sneezed as she slipped on a clean dress. She was tired after thoroughly cleaning Elmer's living room, but she'd also been satisfied with the results. Seeing a flicker of a smile on the man's face when he saw how neat and tidy his living space was had filled her with happiness. She'd helped some people in the past, but sparingly — and mostly out of duty because of her faith. But it was much more gratifying to make someone happy because she wanted to. She just had to take her carpet sweeper next time.

She made her way downstairs, then ate a quick sandwich, glad her parents had already eaten. Then she left for the small mercantile where she'd been employed part-time for the last several weeks. When she arrived, Abigail, the oldest daughter of the Amish family that owned the store, came from behind the counter, gesturing toward the front shelves. "Those need straightening," she told her.

Nettie glanced toward a few customers shopping a couple of aisles away. Abigail's father had hired her with some sympathy in his eyes, but Abigail had only looked at her with suspicion from her first day. At one time she would have told off anyone speaking to her like that, but she deserved terse instructions with no cordial greeting. She just didn't relish anyone witnessing that. "I'll take care of them right after I put *mei* belongings in the back room."

The two of them had been friends when they were very young, but once they'd reached their preteens, their relationship changed. Nettie had become quite aware of her beauty. Abigail, on the other hand, was plain — some would say even by Amish standards. While Nettie was popular with the boys, Abigail wasn't, and at the time, Nettie wasn't about to hang around with someone she considered a loser. Yet today Abigail was happily married and working in her family's successful store. Nettie was alone with no romantic prospects, dependent on a part-time job.

Who's the loser now?

Then Abigail tilted her head, effectively stopping Nettie from going. She squirmed under Abigail's scrutiny. "Is something wrong?"

"I'm not sure. You've changed. I didn't believe it at first, but I'm seeing it more and more."

Glancing at the floor, Nettie mumbled, "I

hope I have." Then she looked at Abigail, her stomach twisting into a knot. Now was the time. "I'm sorry for how I treated you when we were in school."

Abigail put her hands on her hips. "What about everywhere else?"

Her former friend wouldn't make this easy for her, and she shouldn't. "That too. I was a terrible person, and I hope you can forgive me someday."

Abigail's expression immediately softened. "I forgive you, Nettie. I don't understand why you turned on me back then, just like I don't understand why you've decided to apologize to me now." She paused. "But I'm grateful you are, for *yer* sake."

The knot untwisted, and Nettie half-smiled. "I needed to change," she said. "And you deserve an apology. I should have given you one a long time ago. Actually, I shouldn't have treated you poorly at all."

The bell above the door rang as two *English* customers entered the store. Abigail nodded at Nettie, then left her to greet them. Nettie stored her purse and light jacket in the back room, then went to work straightening the shelves. In the past, she would have found such work boring, but now she took great care making sure the items were all evenly spaced and organized.

Again, she experienced joy in doing a task well, even such a simple one.

Nettie continued her work, mostly dusting, stocking and straightening shelves, and sweeping the floor and small front porch. When she'd finished for the day, she collected her belongings.

"Nettie, I'd like for you to join Jonah and me for supper one evening when he returns from visiting his sick *onkel,*" Abigail said, catching Nettie as she opened the front door to leave. "If you want to, that is."

Nettie smiled. She couldn't remember the last time she'd been invited to someone's home. She'd convinced herself she was far too busy with her own pursuits to spend time with friends. But the truth was she didn't have any friends left. She'd ruined her friendships one by one. Of course, everyone was polite on the surface at church or around the community, but she hadn't realized until that moment how starved she'd been for companionship — even though she now understood that she'd never been a true friend to anyone. "I would definitely like to," she said, joy welling inside.

"*Gut.* We'll set a time soon."

Nettie walked home, her feet light and her heart happy. It was nearly dusk by the time she entered her house, but the sun was setting later with each passing day.

As she removed her jacket in the mudroom, she heard her parents' voices coming into the kitchen from the living room. But then she heard how angry her mother sounded, and she stopped to focus on what she was saying.

"I don't understand, Samuel. How can you have suddenly lost *all* our savings?"

All their savings? Coupled with the income from her job, she'd assumed her father had at least enough money to get by until he was well and could determine what to do about his failing business. She'd assumed their finances were tight but not gone.

Her father's weak, weary tone contrasted with *Mamm*'s shrill accusation. "I used most of it to keep the lumberyard afloat. But today I had to tell *mei* manager to let the rest of our employees *geh* and pay them their final wages. That took the rest. This is all *mei* fault. I panicked when the business took a downward turn, and then I made some poor decisions, more than I let on. I didn't want you to worry."

"*Some* poor decisions?" *Mamm*'s footsteps sounded against the wood floor as she paced. She always paced when she was upset, but Nettie had never known her to be *this* upset.

"Sarah, can we please talk about this later?" *Daed*'s voice had turned scratchy, another indicator he still hadn't fully recovered from the illness he'd so recently suffered. It had been scary to see her father so sick, and she'd prayed for his complete healing. But it was coming at a slow rate. Stress over his business hadn't helped.

"We need to talk about it now." The pacing stopped. "What are we going to do? We need money."

"God will provide." He paused. "Remember the Bontrager *familye*? I've heard they're doing well now. God took care of them."

Nettie stepped closer to the kitchen. She shouldn't be eavesdropping, but she couldn't help herself.

"Not until they left Fredericktown. And I doubt God had anything to do with their turnaround. They're doing well only because Phoebe was lucky enough to marry into a rich *familye,*" *Mamm* said. "Which is unbelievable considering what she did."

"You don't believe in luck any more than I do. And you know better than to judge others."

Nettie swallowed hard. Had her father been blind to *Mamm*'s doing just that? To *her* doing just that?

Mamm's tone turned sharp. "Phoebe became pregnant by an *English* man and had a *boppli* out of wedlock. Why would God reward her *familye* with provision after that sin? I refuse to believe it."

Nettie's stomach turned sour as she heard the sound of a chair scraping against the wood floor, followed by her father's heavier footsteps. "Sarah, please don't talk like that. Phoebe asked for forgiveness, and she was forgiven. Thomas and his family suffered here for several years. You know that. Why begrudge them their blessings?"

"Because they don't deserve them. And we don't deserve to be destitute. Nettie hasn't been sleeping around, and she isn't pregnant. We didn't have a dozen children when we couldn't afford them. We've given generously to the community fund —"

"We should have given more," *Daed* interjected.

"We gave enough. You've worked hard, and we've followed all the rules. How can God take away our success like this?"

"He didn't. I told you. I made some bad decisions. And you're speaking nonsense. God is in control even in times like these. I have faith."

"Not enough, according to what Bishop Weaver teaches."

Daed sighed. "I'm not so sure he knows what he's talking about."

"Now who's talking nonsense?" *Mamm*'s voice rose. "He's God's chosen. Of course he knows what he's talking about."

"Shh. Nettie's due home any minute. We don't want her to hear us arguing."

"She's not a *kinn* anymore," *Mamm* shot back. "She won't fall to pieces if she does."

As Nettie listened to her mother march out of the kitchen, she swallowed the lump in her throat. Every word *Mamm* said about the Bontragers, and particularly about Phoebe, had stung. She had no idea her mother had held the family in such low regard. She remembered *Mamm* taking food to them when they lived here, and once she'd taken Nettie along. But they hadn't stayed for more than a minute, and she'd insisted Nettie wash her hands when they got home. She'd been confused by that. The Bontragers were poor, but they weren't dirty.

After a few minutes, she started shivering in the chilly mudroom. She composed herself, then stepped into the kitchen. Her father was sitting at the table with his head in his hands. *"Daed?"*

He looked up and smiled, but the gesture wasn't reflected in his exhausted eyes. He'd lost more than twenty pounds during his illness, even though right now he looked like he carried the weight of the world. "Hi, Nettie. I didn't hear you come in. How was work today?"

Knowing how hard it had to be to put on a brave front after arguing with *Mamm,* she managed a half smile. "I had a great day," she said, happy to see the spark of joy in her father's eyes. "Can I get you something? Some tea or water? I'll start supper in a minute."

"*Danki,* but what I really need is *yer* company. Come sit with me first."

Nettie sat down next to him, and even though she knew it wasn't, she asked him if everything was all right.

"Oh, as fine as it's going to be. But let's talk about you." He sat up straighter, resembling the strong man he was before his troubles hit. "You've taken to *yer* job well."

"It's not difficult work to do."

"Do you enjoy it?"

"Ya," she said, her smile returning. "I do."

"That surprises me." He tugged on his salt-and-pepper beard.

"Because I've never wanted to do anything harder than *Mamm* made me do around the *haus*?"

He frowned. "I didn't say that —"

"You didn't have to." She looked at the polished wood table. It was an expensive piece of furniture, and her mother oiled it every Saturday to keep up its mirror shine. "I know I've been lazy. And self-centered. And uncaring of others."

"Wait a minute." *Daed* leaned forward. "Where is this coming from?"

"You know I'm telling the truth."

His eyes filled with sadness. "I know I've spoiled you. *Yer mamm* has told me enough." He paused, and Nettie waited for him to continue. While they'd always been close, he rarely revealed his feelings. "I'm so grateful God blessed us with you, but since you had no siblings, I guess I poured all the love I had into you, without the discipline you needed. If you've been selfish and spoiled, it's *mei* fault."

"And mine." She wouldn't let her father take responsibility for her actions. "But I'm changing, *Daed.* God is changing me."

"I can see that. Like caring enough about Old Man Elmer to take him food." He blinked, then wiped at his eyes, thankfully saying nothing about Devon. She still wasn't ready to talk about him, especially after she'd just learned what her mother thought of his family. Maybe her parents still didn't know he was in town, especially since they'd been missing church services because of her father's illness. And her father's only visitor, his longtime friend Enos Lambright, wasn't a gossip.

"I believe God is changing me too," *Daed* continued. "It's not painless," he added with a bitter chuckle, "and I've been humbled. But it's necessary. I've been living *mei* life all wrong, too invested in wealth, and I don't want to do that anymore."

Mamm entered the kitchen, her mouth tight. She ignored *Daed* and turned to Nettie. "Help me with supper."

Nettie touched her father's hand, then stood. He rose as well, then left the room. While she and *Mamm* prepared chicken and noodles and green beans, rarely speaking, she hoped her father was resting. When she found him in his chair in the living room later, he returned to the kitchen to eat. The mood at the table was somber.

She considered his words about what they were each going through, and she had to agree with them. She and *Daed* were undergoing change that was far from painless yet necessary. She just prayed her mother would come to understand change was necessary for her too.

■ ■ ■ ■

Two days after Nettie had cleaned the living room, Elmer was still basically banning Devon from it unless he first showered and put on clean clothes. The old man had laid down other ground rules too. "No eating in here," he'd grunted from his favorite chair. "And no drinks. Also, after you take something from its place, put it away."

Devon couldn't hold back laughter. "You're joking, right? You've been eating, drinking, and leaving things lying around in here ever since you moved in."

"Well, that's changing now. I want to keep this room clean and neat." He settled back, a satisfied look on his grizzled face.

Devon could see Elmer's commitment was sincere. The man had showered two days in a row, which had to be a record. He'd also washed at least four loads of clothing, bedclothes, and towels, another surprise since the man had been wearing the same pants and shirt for two or three days, rarely using the washing machine.

Living with Elmer in his *English* house had presented a challenge for Devon when it came to the *Ordnung,* but he'd done his best. He hand-washed his clothes and hung them to dry on a line he'd rigged in the backyard. Wringing them out was a chore, especially his pants, but he refused to use the dryer. His clothes took longer to dry and were stiff in the cooler spring weather. Warmer temperatures were coming, but Devon wasn't sure if he'd be around long enough to see summer. Elmer was gaining strength every day, and after all, Nettie was watching out for him.

"Wonder when that girl is coming back."

Devon raised his brow. This was new. Elmer never mentioned Nettie. Was he looking forward to her next visit? *Easy to do.* He buried that thought and reminded himself she couldn't be trusted, even though she did seem to have changed — *some.* But the woman had made Elmer happy with the simple gesture of cleaning his favorite room. "I don't know when she's coming back."

"Don't you talk to her sometimes?"

He shook his head. "No."

Elmer turned to stare at him, his thick eyebrows knitted together. "Why not?"

"We're not friends."

"Don't you see her at church?"

"I have. I don't hang around for chitchat with anyone, though."

"I ain't much for small talk neither. Never have been." He picked up a crossword puzzle book from a rickety side table, then opened it to the middle and extracted the pencil stuck between the pages. He licked the point and started working. *Conversation ended.*

Devon stretched his legs out in front of him and looked at the threadbare rug in the middle of the floor. Nettie had to have noticed its condition if she was concerned about sweeping it. With the money she and her family had, she could afford to buy Elmer a new rug. Probably a new house. He was sure of that even though he'd overheard Wilma Yoder at the hardware store yesterday telling someone the Millers had financial troubles — something about Samuel's lumber business. He'd wondered why he hadn't seen Nettie's parents with her at church, but he also heard Wilma say Samuel had been ill, so he and Sarah were staying close to home.

Still, he was sure that family would never run out of money, not even with some setbacks.

He sighed. It was pointless to speculate. Wilma, who'd so far only given him some strange looks at church, was the woman who'd told his mother Elmer was sick. And although he'd managed to avoid her so far, it was only a matter of time before she either cornered him or asked his mother why he was here in another letter.

Of course, as far as he knew, his mother didn't know about Elmer. He'd left out the fact that the return address on his cryptic letters home belonged to him, saying only that he'd "found a room." But how long would it be before his deception was revealed, one way or another?

Maybe he should be thinking about leaving before everything hit the fan.

After a few minutes, he got up. "I'm going for a walk." When Elmer didn't even look up, Devon left. He slipped on a pair of tennis shoes and a jacket in the mudroom, then walked out the back door. It was strange not to have a barn to clean or horses and livestock to tend. He also missed his mother's delicious meals and his father's steady company, freely granted him even though he'd disappointed *Daed* by not taking up farming. He missed his brothers, even the younger ones who'd been a pain in his side when he was a teenager. Now that everyone was growing up, though, they all got along much better — or at least they tried to.

He shoved his hands into his jacket pockets and headed down the road, not realizing he was nearing the Millers' large property until he was a good distance from Elmer's house. He had to admit, like Elmer, he'd been wondering when Nettie would come back too. Maybe she'd clean Elmer's bedroom next time. *On second thought, we might need to call a hazardous materials team before attempting that job.*

We. He shouldn't be thinking in terms of a partnership with Nettie. They hadn't spoken more than a few words to each other, even though they seemed to have the same goal — taking care of Elmer. Devon knew why he was taking care of him. He still had no idea what motivated Nettie. But before long, Elmer wouldn't need his help anymore, and then he could go home.

He was about to turn around and head back to Elmer's when he saw a flash of light coming from the roof of a barn in the distance. The Millers' barn. He thought he might have imagined it until he saw another burst. Then he heard an explosion, and the air around the structure filled with smoke and fire.

He sprinted toward the blaze.

CHAPTER THREE

Nettie's parents had already retired for the night, and she sat in the kitchen, draining the last drop from a cup of tea. The whole family was exhausted, not only because of the tension in the house but from caring for the animals as well. She supposed most of their traditionally owned livestock would have to be sold now. Especially since she now understood they had more than they needed. How could they keep horses just because she liked to ride them occasionally or lots of pigs merely to have as much pork as they wanted? Hopefully they could keep their cow and chickens, but she couldn't be sure.

As she yawned and reached for the gas lamp, she heard a sharp popping noise coming from outside. She stood and looked through the window, spotting flames in the roof of the barn. Panicked, she ran to her parents' bedroom. "The barn's on fire!"

"Call the fire department!" *Mamm* scrambled out of bed, *Daed* moving more slowly but as fast as he could.

Nettie dashed to the phone shanty at the end of their driveway, then dialed the emergency number. The dispatcher assured her a fire truck would be there as soon as possible.

She ran back into the house to check on her parents, but neither one was there. Surely they weren't trying to put out the fire. She ran out the back door, into the darkening night save for the glow of the fire. Her mother was on the patio, holding *Daed* back. "There's *nix* you can do, Samuel!"

"The livestock —"

"I'll get them out."

Nettie whirled around to see Devon skid to a stop next to her, his chest rising and falling as if he'd run a great distance. Without thinking, she gripped his arm. "It's too late," she said as burned roof shingles fell into the barn. Sirens wailed in the distance.

But Devon jerked away from her and ran straight to the fire. Nettie chased after him, her skin growing hot from the heat.

"Nettie!" her mother screamed.

Nettie ignored her as she reached the entrance of the barn. Devon quickly brought out two horses, and before he handed them off to her, she ripped the kerchief from her hair so he could block his lungs against the smoke. She released the horses into a nearby field, one of them her favorite, Cherry Blossom. Even if the mares ran away, at least they'd be alive.

Devon brought out animal after animal, and Nettie helped him until the firefighters insisted they both vacate the area, leaving any livestock still there along with her family's two buggies inside. They both collapsed on the ground well away from the barn. Sweat poured down Nettie's back, and Devon was covered in soot.

"How did this happen?" Devon asked after jerking the kerchief off his face.

Nettie stared at the blaze in front of her, strands of hair loosened from her braid. A fire was a common risk, but she'd never thought her family would suffer one. Her father had always been so careful. Tears streamed down her cheeks, and her thoughts raced. At least the chickens were still safe in their coop.

Devon moved closer to her. "Talk to me. Are you okay?"

She turned to him and shook her head. "*Nee*. I'm not."

When Devon put his arm around her

shoulders, it seemed natural for her to lean against him. "I don't know how it happened," she said, fighting sobs. She took a shaky breath, then explained how she'd heard the popping sound and then seen the fire.

"I heard it too," he said in a low voice. "I was close by."

Nettie closed her eyes and wiped the tears from her cheeks with the back of her hand. When Devon held her a little tighter, peace broke through her fear.

"At least I got the animals out," he said.

She lifted her head and looked at him. "All of them?"

He nodded. "It will take some time to track them all down, though. I let some of them out the back of the barn, and I'm sure they ran off. But they'll be looking for food eventually, and they'll come back home."

"Danki," she said as she stared at the reflection of the flames in his blue eyes. His arm still around her, she reached up and touched his hand, then wrapped her fingers around his. "I don't know what we would have done if you hadn't come."

"Then it's a *gut* thing I took that walk." The corner of his mouth lifted with the hint of a smile. "It will be okay, Nettie," he said, squeezing her shoulder lightly. "Our bishop's *familye* back home lost their barn in a fire a couple of years ago. We all helped them rebuild."

She looked at the firefighters still fighting the blaze, which, thank God, hadn't spread to the nearby dry grass. "I don't understand," she whispered. "Why are all these bad things happening to us?"

Despite having worn Nettie's kerchief around his nose and mouth, Devon's throat burned, and his hand stung from grabbing the barn's hot back door handle to let the Millers' pigs out into the night. But nothing could make him move away from Nettie. In the background, the firefighters were still putting out the fire, some neighbors now watching, and he was vaguely aware that Nettie's parents were somewhere nearby, still huddled in the coats they'd thrown over nightclothes. But he didn't care about any of that. His focus was on this woman, and the question she'd voiced — a question he'd asked himself many times during those hard years his family experienced in this community.

Nettie shifted in the curve of his arm, and for a disappointing moment he thought she would move away from him. Truth was he'd been terrified when he saw the fire, and then he'd been running on pure adrenalin when he dashed into the barn. His parents — and probably his siblings and friends, too — would call him insane for doing that. But he couldn't stand by if there was a chance he could help. Now that he was calmer, he needed Nettie's closeness as much as he suspected she needed his.

"*Mei daed*'s business has failed." She glanced up at him, soot smeared across her forehead and cheeks. "He lost everything except our *haus* and . . ." She looked at the barn.

He believed her. Her face told the story. "I'm sorry." Despite knowing he shouldn't, he lightly rubbed her arm again, and he was glad she didn't protest.

"He also got very sick, and he still hasn't completely recovered. Now this." Tears welled in her eyes. "I'm not sure he'll be able to handle it."

"Not by himself." Devon touched her chin and turned her face so he could look directly at her. "The Lord will be his strength."

"But God seems so far away right now."

His heart ached at the sound of her weak voice and the look of pain in her eyes. "Sometimes, *ya,* he does. But that doesn't mean he's not there. The barn can be rebuilt. So can a business. I won't guess about *yer daed*'s health, but he's got the community standing behind him."

She blinked, and then her eyes grew cold. "Oh? Did the community stand behind *yer familye*?"

A muscle jerked in his jaw, and bitterness from the past surfaced. He spoke just as coldly as she had, nearly removing his arm from around her. "Not really. But *mei familye* wasn't the *chosen familye.*" He closed his eyes for a second. "Sorry," he muttered. "I shouldn't have said that."

But the pain in her eyes was back. "Is that what everyone thinks of us? That we're somehow more blessed by God than anyone else?"

He'd opened up this can of worms, and now he had to deal with them. "I can't speak for everyone. But I always thought everything seemed to *geh yer familye*'s way."

"Not anymore." She pulled away from him, then brought her knees close to her chest and hugged them. "I don't think we've been blessed as much as we've been selfishly accumulating everything we could, putting faith in our money and belongings more than in God. And now we're being punished for it." She looked at him. "And in *mei* case, for being an all-around terrible person."

"Nettie —"

"I can't thank you enough, Devon." Nettie's father was suddenly there, and in the residual light of the burning barn, he looked older than Elmer.

Devon scrambled to his feet. "I didn't do much."

"A firefighter told me you got all the livestock out." Tears formed in the man's eyes. "That means everything."

Now on her feet, Nettie stepped close to her father. "You're limping."

"I twisted *mei* ankle running out of the *haus.*" He shook his head. "When it rains, it pours."

"Let's get you back inside." Nettie put her arm around her father's waist. As they walked away, Devon heard her ask where her mother was.

"She went inside a while ago. She couldn't watch."

As the pair headed for the house, Devon wanted to go after them. He wanted to tell Nettie she was wrong about God punishing her family, although he was sure why she would think that. Bishop Weaver had tried to convince his father the bad things happening to him were God's punishment, and Nettie had no doubt heard him teach that same concept for years. Now wasn't the time to address how wrong the bishop was, but before he returned to Birch Creek, he'd set Nettie straight. She couldn't lose her faith now. Not when she needed it more than ever.

Chapter Four

"You ain't gonna stop me."

Devon blew out an exasperated breath as he gripped the back of a kitchen chair. He and Elmer were in a standoff. "Yes, I am. You have no business helping anyone build a barn."

"I ain't an invalid."

"I never said you were. But you're still regaining your strength. You don't want to have a setback, do you?"

The day after the Miller fire, Robert Hershberger, who apparently knew Devon was staying with Elmer, had stopped by to tell Devon about the barn raising scheduled for today, a Saturday. Elmer, who'd been in the living room, of course, had overheard what Robert said through an open window, and for three days he'd insisted he would help. Devon hadn't been able to convince him otherwise, and now he didn't have time. He'd be late to the Millers'.

"You're not a doctor, boy." The old man had an ancient tool belt slung around his waist. Growing up, Devon had never seen Elmer working with tools, only puttering around in his garden. Then again, he hadn't exactly paid much attention to Elmer when he was a kid — except the time he'd had no choice.

He shook his head at the memory and then again at Elmer for good measure. "You're not going. That's final."

Elmer turned, then headed for the back door. Devon heard the car keys jingle as the man snatched them off their hook. He groaned. Clearly, he'd have to physically restrain Elmer to keep him from trying to help the Millers — or more accurately, from trying to help Nettie.

When Devon returned from the Millers' covered in soot and stinking of smoke, Elmer was still up. He'd also looked more concerned than Devon had ever seen him, which was a surprise. Once he told him what happened, though, the old man had an outright conniption, and he'd been even more cranky and stubborn ever since. Devon had suspected Elmer had a soft spot for Nettie; he just hadn't been aware how big that spot was.

Suddenly resigned to the fact that Elmer

would never listen to reason, Devon grabbed his own tool belt and jacket after lifting Elmer's coat from the back of another kitchen chair. It was supposed to be cool all day, and he feared the old man would get cold.

He caught up with Elmer just as he was getting into the driver's side of car. Devon laid the items he'd been carrying on an old bench and opened the garage door. Apparently Elmer hadn't driven in so long he'd forgotten he had to open the garage door. *Potential disaster averted.*

"You forgot this," Devon said as he opened the passenger door and held out Elmer's coat.

"Throw it in the back." Elmer turned the ignition key, and the engine purred to life. "Hmm," he murmured. "I thought the battery might be dead."

Devon half-smiled. But he didn't get inside the car. He figured if Robert knew he was staying with Elmer, others in the community knew, too, and they might all be wondering if he was breaking the *Ordnung* as well. He didn't want to add fuel to any gossip by riding in a car when he could easily walk. "I'll meet you there," he said before shutting the door. Then he barely had time to jump back as Elmer threw the car into reverse.

As Devon made his way to the Miller place on foot, cutting across three fields to avoid seeing how bad Elmer's driving might be, he tried to settle his mind. He had no idea how the community would react to the grumpy old man showing up unexpectedly. Devon's age-mates were grown up now, but that didn't mean they wouldn't treat Elmer with suspicion. He prayed that wouldn't happen.

Then there was Nettie. She hadn't returned to Elmer's, and Devon hadn't expected her to. She had an ill father with a sprained ankle to help take care of, and knowing Nettie the way he did now, he was sure she wouldn't leave his side. But he was eager to see her. He wanted to finish their conversation about God, of course. But he had another, more personal reason too.

By the time he got there, the barn raising was well underway. Elmer's car was parked in the driveway behind quite a few buggies, their horses running loose in a back field. The sky was cloudy, but the air wasn't too cold. It was a perfect day for a barn raising.

As he strode toward the barn, steeled to reengage the community for the Millers' sake, he observed the bustle of activity. The men and older boys were nailing wood together to create a frame. By the amount of lumber he saw, he could tell the new barn wouldn't be as big as the original one. But maybe that wasn't a surprise after what Nettie told him. He looked toward the house where women were setting up tables in preparation for lunch. Children too young to help with the barn played nearby where their mothers could ensure none of them got underfoot. The last thing anyone needed was an injury, especially to a small child.

He looked around, glad Wilma Yoder didn't seem to be there. He still thought she was the one most likely to pepper him with questions, given the chance. He was also looking for Elmer, and he found him talking to Robert by an oak tree. Then he spotted Nettie's father, sitting with his foot propped up on a second folding chair near the building site. Enos Lambright, an old man who'd been a widower ever since Devon could remember, sat next to him. Nettie's mother was with the other women, showing them where to set up tables. However, Devon didn't see Nettie.

"Boy!"

Devon grimaced. Elmer had to be shouting at *him.* He joined him and Robert, the latter sporting a puzzled look on his face. Robert was closer to Phoebe's age, and he hadn't changed much over the years, so Devon recognized him at church right away. He'd just sidestepped any small talk, like he had with everyone.

"Tell this man I'm here to help." Elmer stuck his thumbs into the loops of his jeans.

"I was just explaining we have enough help," Robert said, looking at Devon rather pointedly. "But he's . . . insistent."

Noting Elmer had turned his attention to the barn, Devon stepped away from him and motioned for Robert to do the same. "Don't you have some little job you can give him?" he asked in a low voice. "He doesn't need to be on a ladder, obviously."

"Obviously," Robert scoffed.

"But there's got to be something he can do. He won't leave until he can help. Trust me, the man is as stubborn as the day is long."

Robert frowned, glancing at Elmer over his shoulder, then looked back at Devon. He pushed his straw hat off his forehead. "I gotta say, the thing with you living with Old Man Elmer confuses me — and *mei frau.* It's confusing everyone. Maybe you can explain what's going on sometime, at least to me."

Now Devon knew for sure there'd been some gossip — or at least speculation. He found himself nodding, though. "Maybe I will. But right now we need to deal with the man."

"All right. He can do some sanding."

Relieved, Devon nodded again. *"Danki."*

Robert left to give the assignment to Elmer, who was now staring at them, and Devon turned to head for the construction site. But then he saw Nettie standing near the lunch tables. Her arms were folded over her chest as though she was protecting herself. He joined her against his better judgment. No doubt more speculation would follow if they were seen together, but he had to know how she was.

"Hey," he said.

"Hi." She gave him a weary smile.

"I've been looking for you," he blurted. "I mean, I was wondering how you're doing. Since the fire. And how's *yer daed*?" He wasn't exactly making himself sound any less awkward than he felt.

"He's okay. Enos has been by every day to visit him." She dropped her arms and put her hands into the pockets of her coat. "*Daed* appreciates the company."

"And you? How are you?"

"I'm all right."

Observing the shadows under her eyes, he didn't believe her. But he went along with her. *"Gut."* He gestured toward the construction with his thumb. "I better get to work."

She nodded, and he turned to leave.

"Devon?"

He whirled around. *"Ya?"*

"Please be careful."

He nodded, unable to keep from smiling. "I will."

Nettie watched as Devon joined a group of men sawing boards. She knew she should be helping her mother, but she couldn't stand to be around her. Since the barn burned down, *Mamm* had been difficult to live with despite some good news the day after the fire. With the help of a few of her father's now former employees, they'd tracked down all the livestock, and several farmers volunteered to keep the animals in their barns until this one was built.

But later that day her father made several calls on his business cell phone, and when he announced he'd sold off both his remaining inventory — except for enough wood to build a new barn — and most of the livestock, *Mamm* had been furious. Instead of telling him why, though, she kept up a silent treatment, as far as Nettie knew, even in the privacy of their bedroom.

She sighed. Considering their financial straits, it made sense for her father to sell their animals, and they were fortunate he'd still had lumber for the new barn and a spare buggy at the lumberyard. Why her mother was reacting so strongly, she had no idea. *Mamm* wasn't talking to her either.

Nettie had never felt so helpless. She couldn't remember if her mother had ever acted like this before. Then again, she'd always been such a self-absorbed daughter. Would she have noticed if *Mamm* had?

The tension in the house was stifling, but Nettie was committed to caring for her father. Except for when she was at her job, since her earnings were needed more than ever, she was the one who ensured he elevated his foot, brought him ice for the swelling, and gave him medicine for the pain. At night she asked God to help her parents work things out between them. She didn't see how they could go on this way.

She shook her head, then moved to keep herself busy setting out the food the women there had brought. She didn't want to be caught staring at Devon. Despite the difficulties at home, she couldn't stop thinking about him. How he had run into the barn without a thought for his own safety. How he'd listened as she questioned God — although she thought he'd been about to give her his opinion concerning her doubts when her father joined them. She especially thought about how she'd felt when he put his arm around her. She'd been afraid and shell-shocked, but his steady presence had given her some peace.

"Did you see Old Man Elmer over there?" Abigail said as she set a bowl of ambrosia salad on the table. She jerked her head toward where a few boys were sanding boards.

Nettie looked, her brow lifting. "What's he doing here?" she said, stunned.

"Helping." Abigail moved to the other side of the table to stand by Nettie. "I overheard him talking to Robert, insisting he be allowed to do something. Looks like Robert gave in."

Nettie watched as Elmer gently took a sanding block from one of the youngest boys and showed him how to use it correctly. She couldn't believe it. The children weren't frightened of him. In fact, they seemed to be easily accepting him into their group — an old, crotchety *English* man everyone used to be afraid of.

"You didn't know he was coming?" Abigail asked.

She shook her head. "*Nee.*"

"Don't you take food to him sometimes?"

Nettie looked at her. "How did you know?"

"*Yer daed* mentioned it to Jonas at the shop one day." She smiled at Nettie. "Jonas said he seemed pleased with your thoughtfulness."

A gust of wind kicked up, lifting the corner of the white tablecloth. Nettie moved to tie it back down, grateful for the diversion. While her father would never say he was proud of her, especially to someone in the community, she was pleased to learn she'd made him happy. After securing the tablecloth, she turned around, only to see Abigail had followed her.

"Do you know why Devon came back? And why he's living with Old Man Elmer?" Abigail's brown eyes had filled with curiosity.

Nettie shook her head. "He's never said anything about it to me."

"But you see him when you *geh* to Elmer's, *ya*?"

"Sometimes." Her guard went up. Was Abigail asking out of genuine interest? Or was she after a bit of gossip to spread around? "But there's *nix* else I can tell you."

Abigail paused, still looking at her. Then

she shrugged. "It sure is strange. But I have to say, Devon's had a positive effect on the old man. Elmer looks better now than when we were *kinner.*" She turned to Nettie with a smile. "Clearly, he likes the food you take him. I always wondered why we never saw anyone visiting him. And I still wonder why we've never known what he did for a living before he moved here. Or why he decided to live here at all when he could be living around more *English.*"

"I have *nee* idea," Nettie said, hoping to stave off any other questions about Elmer — even though Nettie had many of the same ones over the years.

"Oh well. It doesn't matter. Everyone's entitled to their privacy. I better check on the roast beef I put in the oven. With the chilly weather, I thought the men might want warm sandwiches today." Abigail turned and headed toward the house.

Nettie pondered what Abigail said about privacy. She had her own secrets, especially the one about how she'd treated Zeb and Zeke. She wondered again if Devon knew about that episode. She doubted it, though. If he did, he wouldn't want to have anything to do with her.

Her face heated as she remembered how she'd felt leaning against him the night of the fire. How he'd gently touched her chin, making her breath catch. But his actions toward her that night couldn't have meant anything other than kindness. She'd been scared, confused, and in need of comfort. He, being the good man he was, had provided it.

But, oh, how she wished they'd meant something more. And that was a problem. She couldn't keep pining for Devon. There would never be anything between them. Even if there were a chance, he'd eventually find out about what she did to his brothers and reject her.

A strange sensation overcame her, as though a simmering, bubbling resentment had erupted inside, a resentment brewing ever since Devon revealed what the community really thought of her family. Weren't all these people here only because this was the Amish way, not because they really cared? Didn't they all believe, like she did, that her family was being punished?

She didn't blame Devon for telling her the truth, and she thought Abigail's offer of a renewed friendship might be sincere. But what was the point of changing when it didn't make any real difference? She'd been trying to live a better life, to be kind and generous as her faith dictated, and for a while she'd felt some peace. But that peace was shattering. Her parents were at odds, the family was broke, and even her favorite mare had been sold.

To top everything off, she'd fallen for a man she could never have. Her hands balled into fists, and she let the resentment flood her soul. But she was angry with herself too. *Of course* God was punishing her. She, more than anyone, deserved it.

Chapter Five

The barn was finished just before suppertime, and Devon was making one last inspection up on a ladder.

As soon as the frame was built, he'd worked on the roof, giving pointers to the men who were inexperienced with the job. Later, Mervin Mullet, a farrier close to his father's age, told him, "You've grown into a fine *mann,* Devon. *Danki* for *yer* help."

Devon had shaken Mervin's hand, gratified by the compliment. Especially after being so standoffish since his return, he hadn't expected to hear anything like it from this normally stoic group. Then again, both the men working and the women who provided lunch had seemed more relaxed today, perhaps because of the sense of togetherness that usually occurred when neighbors and friends helped each other. Or, as Devon expected, it might be because Bishop Weaver wasn't there. Regardless of the reason, for the first time since he returned to Fredericktown, he didn't feel like an awkward outsider. Although he did wish Nettie had talked with him. But she'd kept her distance as the women served the noon meal.

He shimmied down the ladder and joined several men now gazing up at the new barn. It would need to be painted on a warmer day, but Samuel Miller had provided treated wood, which would withstand the elements until the weather cooperated.

Elmer appeared next to him. "Nice job."

Devon looked down at the old man. "Thanks. You too."

"Never seen anyone put up a barn faster than you Amish." He swiped beneath his nose with one thick, dusty finger.

"Many hands make light work." He grinned. "Thanks for lending us your hands, Elmer."

If Devon didn't know any better, he would have thought the old man blushed. "Didn't have nothing else to do today," he muttered, then turned and strolled toward his car.

Chuckling, Devon turned to look at the barn again and saw Nettie and her father standing near it. Everyone else was clearing out, and as he heard Elmer's car engine roar to life, he joined the pair. "Will it do, Samuel?"

"Ya," he said, emotion thick in his voice. "It will more than do." He put his hand on Devon's shoulder. *"Danki."* Then he dropped his hand, leaned on his cane, and said to Nettie, "I better *geh* inside to see if *yer mamm* needs any help."

Nettie's lips pressed together until they turned white. She only nodded, then faced the barn again.

"You're welcome to join us for supper, Devon," Samuel said, then limped away before he could respond.

He glanced at Nettie to see what her reaction to her father's invitation might be. She was still staring at the barn, but her jaw set as another strong breeze lifted the white strings of her *kapp.* Clearly upset for some reason, she was still beautiful.

"Don't you like the barn?" he asked, then cringed inwardly. He sounded like a puppy eager for his master's approval.

She didn't say anything for a moment, then said, "It's adequate."

Adequate? He saw her lift her chin in the haughty way he immediately recognized from their childhood. He just hadn't seen it since returning to Fredericktown. "What?"

"It's . . . all right." She rolled her eyes. "But the roof is ugly, and the barn is far too small."

"Both are what *yer vatter* wanted," Devon said, stunned by her change in attitude since he last saw her. And how dare she insult the roof? He looked up at the plain shingles covering the trusses. He'd inspected each one before coming down the ladder.

"He's being shortsighted." Her eyes narrowed. "We'll be back on our feet soon. Like you said, everything *mei familye* touches turns to gold, right?"

"I never said that." Devon grimaced. "What's gotten into you?"

She whirled around and faced him. "Don't bother staying for supper. *Mei vatter* was just being polite." Then she turned and strode toward the house.

Devon started after her. Something was wrong for her to act like this . . . like she used to be. "Nettie," he called. When she didn't slow or answer, he hurried his steps and caught up to her. Without thinking, he grabbed her elbow.

"Leave me alone!"

His heart ached at her tone. Was she angry? Or was she in pain? With one quick movement, he leapt in front of her, blocking her path.

Despite tears blurring her vision, Nettie tried to move past Devon. But he blocked her way again. Hadn't she been sufficiently cruel for him to get the message? She'd even disparaged his roof, which, of course, was perfect. But something cracked inside her when her father invited Devon to supper. She was still angry with God for punishing her and her family, but how could she hold in her feelings for Devon if he joined them for supper, especially as her parents' ongoing silence suffocated the room? She couldn't. She wasn't strong enough. So she did what she did best. She tried to drive him away. For some reason, though, that hadn't worked.

"Nettie."

Tears slipped down her cheeks as she stilled. "What?" she snapped.

"Don't be like this."

"Like what?" She crossed her arms over her chest. "Like *me*? The real me?"

"This isn't you." He took a step toward her. "I know the real you."

"You don't know anything." She averted her gaze, unable to look at him. The remainder of her resolve was crumbling, which just infuriated her more. "*Geh* away, Devon. Just . . . *geh* . . ."

He took her hand. "I'm not leaving you. Not like this."

Her shoulders slumped. "I . . . can't . . ."

"Can't what?" he asked gently.

"I can't do this." Nothing was left for her to do but tell him the truth, even though he might laugh in her face. "I can't be around you. Not when I . . . care for you so much."

His jaw slacked. "You what?"

Of course he'd be stunned. She would have laughed at his expression if she hadn't gone numb inside. "I have to check on *mei vatter.*" She jerked her hand away, then took advantage of Devon's shock to push right past him.

"Nettie . . ."

She ran inside the house as fast as she could and slammed the door. The mudroom was chilly, but not as cold as her heart. She fought to catch her breath, then heard a knock. She ignored it and took off her coat.

The door opened, and a swoosh of cold air came into the room. She swung around to see Devon stepping inside. "What are you doing?" she said in a loud whisper, unwilling for her parents to hear her. They had enough problems.

Devon smiled at her coolly. "I'm here for supper."

"I told you not to come."

"*You* weren't the one who invited me." He slipped off his jacket and hung it on one of the empty hooks by the door, his movements sure and confident — the opposite of what she felt inside. "Where can I wash up?"

"Are you serious?"

"Of course I am."

Had revealing her heart meant nothing to him? From his blank expression, it seemed it hadn't. But if that was the case, why was he doing this? She couldn't decide which she was more — angry, confused, or hurt. Definitely a large dose of all three.

He opened the door to the kitchen, then looked at her over his shoulder. "I don't know about you, but I'm starving." Then he disappeared inside.

It was an evening of firsts for Devon Bontrager. He'd never barged into someone's house before. He'd never seen Nettie Miller so flustered, which would have amused him any other time. And most importantly, he'd never had a woman confess her feelings about him like that, which had made him both confused and elated.

But he didn't have time to dwell on any of that. He had to get control of himself as he walked into the Millers' kitchen. He had no idea how the evening would go, and Nettie was probably furious with him, but he refused to leave until they talked this out. If they didn't do it tonight, she might shut him out permanently, and he couldn't let that happen.

"Devon," Samuel said, smiling. He was sitting at the end of the table already filled with leftovers from the scrumptious lunch served earlier. "I'm glad you decided to join us."

Devon nodded as he heard Nettie come into the kitchen behind him. "*Danki* for having me."

"You can wash up at the sink."

He glanced at Nettie's mother, who didn't even look at him. But her sour expression told him she wasn't so eager to have Devon as a guest. "Set another place, Nettie," her father said when Sarah didn't rise or even say a word.

As Devon washed up, Nettie remained silent. From the corner of his eye, he saw her open a cupboard door and take out a plate and glass, then some silverware from a drawer. Then she set all the items in front of him as he sat down in the chair opposite the place obviously hers. Her mother poured him some iced tea from a pitcher on the table, still without saying a word.

Nettie sat down but refused to look at him. Not that he blamed her. He had barged in, with little explanation.

Her father led them in a silent prayer of

thanks for the meal, then told Devon to dig in. Oddly enough, Devon was hungry even though tension covered the room like a thick woolen cloak. He helped himself to servings of red-skinned potato salad, cold roast beef, buttered bread, and red cabbage slaw, a dish his mother also made. "I haven't had this kind of slaw in a long time," he said.

"Nettie made it." Her father beamed. "It's one of her specialties."

Devon looked at Nettie, who kept her head down. Regret suddenly ran through him. She was clearly miserable, and he was making her feel worse. He shouldn't be here, and now he wished he'd taken a minute to think before he'd so hastily acted. Nettie's mother was still silent, also keeping her head down as she took a tiny bite of buttered bread.

After a few minutes of complete silence, Nettie's father slammed down his fork. "Enough!"

Devon flinched as both women's heads jerked up.

"Sarah, I will not allow this to *geh* on. I know you're angry . . ." His bluster faded as his tone tempered. "And you have a right to be. But you will not behave like a *kinn* in this *haus*."

Sarah's face turned ashen. "And I can't believe you would talk to me like this in front of company."

"I'm glad someone is here, because now I have *yer* attention." He turned to Devon, his expression apologetic. "I'm sorry you have to witness this, but I can't take it anymore."

"Daed," Nettie said with a frightened tone. "Don't be upset."

"Too late for that." He tossed his cloth napkin on the table. "Sarah, I will have a word with you. Now." He got up from the table and grabbed his cane, then limped out of the room.

Sarah's granite expression didn't change as she dabbed the corner of her mouth with her own napkin. "If you'll excuse me . . ." She rose without looking at him or Nettie. Then with deliberate steps, she followed her husband.

Devon didn't say anything. Neither did Nettie. The ticking sound of the white-and-black wall clock echoed in his ears.

Finally, she lifted her head, her eyes filled with sorrow. "I'm sorry you had to see that."

"I've seen worse," he replied, trying to lighten the mood, which felt like pushing a boulder up a hill. "The fights *mei bruders* and I have had . . ." He shook his head and let out a low whistle. "You don't want to know."

Nettie twisted her napkin into a knot. "*Mei* parents never used to fight. Now it seems like that is all they do."

He got up from the table, then pulled her father's chair closer to hers before sitting on it. "It's all right, Nettie."

"*Nee,* it's not. *Nix* is. Can't you see that?" Her sad but dry eyes met his. "Everything is falling apart."

"Not everything." He reached for her hand, but she pulled away.

She shot up from the chair, then leaned against the kitchen sink, her back to him. "You can *geh* now, Devon. The show's over."

Chapter Six

Nettie hadn't thought her life could get any worse, but she should have known better. She was just as disturbed by her father's outburst as her mother was. She was also embarrassed that Devon had been exposed to what was happening in her home — possibly more than she was when she admitted her feelings for him. Wasn't it bad enough that he knew how she felt? Why did he have to see her family in shambles too?

She closed her eyes when she heard his footsteps behind her. Why wouldn't he listen? She started to turn around. "Devon, I said *geh* —" Now fully facing him, she realized how close he was to her.

"I know you did," he said. "And I will. But I have something to say first. I don't like to leave anything unsettled."

"What is there to settle?" She tried crossing her arms, to protect herself from what was coming next. But he was too close, and to her dismay she realized she could stand on tiptoes and kiss him if she wanted to. But how could she think about kissing him at a time like this? *Then again, how could I not?*

"We need to clear up a few things. Like what you said the other night after the fire."

Confused, she asked, "What did I say?"

"You said God is punishing you. I'm here to tell you he's not. Life is hard, Nettie. Sometimes it's easy, but most of the time it's not. If we're not fighting outside forces — like fires, for example — we're fighting a battle in our hearts. There's only one reason we can win that battle. Because God is on our side — always. How can a God on our side be punishing us?"

She frowned. This wasn't what she expected, but she yearned to hear more. "Bishop Weaver says we shouldn't experience severe struggles if we don't sin and we have enough faith."

Devon smirked. "He said that about our *familye* as well. He was sure our farm kept failing because *mei daed* lacked faith, and he had no compassion for *mei schwester.* But bad things happen to *gut* people too. *Gut* and faithful people." He met her gaze. "I can't explain why, and I don't think I need to know. I just know God wants me to trust him no matter what trial I'm going through, and that's what I choose to do."

His words sank into her soul. He was right. Ultimately, she had to trust God, during both good times and bad. She'd had a lot of good times in her life, more than she deserved, considering how spoiled she'd behaved for so long. But despite the resentment she'd let take hold earlier, she didn't want to be that bratty young woman anymore. The same feeling had come over her after rereading Zeb and Zeke's letter too. She wanted to be the kind of woman a faithful, strong man like Devon would be attracted to. And above all, she wanted to be a better person for God.

She looked up at Devon with admiration. "I never knew you were such a theologian," she said.

"I'm not." He held up his hands in a gesture of denial. "I'm *definitely* not. I'm simply speaking from experience. I'd like to think I've learned a few things."

"You have." She paused, not knowing what to say next. Devon hadn't moved an inch away from her. She didn't know what else they had to say to each other, yet she couldn't pull her gaze from his. His words had comforted her soul, but they'd stirred her heart too. She would never find a man as wonderful as Devon Bontrager, and she wanted to be with him more than anything. But she wasn't good enough for Devon, a man who had been so kind to her and her family. She had to accept that fact with humility. He also hadn't brought up what she'd said about caring for him, sparing her further embarrassment.

"I should check on *Mamm* and *Daed.*" She scooted past him, away from the kitchen sink.

"Nettie —"

She turned, steadying her resolve. "*Danki,* Devon. I feel better. I'm sorry you didn't get enough to eat, but do you mind seeing *yerself* out?"

"But —"

She should stay to hear what else he had to say, but if she did, she might reveal more of her feelings for him, and she couldn't do that. She'd also have to tell him about what she'd done to his brothers, and then he'd reject her as even a friend. She wasn't ready for him to know.

She turned around and left the room. She'd tend to the kitchen and her heart later.

Devon woke the next morning with a sleep-deprived brain. He'd shimmied up and down ladders at the barn raising more than he was used to, and the muscles in his legs were still aching in protest. Good thing this was an off Sunday with no church service.

He rubbed the back of his neck as he sat up in bed, glad he and Nettie had discussed her misinformed ideas about God. He prayed he'd steered her in the right direction, but he was surprised she'd called him a theologian. Nothing could be further from the truth. Yet he'd felt compelled to share what he knew in his heart — God was for them, not against them. For some reason, Bishop Weaver didn't believe that.

But what had kept him awake was the look in Nettie's eyes right before she slipped away from him to check on her parents. He wasn't surprised she was concerned about them. He'd come to see that side of Nettie, a side he was attracted to. And now that he knew how she felt about him, his feelings for her were nearly bursting inside him. If only she'd given him the chance to tell her how he felt. But despite revealing what she felt about him earlier, she'd rushed him out the door.

How could she turn her feelings on and off like that?

He was still thinking about that as he walked toward the kitchen twenty minutes later. But a new thought stopped him just outside the room. *Wait. Look who I'm dealing with — Nettie Miller. A master at manipulation, skilled at getting people to do what she wants.* She'd pulled that trick on his brothers with those letters. Was she playing with his feelings, too, only to crush them when he responded?

No sooner had he entered the kitchen than Elmer was at him. "You're late."

The old man had showered, dressed in a clean shirt, and, unbelievably, combed his hair. "Sorry," Devon mumbled. "Had trouble sleeping last night."

"Humph. Well, I guess I'll make coffee. Looks like you need it." After rising from the table, Elmer scooped some coffee grounds into a filter in his coffee maker before flipping it on and adding water. Devon just sat there, wondering if Elmer planned to make breakfast next. That would be a first.

But then the old man sat down again, directly across from Devon. "You can go home now."

Devon sat up straight. "What?"

"Your debt is paid."

Scoffing, Devon shook his head. "I don't know what you're talking about."

"Don't play dumb with me, boy. I know

why you've been helping me all this time. I might not remember half of what I did yesterday, but I do remember a skinny, pale, Amish kid sneaking into my garden to steal my vegetables."

"Oh," Devon mumbled, hanging his head. "That."

"Yeah. That." He shrugged. "You weren't the only kid who ever tried to steal from me. Just the only Amish one. I also remember what I used to say to people who stole from me."

Frowning, Devon lifted his head. "What?"

"That I'd call the police, and I'd make sure they'd go to jail for ten years." He scratched his stubbly chin. Apparently, shaving was a bridge too far for Elmer this morning. "Ten years seems like a lifetime to a child. Scared them off too."

"But you didn't say that to me."

He shook his head, averting his gaze. "People think I hole up in here and don't pay attention to what's going on in the world. And for the most part, that's true. It's why I moved here among you Amish. You live separate from all the garbage out there. That's what I needed to do too." He turned to Devon. "But that doesn't mean I didn't notice a family of scrawny, underfed Amish boys walking to school with only apples in their pockets for lunch. Or that haughty Amish girl, full of good health and a bad attitude, whose rich parents' farm stood between your place and mine. I've got eyes and ears, boy."

Devon's face heated. "You were spying on us?"

"Observing. You and your siblings had to walk past here to get to school and back home. That's why I always kept an eye on my garden when I knew you'd be out on the road. Those other kids wanted to steal from me for fun. It was all a game to them. But when I saw you . . ."

Devon couldn't look at Elmer. Shame filled him, even after all these years, even knowing how hungry and desperate he'd been that day. "I knew it was wrong," he said, remembering how he'd grabbed whatever he could from the lush garden — a head of cabbage, some carrots, a few green onions. He'd been about to pick some lettuce when Elmer caught him. The old, scary man had looked him over with those piercing eyes, but then he just turned and went back into his house. Devon had run away with what he'd managed to take, then told his parents he earned the produce in exchange for doing some work. Thankfully, they hadn't questioned him about where or for whom. But not only had he stolen — he'd lied. "I'm ashamed of what I did," he whispered, forcing himself to look up.

"I know, boy. I know. And that's why you're here. You're trying to get rid of that guilt." Elmer shook his head.

"I wanted to make up for what I did."

"But that's just it. You don't have to. I may be a grouchy old hermit, but I've got a heart. At least I think I do. What kind of person would I be to take food from a starving child? What kind of man would I be to demand payment for it?"

A lump formed in Devon's throat, and he couldn't bring himself to speak. The coffee had stopped dripping, and he started to rise, intending to pour some of the brew for them both. But Elmer held up his hand. "I'm getting our coffee this morning."

Devon sat back in his chair, then shifted his weight, not used to Elmer doing anything for anyone but himself — apart from letting a young, hungry boy steal food from his garden that day. A minute later, Elmer placed two mugs on the table, a little of the coffee inside sloshing down the sides.

"I've been doing a lot of thinking." Elmer slowly lowered himself onto his chair. "Like I said, you've got no reason to try to make restitution for cabbage and carrots. But I've been glad to have you here."

"You have? I thought you didn't like me intruding on your life."

"I didn't, at first. I was also too sick to stop you." He took a long swig. "But it's been nice having someone around for a while. And I hate to admit it, but I was letting the place go to pot."

"That's for sure."

Elmer's wayward eyebrows knitted together. "You don't have to agree with me, boy. Still, I feel bad I let you spend money on my place I can never pay back. I shouldn't have let you do that."

"I don't regret it, Elmer. I . . ." Devon quickly took a sip of his coffee. He wasn't ready to admit he'd grown a little fond of the man. He hoped Elmer would let the money issue go.

"All that said, I'm a man set in my ways, and it's time for you to go home now. Nettie will watch after me."

Devon's heart skipped a beat at the sound of her name. "What if she doesn't? What if she's still that stuck-up girl with a bad attitude deep down, and she's just . . . You don't know her like I do —"

"I should hope not," Elmer said, chuckling as he lifted his mug again. "She's a handsome woman and all that, but I'm way past my prime."

"I didn't mean that way."

"Didn't you?" Elmer grinned at him before taking another drink. "You've taken a shine to each other. Remember, I've got eyes and ears, and I'm gonna use them until they completely wear out. I saw the two of you talking at the barn raising."

Devon sat back in his chair. He should be surprised to learn Elmer figured out he and Nettie had feelings for each other, but he wasn't. "It doesn't matter anyway."

"Because you're going home."

"Right." Elmer was giving him an out, and Devon should take it and run. He wouldn't feel guilty, either. The old man was healthier than Devon had ever seen him, and he knew Nettie would keep an eye out for him. She might not have changed as much as he'd hoped just because she cared about her parents and Elmer, but she wouldn't abandon the old man. He was sure of that.

"Are you going to tell her?" For an old guy who made it his mission to stay out of everyone's business so they'd stay out of his, Elmer was being annoyingly nosy.

"That I'm leaving?" Devon shook his head and fumbled with the handle of his mug. "She'll find out on her own."

"So you're going to up and leave without

telling her how you feel?" Elmer barked. "I pegged you for a better man than that, boy."

"It's better for both of us if I don't."

"Why?"

Devon paused. He should have expected the question since Elmer was acting like a dog with a meaty bone. But it threw him off guard. He allowed his mind to wander to a new place. What if Nettie *was* the woman he wanted her to be? What if they had a future together? But Devon wasn't willing to live in Fredericktown, and Nettie would never leave her parents, especially with their current struggles.

That fact and his lingering uncertainties about Nettie left a knot of bitterness in his stomach. Ignoring Elmer's questioning his decision to not tell Nettie he was leaving, Devon shot up from the table. "I'll go pack my things and take the first bus tomorrow." Elmer remained silent as Devon left the kitchen.

In the spare bedroom, not much bigger than a closet, he sat on the edge of the twin-size mattress and frame he'd slept on for weeks. He was eager to get back to his family, and nothing was keeping him in Fredericktown now.

Devon shook his head, then retrieved his duffel bag from under the bed.

Chapter Seven

Nettie poked her sunny-side-up egg with her fork, unable to eat a single bite. Her parents were still at odds, and they both sat silent at the table. She'd tried to stay positive all day yesterday, but she didn't have the strength to do it this morning. It didn't help that she couldn't stop thinking about Devon.

Mamm stood, then scraped her plate before putting it in the sink and walking out of the kitchen. Nettie gripped her fork. Why was her mother still so angry? *Daed* said she had the right to be, but like this?

"You haven't eaten a bite, Nettie."

"I'm not really hungry. How's *yer* ankle?"

He smiled. "Better. The swelling is down, and I'm sure I'll be back to normal in a few days. I'm feeling a little more energetic too."

"That's *gut.*" Now she picked at the biscuit on her plate.

"Are you going to Elmer's today? We still

have some baked goods from the barn raising he might enjoy."

She didn't answer right away. She should go, giving her the chance to thank the old man for helping with the barn. But Devon would be there, and she couldn't trust herself with him. She didn't know how she could avoid him from now on, but she'd figure that out. "Tomorrow," she said, not looking at her father.

"Be sure to thank him for me." *Daed* shook his head. "I never imagined that old man would help out anyone, much less me. Then again, God is always surprising me." After a few moments of silence, he said, "What about Devon? That *yung mann* staying with Elmer."

So he knew Devon was back. "What about him?" Nettie blurted, then averted her gaze again.

"Something is up between you two. I saw it the night of the fire, and then I saw you talking at the barn raising."

Now she looked at him. "Is that why you invited him to supper last night?" When he raised his eyebrows, she shook her head. "I was just scared, and he was reassuring me. That's all."

"It looked like more to me."

"I'm uncomfortable talking about this,

Daed."

"Oh. I'm sorry. Of course." He nodded, then added, "I just want you to know *yer mutter* and I will work things out between us. We're going through a tough time right now, but God is with us."

His positive attitude reminded her of Devon's. "Do you really believe that?"

"I do." He smiled. "And I want you to promise me something, *lieb.*"

"What's that?"

"That you won't let what's happening to our *familye* get in the way of making decisions for *yer* own life."

She frowned. "I don't understand."

"Don't worry about us." He patted her hand, then grabbed his cane. "And don't close *yerself* off from happiness."

Nettie was still frowning after he left. How could she not worry about her parents? Then again, hadn't she decided to trust God with everything? With her parents and their troubles as well as with her feelings for Devon? Eventually, those feelings would go away, especially if she avoided him as much as possible. Never mind the thought of not seeing or talking to him brought a sharp ache to her heart.

She cleared the table and cleaned the kitchen, glad for the distraction. But then she decided to visit Elmer after all. She had started to like the old man, and she'd just have to get used to avoiding Devon. She took out a few containers of baked goods, despite knowing her mother wouldn't approve. *But God does.* She loved her mother, but in this case, and in a few others, her mother was wrong.

She was just about to retrieve the picnic basket when she heard a knock on the back door. When she opened it, she took a step back and steeled her heart. "Devon."

"Do you have a minute?"

His expression was impassive, much like it used to be before the fire happened. Against her better judgment, she let him in. *Keep it together.* She had to, because at that moment, all she wanted was for him to take her hand in his. She needed his comfort more than ever, but she couldn't have it. He'd been nice to her, but that was all.

"Do you want some *kaffee*?" she asked as he followed her into the kitchen. At least she could show some hospitality.

"Nee."

She turned to see him standing barely a foot or two into the room. Now he looked concerned, and panic hit her. "Is something wrong with Elmer?"

"*Nee,* he's fine. More than fine, actually.

But I need to tell you something."

"Oh?"

She noticed his Adam's apple was bobbing. "I'm leaving, Nettie. I'm going back to Birch Creek, back to *mei* home."

Devon hadn't wanted to come here. He'd fully intended to go forward with his plan, returning home without telling Nettie he was leaving. But his stupid conscience wouldn't leave him alone. He thought he saw a flicker of surprise in her pretty eyes, but it was gone in a flash, replaced by the coldness he'd seen before. How could he ever trust this woman?

"I'm sure *yer familye* will be glad to see you," she said, her chin lifting.

"Ya." He was itching to escape, but his feet wouldn't let him. That didn't make any sense. He'd told her what he wanted to say, and she obviously didn't want him here. All he had to do was turn around and go.

"What about Elmer?" she asked, suddenly showing the slightest sign of emotion in her hardened eyes.

"He'll be fine." Devon let out a bitter chuckle. "He even told me to leave."

"He did?" Nettie's demeanor quickly changed. "Why?"

"He says he'll be *gut* on his own."

"And you believe him?"

Devon nodded. "I do. Besides," he added, his own emotion almost choking off his words, "he has you."

Her eyes met his gaze, now in defiance. "What if I decide not to look out for him anymore? I have *mei* own problems, you know. What makes you think you can trust me?"

Was she trying to make him angry? But why? Then again, why should he care at this point? Her motives didn't matter since he'd never see her again. But she needed to hear the answer to her question. "I don't think I can trust you," he said. When he saw her flinch, hurt entering her eyes, he took a step forward. Now he saw through her façade. "I *know* I can trust you. Elmer is in *gut* hands."

The issue was settled. He could leave. But again, his feet betrayed him, along with his mouth. "I just don't understand why you're acting this way."

"I don't owe you any explanations." She lifted her chin again, but it was trembling now, and that was all he needed to convince him she was just pretending she didn't care, trying to make him forget she'd told him she did.

He took another step toward her. "What's

going on, Nettie? Why are you acting like this?"

"Because . . . because . . ." She turned her back to him. "I don't know."

Devon couldn't stop himself from placing his hands on her shoulders. For a moment, he thought she would lean back against him, but then her shoulders stiffened, and she pulled away.

"Don't," she said, still not facing him. "I don't know why you thought you had to come back and take care of Elmer. I don't even know how you knew he was sick. But you've done *yer* duty, and now you're free to leave."

The words came out of his mouth before he could stop them. "What if I don't want to leave?"

Nettie fought not to let Devon see how much she wanted him to stay, but that was becoming impossible. First, because he said he trusted her, then second, because of his gentle touch. But now he was confusing her, suggesting he didn't want to leave immediately after telling her he was. What was she supposed to do now other than turn around and face him? But if she did, her resolve to push him away would crumble.

Then the answer came to her. She had one

sure way to make him go. Slowly, she turned around. "You need to know something."

His brow furrowed. "What?"

"You're not the first Bontrager I've feigned an interest in." She swallowed, trying to distance her shame from her words. "There was Zeb and then Zeke. I wrote letters to them —"

"I know," he said quietly.

She swallowed hard. "You do?"

"You wrote to both of them, first one and then the other, telling them you liked them, waiting to see which one bit the bait you dangled in front of them. That bait was you. Although none of us know why, you tried to play *mei bruders* for fools."

"*Ya.* I did. It was all a game to me. Something to do because I was bored. So you see, I *am* a terrible person." She waved her hand, tapping into her previous callousness, which now made her nauseous. "The single men here are too poor or too dull —"

"Stop." He moved closer. "Nettie, whatever you did in the past doesn't matter. And I got a letter from Zeb and Zeke, telling me you wrote them again, apologizing."

Now she was tearing up at Devon's kindness. But crying was the last thing she needed. When she tried to turn away again, he took her arm, but she squared her shoulders. "Asking for forgiveness is the Amish way, so of course I apologized. But I didn't . . . I didn't . . ." She couldn't bring herself to say the words.

"You didn't mean it?" He scowled. "Because if that's what you're trying to say, I don't believe you. Look, I suspected you might be pretending to be interested in me, using Elmer to have a go at another Bontrager brother. But you're not the same *maedel* you were, Nettie. I've seen that for myself. And I'd be lying if I didn't admit I'm attracted to the woman you've become." His gaze intensified. "Very attracted."

Her heart warmed the coldness she'd tried to maintain. "You are?" she whispered.

"I am," he whispered back, touching her cheek. "I care about you, Nettie. And I want to help you and *yer familye.*"

"Because you feel sorry for us."

"Haven't you been listening? I don't feel sorry for you. Despite this rough patch, *yer familye* is strong, and *yer* faith will see you through. Most important, God is with you, just as he's always been with me and *mei familye* during our troubles." He leaned forward and touched his forehead to hers. "You said you care for me, and now I'm telling you I care for you as well. What do I have to do to convince you? Kiss you?"

Her breath caught as she tried to process his words. "You want to kiss me?"

"*Ya.* And not only do I want to kiss you now, but I've been wanting to kiss you for a long time." He moved a few inches away and cupped her face with his hands. "Is that okay?"

She nodded, unable and unwilling to think anymore. His kiss was gentle and told her everything she needed to know. His words were true, his feelings genuine. That knowledge not only further warmed her heart but melted away the last trace of the old Nettie. If a wonderful man like Devon could care about her, she was worth caring about.

When he pulled away, he still held her face in his large, work-callused hands. "Wow," he said, breathless. "That was better than I imagined."

Her heart swelled, but had he just kissed her good-bye? "Are you still leaving?"

He laughed and let her go. "After that kiss? Absolutely not. And I can't help you if I'm not here." His expression turned serious. "You do want me to stay, *ya*?"

Nettie wrapped her arms around his neck and looked up at him, finally feeling free. God had redeemed her, and Devon and her father had seen it. Abigail too. Yes, she'd let old fears and resentment come into her heart again when her troubles seemed overwhelming. But now she could see her future was filled with love. "*Ya,* Devon. I want you to stay."

To Nettie's delight, Devon stayed for the rest of the morning. They took a leisurely walk around the property, and among other things, he told her what Elmer had done for him when Devon was a child, along with the reason he'd come back to Fredericktown and moved in with the old man. They also talked more about God and his provision, leading Nettie to a new level of peace.

After Devon left, taking the basket she'd filled with food with him, she went back into the house to make lunch. She was surprised to see her mother sitting at the kitchen table, her head down. She hadn't been there ten minutes ago. When *Mamm* looked up, Nettie could see she'd been crying.

She rushed over and put her hand on her mother's shoulder. "*Mamm?* Are you okay?"

Mamm pressed her lips together and started to nod, then stopped. *"Nee,"* she whispered, emotion heavy in her voice. "I'm not."

Nettie sat down, dread pooling in her stomach. She steeled herself for more bad news. "What happened?"

"I overheard you and Devon talking. During the barn raising, *yer vatter* told me he'd learned that young *mann* had been living with Elmer and, for some reason, helping him. He also said he thought you'd developed feelings for each other. I didn't want to believe it. I hoped Devon would go away again, and I was angry when *yer vatter* invited him to supper." For the first time in ages, *Mamm* cupped Nettie's cheek. "But he really does care about you, doesn't he?"

Nodding, Nettie covered her mother's hand with her own. "*Ya.* He does. And he's been helping Elmer for a *gut* reason — besides being a kind *mann.*"

Mamm removed her hand and sighed, touching the corner of her eye with her handkerchief. Her gaze dropped to the tabletop. "I'm ashamed, Nettie. I've been full of pride all these years, even though I pretended not to be. I looked down on Elmer because he wasn't one of us. And I looked down on Devon's *familye* because they were poor, beneath me. I also had no compassion for their *dochder* and her *sohn.* And how I've treated *yer vatter,* blaming him . . ." She started to cry.

Nettie was touched by her mother's confession. "It's all right, *Mamm* —"

"*Nee,* it isn't." She looked up, wiping her

face. "I agreed with Bishop Weaver when he told us people suffer because their faith is weak, and I thought God rewarded me with such a *gut* life because *mei* faith was strong. And then *yer vatter*'s business started to fail, and he got sick . . ." She grimaced. "God is punishing me for how I've treated others and for putting *mei* trust in things, not in him. And now you and *yer vatter* are suffering for *mei* sin."

"God isn't punishing you, *Mamm.* Bad things happen to everyone. But Devon has helped me see God is for us. I'm not the selfish, prideful person I used to be, and I know we can trust the Lord to help us get through these hard times."

Mamm gripped Nettie's hand. "Can you help me change like you have?"

Nettie squeezed her hand. "God changed me, *Mamm.* No one else could. But I'll be by *yer* side as he changes you. All you have to do is tell him you're sorry for what you've done and ask for his help. He's the one you need most of all."

Mamm nodded, her lower lip trembling as she seemed to be taking in what Nettie said. "*Danki, dochder.* I'm sorry I ever called you spoiled."

Nettie chuckled. "You had a right to, because I am."

"Not anymore." In a rare show of affection, *Mamm* leaned over and kissed Nettie's cheek. Then she wiped her eyes again and rose from the table. "You and *yer vatter* have lunch without me. I'll be in *mei* room for a while, gathering *mei* thoughts. Then I'll be able to apologize to him later." She smiled, then left the room.

Nettie closed her eyes, her heart swelling with joy. Months ago she'd been a miserable, lonely woman. Now she was full of peace despite the storm still surrounding her family. But God was with them, and now she knew it.

Thank you, Lord.

Epilogue

Six months later

Nettie stood gazing out the living room window as fluffy snowflakes fell in the twilight. Several inches already covered the ground, no surprise for early November. Devon came close and slipped his arms around her waist, and she leaned back against him.

"I should *geh* back to Robert's before it gets too late," he said, giving her a squeeze. "*Danki* for supper. It was *appleditlich,* as usual."

She turned to face him. "*Mamm* wanted us to make *yer* favorite meal to thank you for repairing the hole in our roof."

He gave her a half-smile. "She didn't have to do that. And I'm afraid *yer* folks will need a new roof soon anyway."

Of course they would. But she wouldn't complain. Over the last several months, Devon had been true to his word, helping her family as her father set up a new business. He'd had just enough proceeds from the sale of their excess livestock to buy a small leather goods store in a nearby district. Then Devon had taken over the chores Nettie and her mother would have struggled to manage alone while her father put in many hours getting the store back on its feet. He wasn't making close to the income he'd had with his lumber business, but he could pay their bills, and he was satisfied. His former employees had found other jobs, too, which had taken guilt from his shoulders.

Her mother had changed, although it had taken some time along with a new humility and lots of prayer. Now she visited Elmer too. He was doing fine, and he was even a little more engaged with his neighbors after meeting some of them at the barn raising. *Mamm* had also been visiting a few of the older members of the district on a regular basis, staying to talk to them instead of rushing off to her own pursuits. "I didn't think I'd ever say this after our financial troubles," she admitted as she and Nettie recently walked home from Elmer's, "but I'm happier than I've been in a long time."

Devon had told Robert why he'd come to Fredericktown, but Robert didn't see any reason to tell anyone else. And the community had accepted Devon anyway, especially after they'd seen how he'd helped both Elmer and her family. Abigail and Jonah had also become friends, enriching both their lives.

Needs like replacing the roof, a significant expense, had continued to plague her family, but they didn't worry. She and her parents had learned to trust God like never before. So far they hadn't found out who had thrown a box of lit matches into their barn that night, causing the fire. Although the authorities suspected a gang of kids who'd been vandalizing homes in some other towns close by, they had no proof. It didn't matter. Whoever did it was forgiven.

"Nettie?" Devon said.

"What?" She shook off her thoughts and looked into his eyes.

"You're a million miles away. What are you thinking about?"

"How things are better than they were a few months ago."

"That they are." He glanced out the window and then back at her. "I didn't want to rush this, but I think I have to."

"Rush what?"

He took her hand and led her to the couch. Her parents were out in the barn, feeding the animals and tucking them in for the night, something they'd started doing together shortly after working out the struggles in their relationship.

"Things are more than better, Nettie," Devon told her. "Elmer is well, and *yer familye* is stronger than ever. *Yer vatter* is happy with his leather store, plus he's able to handle chores around *yer* property again. *Yer mamm* even enjoyed taking care of the garden you two planted together —"

"With *yer* help," Nettie added. "She's so happy she's already planning one for next spring.

"See? *Yer mamm* is excited about gardening. That's how *gut* things are." He paused. "Of course, other than replacing the roof, I've run out of work to do here."

Where was he was going with this conversation? He'd had plenty of work at construction sites in the area, earning enough money to rent a room at Robert's and buy his own horse and buggy. So it wasn't as though he'd be idle now.

"Remember that day I told you I was returning to Birch Creek?"

Nettie nodded. "You said it was *yer* home." Her stomach turned sour. She'd thought about that for months, hoping he'd never leave.

"I've realized *mei* home isn't a town or district. *Mei* home is wherever I am with you." He squeezed her hand. "Will you marry me, Nettie?"

Her heart immediately said yes, but she had a question of her own. "Do you mean you'd live here in Fredericktown? For me?"

He nodded. "I don't know if I'll ever see eye to eye with Bishop Weaver, but that won't keep me from respecting him as a bishop. God chose him for that job for a reason, and I trust that whatever that reason is, God will see it through."

"What about what he did to *yer familye*?"

"I had to let that *geh*. *Mei* resenting his actions needed to change. Besides, you've taught me people can change too."

She was happy to hear that. "And what will *yer familye* think?"

"They'll support me, like Zeb and Zeke did when I wrote to them about us."

She looked down at their hands clasped together, remembering when he told her he'd written to his brothers, telling them about their relationship. She'd been hoping they'd accepted her apology, and when Devon told her they had, she'd been thrilled. His parents were supportive as well.

But she didn't want him to sacrifice being with his family. She also didn't think she could love him more than she did right now. "I can't ask you to permanently leave them for me."

"You're not asking." He gazed into her eyes. "I'm offering. There's a big difference."

"Maybe I want to move to Birch Creek," she said. "Did you ever think of that?"

His eyes widened. "I didn't. You'd live there? You'd leave *yer* parents?"

At one time she couldn't imagine leaving. But now it wasn't the impossibility she'd always thought it would be. "*Mei* home is with you, too, Devon. Wherever that might be. Here or in Birch Creek. The place doesn't matter to me either."

He grinned. "I'm happy to hear you say that, and we can discuss it later. But first things first." He moved closer. "You still haven't answered *mei* question."

"You're right," she said, leaning forward until only inches hung between them. "I haven't."

"Are you going to keep me in suspense? Will you marry me?"

Nettie kissed him, giving him her answer in a way she knew he'd appreciate more than words.

Devon hugged her. "I love you, Nettie. *Nix* will ever change that, and I'm ready to make you *mei frau.*"

"I love you, too, Devon." Her heart filled with the love she had for this man, a love out of reach months ago but now hers to treasure.

ACKNOWLEDGMENTS

Thank you to my editors Becky Monds and Jean Bloom for their valuable insight and amazing editing skills. A big thanks to my agent, Natasha Kern, for her endless support. And above all, thank you, dear readers. I hope you enjoyed Nettie and Devon's story and that it encouraged you. We can all use encouragement!

DISCUSSION QUESTIONS

1. When Devon arrives in Fredericktown, he muses about God changing well-laid plans. Have you ever experienced God changing your plans, and how did you react?
2. How did Nettie show Devon and her parents that she had changed?
3. Nettie and Devon have both struggled at various times with whether or not God was punishing them for the bad things that happened in their lives. Is this true? Why or why not?
4. The Amish believe that bishops are chosen by God to lead their communities. How should the community address Bishop Weaver's incorrect teaching about bad things happening to people who don't have enough faith?
5. Elmer discovered that he did need community, even though he had lived for years without it. In what ways does having a reli-

able community of family and friends help us in our lives?

ABOUT THE AUTHORS

Amy Clipston is the award-winning and bestselling author of the Kauffman Amish Bakery, Hearts of Lancaster Grand Hotel, Amish Heirloom, Amish Homestead, and Amish Marketplace series. Her novels have hit multiple bestseller lists including CBD, CBA, and ECPA. Amy holds a degree in communication from Virginia Wesleyan University and works full-time for the City of Charlotte, NC. Amy lives in North Carolina with her husband, two sons, and five spoiled rotten cats.

Visit her online at AmyClipston.com
Facebook: @AmyClipstonBooks
Twitter: @AmyClipston
Instagram: @amy_clipston

Kelly Irvin is a bestselling, award-winning author of over twenty novels and stories. A retired public relations professional, Kelly lives with her husband, Tim, in San Antonio. They have two children, three grandchildren, and two ornery cats.

Visit her online at KellyIrvin.com
Facebook: @Kelly.Irvin.Author
Twitter: @Kelly_S_Irvin
Instagram: @kelly_irvin

With over a million copies sold, **Kathleen Fuller** is the author of several bestselling novels, including the Hearts of Middlefield novels, the Middlefield Family novels, the Amish of Birch Creek series, and the Amish Letters series as well as a middle-grade Amish series, the Mysteries of Middlefield.

Visit her online at KathleenFuller.com
Facebook: @WriterKathleenFuller
Twitter: @TheKatJam
Instagram: @kf_booksandhooks

The employees of Thorndike Press hope you have enjoyed this Large Print book. All our Thorndike, Wheeler, and Kennebec Large Print titles are designed for easy reading, and all our books are made to last. Other Thorndike Press Large Print books are available at your library, through selected bookstores, or directly from us.

For information about titles, please call:
(800) 223-1244

or visit our website at:
gale.com/thorndike

To share your comments, please write:
Publisher
Thorndike Press
10 Water St., Suite 310
Waterville, ME 04901